# THE YEAR OF THE RAMS

*By the same author*
EWES AND I

# THE YEAR OF THE RAMS

**Elizabeth Arthursson**

*illustrations by*

*DAVID BARLOW*

*SOUVENIR PRESS*

For
my special friends
Sally and Tim
with love

## CHAPTER ONE

It was a morning of pale spring sunshine. The fat green buds on the daffodils were ready to open, and long purple catkins hung from the tall poplar trees in the hedge beside the garden. Behind the old thatched barn the branches of the willow trees, grey-green in summer, shone golden yellow in the clear, bright morning. The air was warm and smelled of primroses.

Gilbert and Polly, our geriatric geese, carefully picked their way through the flower bed under the kitchen window on their rubbery orange feet, treading now and again on a crocus flower or on the new shoots of the Michaelmas daisies.

I drove down the lane from our little Tudor cottage, between wide fields of pale green wheat, towards the line of blue-grey hills that I could see from the meadow behind our house. I was filled with happy anticipation: I had been promised a lamb — a tiny warm scrap of life to bring up on a bottle — and I was on my way to collect it. Lambs were so appealing and somehow so vulnerable. I could not imagine that their charm would ever fade.

It was a year since I had been given my first lamb, a four-day-old black and white Jacob ewe, so small that I had never believed I should be able to rear her. Now she was a huge, shaggy brown and white beast with horns, and a passion for roses and wallflowers and digestive biscuits. I had called her Pandora and just as, in Greek mythology, Pandora with her box had changed the world, so my Pandora had changed my life: I had fallen hopelessly and irrevocably in love with sheep and their ways.

I had left her that morning wandering about in the meadow behind the cottage with Berkeley, the black sheep I had bought as a weaned lamb to keep her company. Berkeley was big and bold and very greedy. She had nearly killed herself last summer eating half a sack of chicken food; she had devastated the vegetable garden; she had wandered into the house and chewed through the telephone wire, cutting us off from the outside world.

They had both been nibbling at some fresh young blackberry shoots in the hedge when I left, and I hoped that they would not manage to escape from the field or the garden before I was home again. Berkeley had a very bad habit of hoofing it off up the lane if she got bored, and Pandora always went with her.

I thought back over the year as I drove along the winding lanes, and of all the pleasure I had had from my first attempts at sheep-keeping. It had certainly been far from dull. The sheep had, by turns, delighted, amused and exasperated us. The rest of the family — my husband Gerald, daughter Katy and son Tom — had helped with hoof trimming, worm dosing, mending holes in the hedges where the sheep had eaten their way out and generally rounding up and fussing over the two unruly woolly beasts.

I thought about David Roberts, the tall, dark-haired farmer I had last seen at one of the autumn sheep shows. It was David who had promised me a lamb, and now I was on my way to his farm. It was about thirty miles from Monks Green, the hamlet where our little cottage stood among the fields, on the other side of the market town of Wetherbury where I went to do my shopping or take my cats and dogs to the veterinary surgery.

The road ran across country and the traffic and houses disappeared. Before me was an undulating patchwork of fields — pale green, grey, and in the distance purple; some in shadow, some in sunshine. My route was little more than a lane flanked by hedges. Here and there were poplars, their branches ochre-coloured in the sun, and grey-green ash trees, their upturned branches tipped with soot-black buds.

The road dipped and turned, sometimes running between flat fields bordered by elms, then turning a corner to reveal an unexpected view across miles of rolling countryside to distant hills. For some miles it hugged a stream, and I saw that the fields were stony, littered with flints. In the next village several of the cottages were built of flint; there were flint walls everywhere and an enormous flint barn, its ancient tiled roof covered with orange lichens.

The road then passed through an avenue of giant beech trees: their smooth grey trunks were like polished marble. After about a mile they terminated in a beech wood spreading out on either side. There was a bold notice, saying 'Strictly Private'. I imagined the wood in May: carpeted with bluebells, for the green spikes of their leaves were now showing through the leaf mould, and the trees with their newly unfurling leaves of that lovely, almost translucent green.

I turned a corner. Ahead of me stretched a wide valley wooded with purple trees and in the distance were dark blue hills. The road ran straight ahead between neat hedges, slipping down into the valley like a ribbon of grey smoke. And below was the village I had come to find.

At its centre was a crossroads where stood a large Norman church, the clock on the tower showing ten twenty-five. 'Come about ten-thirty,' David had said. I glanced down at the directions I had scribbled: 'Turn right by the church — 100 yards, then left into Mill Lane.'

Following these instructions, I saw ahead a group of farm buildings — large grey barns and stables and a square, grey-brick farmhouse with white painted windows and a dark blue front door. I turned into the wide gateway and drove round to the buildings.

As I got out of the car I could hear the bleating of young lambs and the deeper 'baas' of the ewes. I followed the sound and came round a corner to the lambing yards. There were long brick barns open on one side, the floors spread with straw, and filled with sheep. Some of the ewes were lying down in the sun, contentedly chewing their cud, their lambs curled next to them. Some of the bolder lambs were jumping and twisting in the straw, or chasing after each other.

I stood and watched them for a while They were all Ryeland sheep, white and well-woolled. The faces and legs of the ewes were covered with wool, just their eyes showing and smooth patches round their noses. The lambs had the appearance of little soft teddy bears, so white and fluffy as they jumped about in the straw or lazily dozed in the sun.

David appeared round the corner of the sheep pens and walked up smiling. He was dressed in dark blue nylon overalls, from under which bulged a thick knitted jersey, and had a checked cap on his head. Straw and mud stuck to the bottom of his large wellingtons.

'Hello, you found us all right, then? You've arrived just in time for coffee.'

'Hello, David, your directions were perfect. I was just looking at all the lambs. They are beautiful. How many have you got now? Is lambing nearly over?'

'I've only got sixty ewes left to lamb, just over three hundred lambed already. Quite a few sets of twins this year and not many losses. It's been a good lambing, but I never count the lambs until all the ewes have lambed: it's bad luck. No shepherd counts his lambs until lambing's over.'

'Oh, I didn't know that. Have you got many orphans? Have any ewes died?'

'We haven't lost any ewes this year so far, but several have got mastitis, so that means bottle lambs, like the one you're having. And a couple of my old girls just haven't any milk. Cup of coffee? or do you want to see your lamb first?'

'Oh, I'd love to see the lamb, please.'

We walked the length of the sheep barns and then into a large high barn stacked in one corner with bales of hay. Sunlight filtered in through cobweb-covered windows and from a skylight in the roof. Six large Ryeland rams were penned into an enclosure made from hurdles and straw bales. Some purple and white

turnips, still with green tops, lay in the straw and the rams
nibbled idly at them, while some red-gold bantam hens scratched about at their feet. A bright chestnut-coloured bantam cockerel, with large red comb and trailing green and blue iridescent
tail feathers, sat on top of one of the hurdles, watching over his
wives.

Next to the rams was another pen of straw bales containing
eight lambs, skipping about in the straw or pretending to nibble
at the bales. We walked up to the pen and looked over. Some
of the lambs were pure white, some had brown speckled faces
and spotted legs. One lamb, smaller than the others, was sitting
in a corner against a straw bale. He had an almost round face,
with a turned-up mouth as if he was smiling, little teddy-bear
ears and pale brown eyes shining out of the white woolly face.
David lifted him out and handed him to me. He was small, but
felt quite heavy and solid, and his wool was as soft as thistle-
down. He nuzzled his warm nose into my neck and pushed it
forward as if he were hungry. He was captivating.

'Oh, he's wonderful. Can I really have him?'

David laughed. 'Of course. Come and have some coffee, then
I'll show you round the farm. You can come and fetch him
afterwards.'

He took the lamb from me and put him back in the pen. I
was loath to let him go. I would have liked to carry him round
the farm all morning, but I followed David down the concrete
path that led from the barns round to the back of the house,
where a large, ancient japonica bush covered the wall near the
kitchen door with dark red, waxy flowers.

David opened the door and stepped out of his wellingtons,
leaving them on the doorstep and padding into the kitchen in
thick grey woollen socks. I followed in my blue canvas boots,
having quickly checked the soles for mud or straw.

'This is my wife, Pamela,' and David waved his arm in the
direction of a tall, fair haired woman sitting at a pine table
reading a copy of *Horse and Hound*.

'Elizabeth,' he said to her, and she smiled and got up, moving
towards a dresser hung with blue and white china. 'She's come

for a lamb,' he continued, going across to the kettle and switching it on, while Pamela took three mugs off the dresser.

'Are you having one of the bottle lambs?' she asked as she made the coffee, and David, after pulling out a chair for me, sat down at the end of the table in front of a pile of papers, copies of *Farming News* and *Farmer's Weekly* and a catalogue of sheep-handling equipment.

'She's taking the little runt,' said David laughing, 'saving him from the pot.'

'He's lovely,' I said. 'All baby animals are hard to resist, but there's something special about lambs.'

'How many sheep do you have?' she asked.

'Two, that's all at the moment. They're just pets really, but I spin so I shall use their wool.'

'My sister-in-law spins, but it's never appealed to me. She keeps a few Hebrideans and has a fleece from David now and again. I have to admit I prefer horses. I suppose a few sheep might be fun, but having as many as David has just seems to be hard work.'

'It gets busy at lambing,' admitted David. 'I've only had a few hours' sleep a night for weeks, but we've nearly finished now.'

'What about shearing? Do you shear them yourself?'

'No, I get contractors in.'

'I thought I'd try to shear my two myself this summer. Someone told me that the Agricultural Training Board runs classes, so I thought I might go to some.'

'Yes, they're very good. They run lambing courses as well. There's an office near you at Wetherbury. I know Andy there — he's a good chap — keeps some Suffolks himself. I've got a few and half a dozen Suffolk rams, but Suffolks are notorious for foot problems. One thing you don't get with Ryelands,' he added.

'Ryelands are a nice size to handle as well,' I said. 'Suffolks are so heavy. I can't imagine being able to turn one over to trim its feet.'

'Where did you get your lambs last year?'

'From Ian Boyton, he lives in the next village. Or used to,' I added.

'Oh, I know Ian. His father used to have the best herd of Friesian cattle in East Anglia. What's he doing now?'

'He left the farm last autumn. He's gone to Scotland to their farm up there. I used to watch the shearing every summer. Ian had shearers in, but his father used to shear alongside them with hand shears. He was amazing — he could clip sheep by hand as fast as the contractors with their machines.'

'I've done a few by hand, but it's hard work,' said David. 'D'you think you'll manage it?'

'I don't know, but at least I've only got two to shear this year, thank goodness.'

David laughed. 'Go to some classes and see how you get on. Come on, let's go and look round the farm. I can't sit here all day — work to be done.'

We went back to the lambing pens. David climbed over the hurdles and I followed him. He walked about among the sheep, picking up a lamb now and again, catching a ewe to check her udder.

'You must make sure that all the lambs are feeding properly, also that the ewes aren't getting mastitis. This old girl is seventeen —' he pointed to a ewe with a sagging back like an old horse. 'Hardly a tooth in her head, but she's got a good lamb on her, and milk for it. She lambs every year and always produces a good one. The ram lamb she had last year I'm keeping on for show, taking him to the "East of England" in the summer. I think he'll do well.'

'How long do sheep live?'

'It depends where they're kept. Out on the hills where food is scarce they wouldn't live that long. They're usually kept on hill farms for four or five years and then sold to lowland farms as draft ewes for another three or four years. At eight or nine ewes can be old, but I've got several of fourteen and fifteen and two more of seventeen. Most sheep never get the chance to live to a ripe old age, though. Three or four months is all they're allowed.'

'It seems such a shame.'

'Sheep are kept for meat, remember.'

I thought of my two ewes at home, my lambs of last year, and the adorable little lamb I was to take home with me to join them. It was a great sadness to me that all these gentle creatures should end up in some butcher's shop, especially as I was a vegetarian. At least there would be three sheep that would not end up like all the others, but what were three in a world of millions of sheep?

We spent a pleasant morning among the ewes and lambs. After looking at the newest arrivals in the barns, we went across the farmyard to a field at the back, where about fifty ewes were penned with their lambs. There were some Ryelands here but also some crossbred ewes with dark faces and legs, the lambs either dark faced like their mothers, or with speckled faces and spotted legs.

'These lambs are getting on for four weeks old now. I keep them in the barns for a couple of weeks depending on the weather, then get them outside. I've got another hundred ewes with their lambs at the other end of the farm, and some more in the field the other side of the house.'

'It's surprising how quickly they grow. Some of these lambs are quite big.'

'They're on creep feed now,' and David waved his hand in the direction of a metal feeder standing in the middle of the field, surrounded by hurdles and a gate with bars wide enough for the lambs to get through and eat the concentrates, but not the ewes. There were lambs all round the feeder, pushing and jostling each other.

'If the ewes had access to the food as well, the lambs would be pushed away and some, especially the weaker lambs, wouldn't get any at all. And they are just the ones who need it. Sheep are greedy and can be surprisingly aggressive when it comes to food.'

'Yes,' I laughed, thinking of big, bold Berkeley and her prodigious appetite, 'I've already found that out.'

As well as the sheep David also farmed five hundred acres

of cereals. We walked beside wide, treeless fields of pale spring barley and blue-green winter wheat. The sun felt warm on my back and skylarks were singing above the corn. The air was fresh with the honey smell of spring.

We returned to the farmyard and back to the barn where my new lamb was waiting to be collected. David lifted him out of the straw bale pen and gave him to me.

'Have you got milk for him?'

'Yes, proper ewe-replacer — I went to the mill for a bag on my way here. He's lovely. Thank you. I'm going to call him Rupert.'

'Rupert? That's an odd name for a sheep.'

'But he looks just like a teddy bear. Rupert Bear.'

I drove home through the spring day with my wonderful lamb. He stood quietly in the back of the car as I turned out of the farm gate and then sat down for the rest of the journey. Every time I looked in the driving mirror, I could just see the top of his woolly head and little rounded ears.

When I reached home, I carried him into the house. At this time we had three dogs: a red cocker spaniel of uncertain temper called Sophie, a black labrador, Henry, and Wolf, a large, yellow hairy beast with three legs. The dogs came up to sniff and inspect the new arrival. I wondered if Rupert would be afraid of them, but he stood quietly in the middle of the tiled floor showing no signs of anxiety as they nosed around him. They had all been very good with Pandora as a lamb, when she had slept here in the farmhouse kitchen, in a straw-filled box beside the Aga, and I was sure now that they would accept Rupert in the same way. Henry had become very attached to Pandora, and before Berkeley joined her she used to follow Henry round the garden and share his large basket with him.

After the introductions I let the dogs out into the garden and mixed up some milk for Rupert. He took it quickly and eagerly from the bottle, then I lifted him into the straw-filled box that I had made ready before I went out. He looked around him for a few minutes, then folded up his legs and sat in the straw, the little round face and shining eyes watching me.

'You are beautiful, Rupert. You're the most wonderful lamb. Just wait till Tom and Katy see you.'

With two biscuits in my pocket, I went out to the garden and round the back of the cottage to the gate into the meadow.

'Pandora! Berkeley!' I called.

They were near the top of the meadow, nibbling at cowslip leaves under the oak tree. They put their heads up and began running towards the gate, Pandora in the lead, jumping and skipping as she ran, her tail swinging behind her. Berkeley was a good deal heavier, and slower, and arrived at the gate somewhat breathless. I went into the meadow with them, stroked their soft noses and rubbed Berkeley's head behind her ears. Pandora tossed her head and Berkeley nosed at my pockets. They were impatient for the biscuits that they knew I would have for them.

The biscuits were soon eaten. Berkeley licked her lips with her purple-black tongue and looked hopefully for second helpings.

'I've got a surprise for you two. You're going to have a new friend called Rupert.'

Pandora put her head on one side and looked at me inquiringly. Berkeley licked her lips again. I walked up the meadow and they followed back to the oak tree. The cowslip leaves were growing in pale green rosettes near the hedge, and in the ditch the other side were soft yellow primrose flowers.

The ground rose behind the house in a gentle slope to the oak tree. I turned and looked back. From here the house seemed to nestle in a hollow, only the upstairs windows and the roof of old mossy tiles visible. Trees clustered round it — the tall poplars in the hedge with their long purple catkins, and the willows behind the barn, now shining bright yellow-green in the sunlight. The little house had sheltered us all through the rain and snow of winter, and the barn had kept my two beloved sheep and the ageing geese warm and safe; now we had a whole long summer ahead, of walks up the lane and picnics in the meadow with Pandora and Berkeley, and also now little Rupert.

I walked back towards the gate, but Pandora and Berkeley

stayed near the oak tree nibbling at the fresh shoots of grass growing along the hedge.

The hens were scratching about under the old apple tree near the gate. Looking at them now, plump brown birds making happy clucking noises at each other, it was difficult to remember how pathetic they had been last summer when they first arrived, pale and almost featherless from the horrors of a battery unit. One of them had found some dry, dusty earth near the base of the apple tree, and was fluffing up her feathers and churning the earth through them with her yellow legs.

The school bus trundled to a halt at the gate, and Tom and Katy climbed down, followed by Tom's friend Alex. Katy had a bag of school books over her shoulder and her large blue art folder under one arm. She was fifteen now, and working hard for her 'O' level exams, which meant hours of study every night, and weekends shut away in her bedroom with her books.

Tom, who was three years younger, with a mop of fairish hair and a cheeky grin, pushed open the gate and they came up the path, followed by Gilbert and Polly who had sidled round the corner of the house and appeared silently to torment Katy. Katy was not fond of Gilbert; in fact she detested him. Every time she went into the garden he would creep out from behind a bush or round the house and walk towards her, with his neck outstretched like a snake, hissing and scolding. Polly was very gentle, just padding amiably after Gilbert, but he seemed to have a great dislike of women and always teased Katy. I never had any trouble with him but he had chased several of our women friends. On one occasion, when an unfortunate woman who had run out of petrol in the lane had been standing on our doorstep, asking to use the telephone, he had crept up behind her and bitten her on the leg. It had made a large, spreading red and purple bruise, and looked very painful.

'Go away, you horrible goose,' said Katy, 'or you'll get a broom up your rump.'

Tom and Alex laughed. Alex was the same age as Tom, and lived in a cottage a mile farther up the lane. He was a good looking boy, dark haired, and with a very willing nature. He

was always ready to help if anything was needed, and he and Tom were firm friends. They had made chicken houses together, tree houses and camp fires; helped with gardening, decorating and playing shepherds.

The dogs bounded up, sniffing and wagging their tails as Katy, Tom and Alex came in through the heavy oak door and dropped their bags of school books on the tiled floor.

'Hello, darlings,' I said. 'Had a good day? What do you think of Rupert?'

They were already half-way across the kitchen to his box. He had been sitting in the straw, but now he got up and stretched his back a little, then looked at them all in turn.

'He's lovely,' said Katy, 'just like a little toy. He's got such a funny little face, and he's so woolly. Can I pick him up?'

'Yes, of course. He's so quiet and good, he doesn't seem to mind anything at all. Not even the noisy hounds.'

'He's not bad, Mum,' said Tom. 'Does Father know you were going to get him?'

'No, not yet. But I'm sure he won't mind. Rupert's so adorable, how could anyone not like him? And he's very small. He won't be any trouble.'

I made them all a cup of tea, and they sat round the Aga, eating chocolate cake and taking it in turns to have Rupert on their knees. He went from one to the other happily, sniffing at their faces, nibbling at their hair, while I mixed up another bottle of milk for him.

'Can I feed him?' asked Tom.

'Yes, if you want to.' I handed him the bottle. 'He's no problem. He's used to a bottle. Do you remember how difficult Pandora was when we first had her?'

'I remember you kept thinking she was going to die because she was so small,' said Katy. 'I wonder what Father will think of Rupert.'

'My Mum would like him,' said Alex. 'She's been learning to spin and she keeps trying to persuade my Dad to let her have a sheep in the garden.'

'Tell her to come down and see Rupert. And there are more where he came from if she really wants one.'

After Rupert had finished his milk he wandered round the kitchen, sniffing at the dog baskets and the grandfather clock. One of the cats was sitting on a chair watching him, and as he passed she put out a playful paw and patted at him. He pushed his head against the chair. She looked very affronted and got off the chair in disgust, and went and sat on the windowsill among the geraniums.

When Gerald came home, Katy was at the kitchen table, her homework books spread out round her. Rupert was back in his box, asleep, his legs folded up underneath him and his head down in the straw. With his eyes shut, I saw that he had long white eyelashes.

'Well,' asked Gerald, 'what's this?'

'Rupert. Isn't he sweet?'

I picked Rupert up and he opened his eyes and stretched out his front legs. He sniffed at Gerald's arm. Gerald laughed.

'Yes, he's a lovely little lamb. But where did you get him from? I was quite thankful that Ian had gone to Scotland, as I thought you'd want to get more lambs this year and had visions of the house filling up with them. But I see Ian's departure hasn't stopped you.'

'You remember Katy and I went to that Autumn Show at Peterborough? We met some sheep farmers there and one of them promised me a lamb, so I went to fetch him this morning. The farm's just the other side of Wetherbury. Rupert is a pure-bred Ryeland, a very special breed.'

He stroked the soft wool on top of Rupert's head.

'What's so special about Ryelands, then?'

'They are one of the oldest breeds in England. In the Middle Ages their wool was considered superior to that of any other sheep, and so valuable that it was called Lemster Or. They come from Herefordshire; the monks there used to breed them around Ledbury and Leominster.'

'Ledbury? That's the place you like so much, isn't it, with all those black and white timbered houses?' He looked down at Rupert and rubbed one of his little round teddy bear ears.

'Well, Rupert, welcome to this madhouse.'

I put Rupert down while I went to make Gerald a cup of coffee, and he wandered round, sniffing at Gerald's shoes and nibbling at his shoelaces. The dogs were lying quietly in their baskets, and after their initial interest in the new lamb had taken no more notice of him.

While Gerald sat and drank his coffee I gave Rupert another bottle of milk, which he took quickly and eagerly, flicking his little tail as he drank, as if by clockwork. I heaved a sigh of relief that Gerald had taken the new addition so calmly. But Rupert was so angelic that he seemed to put a spell on everyone who saw him.

I thought it prudent not to mention another plan I was considering. I had read in the National Press about a 'Lambs' Orphanage' in Cambridgeshire, run by a veterinary surgeon who had developed a new feeding system for orphan and rejected lambs. It seemed the ideal place to go in search of a little friend for Rupert, so that they could grow up together. I had telephoned the orphanage and arranged to go and have a look round, explaining that sex and breed were unimportant to me.

On Saturday morning Tom and I left Katy in charge of Rupert and set off on our secret quest. We drove through Wetherbury and then across the rolling green and brown hills on the border of Cambridgeshire. It was another beautiful spring day, the air warm and still. Now the hills were turned to silver and gold in the sunshine and there was a blue-grey mist in the distance.

We found the orphan lambs housed together in a large barn, which had been divided into pens by straw bales. Along one side was a wire mesh fence and the feeding system consisted of a number of rubber teats on the end of long tubes. The teats were fixed to the wire at a height level with the lambs' faces, and the other ends of the tubes went into buckets of ready-mixed milk. There were several buckets along the length of the wire, one for every five feeders, and the lambs were supposed to go to the feeders whenever they were hungry and help themselves.

A lamb with its natural mother will take small feeds often, suckling sometimes for only a few seconds, but when artificially fed on a bottle it is expected to take more milk at each feed than it would from its mother, and to have fewer feeds. So this new idea of feeding them was to be more as they would be fed naturally. But the milk in the buckets was cold, and there was no warm body to push against, to make them feel safe and loved.

I had already explained to the veterinary surgeon who owned the lambs that I simply wanted a lamb to love as a pet. There were about thirty of them in the straw pens, jumping about with each other, or sucking from the feeders. Some of them were white, some speckled, and a few were black. They were all crossbred lambs, the crossing chosen to provide quickly maturing animals and multiple births. Most of the lambs had been triplets or quadruplets, and the mother ewe, having only two teats, would be unable to feed so many babies.

One of the lambs was much smaller than the others and was not happy with the artificial feeding system. He would obviously benefit from being taken into a house and given some special attention, so he was going to be ours. He was soft and white, with a smooth face and a pink nose. His ears, longer than Rupert's, showed pink in the light. I held him against me and he kept very still, his front legs over my arm, his face against my shoulder. His back was covered in tiny white curls, through which his pink skin was clearly visible. He was ten days old.

He sat on Tom's knee on the way home, wrapped in a blanket. I glanced across at them as we drove back over the gold and silver hills. Tom had a large smile on his face as he held the warm, woolly bundle.

'He's great, isn't he?' he said. 'What are we going to call him? Do you think Rupert will like him? I hope they'll be friends.'

'It will be fun for Rupert to have another lamb to play with. They'll be able to chase each other round the garden.'

I looked down at the lamb, sitting so quietly on Tom's knee, looking so innocent and gentle. He had a completely different face from Rupert. Rupert's face was round and covered in woolly curls, and he always looked happy. This lamb had a longer face, covered in smooth white hair, and there was a sad expression on his face. There was something pathetic about him: he really did look like a little lost orphan.

'Let's call him Adam, shall we?' Adam seemed a fitting name for something so beautiful and pure.

'OK,' said Tom, 'Rupert and Adam.'

*CHAPTER TWO*

The two lambs were very different in appearance, and it soon became obvious that they were also completely different in character. Rupert would trot happily round the kitchen, inspecting any boxes or bags left lying about, running after the cats with hops and skips that made us all laugh. But Adam was very quiet and shy, and would retreat under the kitchen table as often as possible. Rupert was bouncy and full of life; Adam seemed almost to drag his back legs, as if they did not work properly.

Although he spent a good deal of time trying to hide himself under the table, Adam liked being picked up and cuddled. I would take him on my knee when he had finished his feed, and he used to put his head down along my arm and go to sleep. It always surprised me how quickly he would shut his eyes and doze off. He obviously liked the warmth and felt safe, as he would sleeping next to his mother. Rupert was quite happy to climb into their straw-filled box and settle himself in one corner on his own. There were usually one or two cats in the box, in permanent occupation, and Rupert sometimes nosed them out of the way. They would stir and stretch lazily and then curl up again in the straw as soon as Rupert had made himself comfortable.

In the afternoons I took the lambs outside onto the front lawn. The first time, Adam stood on the grass, looking round, and then came and stood next to me as I sat on the doorstep

24

watching them. Rupert inspected the flower bed under the kitchen window, and nibbled at the primroses. He was delighted to find one of the cats in the middle of the old straggly lavender bush and did a few ridiculous jumps, like the beginnings of a lamb's jump for joy. The cat watched him sleepily for a minute, then closed her eyes and went back to her dreams.

By the end of the following week Adam had lost some of his shyness. He and Rupert began running after each other in the garden, first one in the lead, then the other. They became more adventurous. They ran after the chickens, but stopped in their tracks when they rounded a corner and met Gilbert. The gander stretched out his neck and made some scolding noises. They looked at him in surprise and I waited, ready to go to their help if Gilbert advanced. He stayed where he was, still scolding, but not making any attempt to attack them.

Then Rupert did one of his jumps, turning in the air and landing facing in the opposite direction. He ran back to the front lawn followed by Adam, and left Gilbert and Polly scolding and squawking near the hedge.

I thought it was time that the lambs met Pandora and Berkeley, so I walked up to the gate into the meadow and they followed behind me like two little dogs. The sheep were at the far side of the meadow, but when I called them they put their heads up and then came running towards me, Pandora in the lead as always. When they saw the lambs, they stopped and Pandora put her head on one side.

I held out the biscuits I had brought for them.

'Come on, Pandora,' I called, 'don't you want your biscuits?'

They came running up then and gobbled up the biscuits, nosing in my pockets when they had finished to see if there were any more. Then they stopped and looked at the lambs. Rupert and Adam had been standing next to me under the apple tree, watching the big sheep with interest. Berkeley went up to Adam and put her head down to him. How nice, I thought, she's going to mother him. She moved her head slightly and gave him a large knock so that he fell right over and sprawled on the grass, his feet in the air.

I picked him up quickly.

'Berkeley, how could you? He's only a baby. You should be nice to him.'

Berkeley stood looking at me as if she was smiling. The meadow belonged to her and Pandora, she seemed to be saying, and she didn't want any miserable little lambs in her field, eating her grass. Pandora moved closer to Rupert. The horns, sticking straight up out of her head, were now about six inches long. I didn't want her to start on Rupert with such formidable weapons, so I decided it was time to take the lambs back to the garden.

'Come on, boys,' I said. 'We'll come back later. I think it's time for your milk.'

The next afternoon I took the lambs back to the meadow. It was a beautiful spring day. The air was really warm, and the wild cherry trees in the hedge were covered with blossom. Half a dozen greenfinches were hopping about in the branches, their feathers bright olive green in the sunlight.

I walked up towards the oak tree followed by Adam and Rupert. Pandora and Berkeley came running down to meet me as soon as they saw me. This time I was ready for their unfriendly reaction to the newcomers. I gave them their biscuits as usual, and then, holding Pandora's collar, took her to her favourite eating place near the hedge, Berkeley following close behind, and the two lambs running and skipping after us. Berkeley turned round and watched them several times, but as soon as she reached the hedge she and Pandora started eating again. The grass here was a very bright green, and interspersed with wild mint, so that the smell of the mint drifted on the air as they walked.

I walked slowly along beside the hedge and Adam and Rupert followed me, now forgotten by the others. They sniffed at the rosettes of cowslip leaves, and the dried leaves under the hedge. The elder bushes already had new leaves all over them, and the oak tree was covered in blossom, tufts of pale green flowers clustered all over the branches.

Adam was quickly changing from a shy, timid lamb into a

much bolder, adventurous creature. He chased the cats and formed a great affection for one of them, a pretty long-haired black cat called Fiona. Every time he saw her, he ran after her and tried to climb on her back. He chased her all round the kitchen until she jumped onto a chair or up onto the windowsill out of his way. Rupert just stood in the middle of the floor watching him, although sometimes he would join in the fun and run after Adam.

Whenever Fiona ran away and jumped out of reach, Adam appeared to become very angry and would turn his attention to the kitchen chairs, butting them and the table legs. Sometimes he would put his head down and take a run at the unsuspecting Rupert, charging at him and knocking him in the side. Rupert turned in surprise and put his head down to Adam, who would then take a few steps backwards and charge again, hitting him on the head.

Rupert had already been castrated before I had collected him from David, but Adam had not. I knew that rams that have been bottle-fed can become quite aggressive and eventually unmanageable, so I phoned the surgery at Wetherbury and made an appointment.

When I took him in a few days later, he sat on my knee in the waiting room, eyeing all the cats and dogs around him with interest. He looked very good and well-behaved, the picture of innocence, and everyone wanted to pat him.

'Isn't he sweet,' said one woman. 'Has he come for his jabs?'

'No,' I replied, 'he's come for a nasty experience.'

'Oh dear,' she said, turning pale, obviously sorry that she had asked.

A pleasant girl named Louise called us into the consulting room. The vet, Will, a tall good-looking man with reddish hair and a beard, had already heard, and helped with, some of my sheep problems of the year before.

'Hello, Lizzy,' he said, 'this is the latest addition to the flock, is it?'

'Yes, he came from John Philips at Bennington, who is running a lambs' orphanage.'

'I know John, we were at college together. I've heard about his new feeding system. He's been getting some very good results there. Most of the lambs come from a Finnish Dorset cross. The Finnish sheep are renowned for having multiple births. Triplets are usual, but they are known to have quads and quins. What have you called this one?'

'This is Adam. I do feel mean bringing him in, but I'm sure I'm going to have problems with him later on if I don't have him castrated, apart from the fact that I don't want Pandora and Berkeley having lambs all the time. I've got another little bottle lamb at home, a Ryeland wether, and he's already much quieter than Adam. Adam has started butting the chairs and even has a go at the labrador sometimes. It's lucky that Henry is so good-tempered and doesn't go for him when he gets butted in the side.'

Will laughed. 'You're doing the right thing. Don't worry about him. In a day or two he'll have forgotten all about it. I'll give him a local anaesthetic, so he won't feel anything. Just sit outside while we see to him, it won't take long.'

I went back to the waiting room. I heard Adam bleat several times as I went out and shut the door on him, and felt very guilty. I sat near the window and picked up a pile of pamphlets lying on a low table. There were detailed descriptions of the inner workings of a cow's stomach and all the revolting parasites to which they were prone; a leaflet on the care of the ageing dog; cat behaviour explained; how to look after your goldfish; first aid for pets. The list seemed endless but I found it hard to sit calmly, thinking about my unhappy lamb.

I got up and inspected the notice board, then went to the window. Outside under the window was a wide bed of wallflowers, a beautiful display of dark red, peach, cream, pink and apricot. The window was open and their sweet, heady scent drifted in. I have always been fond of these flowers. In the Middle Ages, the troubadors used to wear wild wallflowers in their hats — they were a symbol of love because they grew so constantly, sometimes growing out of walls or on any waste patch of ground. I thought ruefully of the wallflowers I had so carefully planted last November on an icy-cold day, all along the flower bed under the kitchen window. It had been a sunny day, but the air was so cold that by the time I had finished my hands were numbed and I had been thankful to sit by the Aga and slowly thaw out. But it would be worth the effort, I thought, when they were in bloom the following spring. Two days later Berkeley had found the wallflowers, and in ten minutes had disposed of my afternoon's work. So we had no sweetly scented wallflowers in our garden this year.

After what seemed hours but was probably about ten minutes, the consulting room door opened and Will appeared in his dark green operating apron, holding Adam.

'Is he all right?' I asked anxiously.

'Of course. Feed him as soon as you get home. That will take his mind off his troubles. He'll be a bit quiet for a day or two, but after that he'll be running about again and chasing all the cats.'

For the rest of the day Adam looked very unhappy. He stood in a corner of the kitchen near the Aga. Rupert seemed very concerned and kept going up to him and putting his little woolly face up to Adam's. Adam tried to sit down several times, folding his front legs and slowly lowering his back ones, but then getting up again.

I gave the lambs their bottles last thing before I went to bed. I put them into their straw box, and Rupert immediately sat down in a corner and settled himself for the night. But Adam stepped out, carefully and slowly, and went back to his place by the Aga where he had been standing all day.

The next morning I was very relieved to find the two lambs sitting together in the straw box. They both jumped out and followed me across the kitchen, Adam pushing his head against my legs, and then scraping at me with one of his hooves, demanding his breakfast.

I put the kettle on, then opened the door. The sunlight flooded in, lighting up the heavily beamed oak ceiling and making patterns on the flagstone floor. The dogs ran out into the garden, Sophie's little stumpy orange tail wagging happily, the tails of the two big dogs waving about as they sniffed around.

I mixed the two bottles of milk, and was feeding Rupert and Adam when the door at the bottom of the stairs opened and Tom appeared, whistling.

'Hello, Mum. How are the lambs? Is Adam all right this morning?'

'Yes, he's fine today. It's a lovely day. What are you going to do? Is Alex coming?'

'He'll be down after breakfast. We're going to mend the tree house first, then go into Castle Monkton this afternoon to play football.'

He went to the pantry and found the measure of corn for the hens, then disappeared into the garden. When the bottles were finished I went out and across to the barn to Pandora and Berkeley. They heard my step on the gravel, and Pandora called out as I approached. The barn was warm and dark with the sweet scent of hay. I opened the gate of their pen and they pushed out, trotting into the bright garden and round the corner of the house to the meadow. Gilbert and Polly followed me back to the doorstep and put their orange vacuum cleaner beaks to the pile of corn I had left for them, sucking it up with muffled squawks.

Katy was in the kitchen making tea when I went back inside. She looked up and smiled as she stirred the mugs. She had a lovely face, with fine bones and clear blue eyes. Her hair was thick and dark, and this morning she had it tied with a floppy blue ribbon. She was wearing a white cotton jersey and jeans and black shoes like doll's slippers.

'Adam seems all right this morning,' she said. 'I'm glad he's better, he seemed so unhappy last night.'

'Yes, but he's back to normal now. He made short work of his bottle. What do you want to do today? D'you want to go anywhere?'

'I don't mind. Have you got any shopping to do? I'd like to look for some material. I want to make a skirt for a party next weekend at Julie's. Will you help me with it?'

'Of course. What do you fancy for breakfast?'

'Nice big fried breakfast, as it's the weekend,' said Katy laughing.

'Right, coming up. Would you be a love and lay the table?'

After breakfast we took cups of coffee into the garden and sat on the bench under the kitchen window in the sun. Adam and Rupert and the dogs followed us. Henry and Wolf wandered off to the hedge, pushing their big black noses under the dried leaves, into the clumps of wild violets flowering at the base of the hedge, catching all the smells of mice and cats and birds. Sophie sat down beside me and watched the lambs. They were jumping about on the lawn, stopping to sniff at the grass, and then skipping backwards and forwards in the sunlight.

Gerald leaned back against the wall of the house, cleaning his glasses with a red and white handkerchief. Gerald always wore a tie, even at weekends, but as a concession to being at home he had on a checked sports jacket and twill trousers, instead of a suit. Tom had tried to persuade him into jeans and trainers, but Gerald was very conservative and such things were not his scene.

'Well, my dear,' he said, 'how are all your unruly beasts this morning?'

I laughed. Considering that there were three dogs, seven cats, two sheep, two lambs, some assorted hens and a pair of geese wandering about the place, all was remarkably quiet.

'Just at the moment they're all behaving themselves,' I said. 'What are you doing today? Katy and I thought we'd go into Wetherbury this afternoon to do some shopping.'

'Oh, I've still got some of the finds from the local dig to finish sorting through. If you're going to Wetherbury, would you try and find me a book? It's on Pre-Roman history. I'll write down the title and author.'

We were interrupted by loud honkings from the front of the house, announcing the arrival of Alex. Gilbert really made a very good guard dog.

On Monday morning I telephoned the Agricultural Training Board to make enquiries about shearing classes. I was put through from the switchboard to a pleasant-sounding male voice. I explained that I had some sheep and was anxious to learn all I could about them, including shearing them myself.

'We shall be having some shearing classes, but they won't be until the beginning of May' — it was now the end of March — 'but if you'd like to give me your name and address and details I'll let you know when they are. How many sheep do you have?'

Should I say two and two halves? It was too ridiculous. I was sure I would not qualify for their classes with so few sheep.

'Four,' I replied.

There was a pause while he waited for me to add score, hundred, thousand. 'I see,' he said brightly. 'Would you be interested in a lambing course we're having next week?' Obviously he thought I wished to enlarge the size of my flock and doubtless assumed that I had four pregnant ewes.

'Oh, yes,' I said enthusiastically, 'I would.'

'We have a sheep disorders class, too — a few weeks later,' he added. 'Shall I put your name down for that, too?'

'Yes, please.' Any opportunity to see lots of sheep was exciting and I imagined a day spent on a farm watching hundreds of ewes and their new-born lambs. He took my name and address and said he would post me the details.

My friend Laura arrived later to see the lambs. Laura and I had been to the same boarding school, and as she was several years younger than I we had never really been friends at school. But I had met her by chance a few years ago and discovered that we now lived in neighbouring villages. So we had become now the friends that we never were before. We sat at the kitchen table while the lambs nosed around us. Laura stroked their soft backs and agreed that they were very lovable. She had become quite converted to sheep, although I was still trying to persuade her to become a vegetarian. However, I had got her addicted to sunflower seeds and kept trying.

I picked up Adam. 'Do you want to hold him?' I asked. 'I shan't be offended if you don't. I always dread people offering me their babies. I really don't like babies at all, only ones with fur and four legs. Adam is lovely and cuddly, and very good.'

Laura laughed. 'Yes, I'd like to have him on my knee.'

I handed him over and he sniffed at her chin. I picked Rupert up and he settled himself on my knee, folding his little legs underneath him.

'Adam's quite heavy, and so warm. Yes they are lovely. I was going to ask you a favour actually,' she continued, 'but say no if you don't want to.'

'Oh God, what is it? Not give a talk to someone?' Laura was involved with several village groups and I thought with horror of telling a collection of blank-faced strangers what they could do with herbs, or how to make soup from elm bark or daffodil bulbs, or the delights of nettles.

'No, nothing like that. It's just that I wondered if we could bring the play-group children up to see your sheep and the cats and watch the lambs have their bottles. Most children only see sheep the other side of a field and they can't get near them like you can yours.'

'Oh, that's all right.' I was highly relieved. 'How many will there be?'

'Well,' she hesitated, 'about twenty, and six or seven mothers. But we wouldn't stay long.'

'I'll get some lemonade, then, and lots of biscuits.'

'No, I'll take them back to the play-group for their usual bottles of milk.'

It sounded fairly harmless. 'You'd better make sure they all have wellies. It's a bit muddy at the moment, especially if they want to go into the field with Pandora and Berkeley.'

'My thoughts entirely,' she agreed.

The lovely spring weather deteriorated into several days of heavy rain. The morning that the play-group were due to arrive there was a fine rain falling and an icy wind blowing round the house. The ditch at the back of the garden by the meadow, which had held only dry leaves and twigs all winter, now had several inches of water in it, much to Gilbert's delight. He and Polly splashed about in it calling to the hens and each other and anyone else who was near. I shut the geese into the barn for the morning and hoped that the children would remember their wellies.

I shut the dogs upstairs in the bedroom. Sophie, I knew, would growl at them all, and was quite likely to bite someone if she felt like it, so they were all better out of the way. Having swept the floor and mopped it as I did every morning, I decided to mop it again and opened all the windows to dispel the smell of sheep.

Rupert and Adam followed me round the kitchen, sniffing at the mop and trying to stick their heads into the bucket. I bent down to mop under the table and Adam put his head down to the bucket and gave it a shove, spilling about two gallons of soapy water all over the floor.

'Oh, Adam, how could you?' I was exasperated. They were due to arrive in about five minutes. The water spread out in great pools, running towards the grandfather clock and the dresser, showing up the uneven undulations of the floor. I had just finished mopping it all up again when loud barkings from upstairs indicated that the children had arrived. I pushed the mop and bucket into the pantry to empty later, and shut the door.

The children trooped in, twenty of them between the ages of two and five, followed by Laura and six of the children's mothers. They all stared at Rupert and Adam standing in the middle of the floor, and pushed forward. Adam looked horrified to see so many people and retreated under the table, while Rupert hid behind me.

Laura produced a packet of biscuits and Adam ventured out rather uncertainly and took one from her, then quickly backed away again from the eager children. Luckily they all had wellies on, although most of the mothers had not brought any, so we went out into the garden to see Pandora and Berkeley. Rupert and Adam followed me, one each side, staying as close to me as they could.

'I was chased and butted by a ram once,' said one of the women. 'They can be nasty — just like bulls.' I had a feeling that she did not care for sheep much.

'Pandora,' I called. There were answering bleats, and Pandora and Berkeley came running across the meadow to the gate, but when they saw the army of visitors approaching they backed away again. The children were now all clutching biscuits and jostling to feed them. Berkeley, normally so greedy, was undecided. She eyed the biscuits and licked her lips with her black tongue. Finally she took a biscuit from one of the children. The other children pushed forward, but Pandora and Berkeley retreated. Adam took a couple of biscuits, but after sniffing at the other pieces for several minutes, refused to have any more.

The children ended up throwing the biscuits to the hens who were less fussy. They ran up clucking and scratching and pecking at the pieces. Pandora and Berkeley disappeared to the top of the meadow in disgust. Henry stood with his paws on the bedroom window sill, barking at the invasion. The children looked up and, seeing his big black face, 'wanted to see the doggies'. 'I don't think you'd really like that,' I said.

Two of the little boys made for the ditch and began splashing around, getting themselves thoroughly wet and muddy. Another child fell face down in the mud and wailed loudly. We took them all back to the house and into the bathroom which, as in many cottages, was downstairs. To the children's delight, five of the cats were asleep in there. However, they scattered like shrapnel, shooting out of the window and the back door in all directions, and did not return until supper time.

While the children were being washed of some of the mud, I mixed up the milk for Rupert and Adam and put it into their bottles. They gathered round while the lambs had their elevenses, and watched in hushed silence. Then they all departed, wet and muddy. I felt it had not been exactly a success.

I found the mop and bucket and redid the floor while the lambs sat by the Aga and nibbled at a bowl of sheep nuts. I went out to see Pandora and Berkeley, taking some biscuits in my pocket. This time they ran up and gobbled them, and seemed to have forgiven me for the recent invasion.

Laura had asked me to go and have lunch afterwards when the children had all gone. We discussed the morning over gin and tonic, and I apologised for the mud and rain and my standoffish sheep and the fact that the rabbit had bitten one small boy very hard on his finger. But she seemed to think that they had all enjoyed themselves. It had certainly been a change from their usual mornings of playing shops or painting in the village hall.

# CHAPTER THREE

The details for the lambing class arrived next morning, with the time, place and what to wear. Protective clothing was called for. I could not see myself in a boiler suit or a chain store nylon overall, so the obvious thing was a genuine shepherd's smock. I had a book on old smocks and had been meaning to make myself one for years. Now was the perfect excuse. After I had given Rupert and Adam their lunchtime bottles, I left them in the kitchen with the dogs and drove to Wetherbury to look for some suitable material. I went to several shops and eventually found some heavy cotton canvas in a dull greenish colour and some matching linen thread for the smocking.

When I got home I heard frantic bleats coming from upstairs as soon as I opened the door. The little pine door at the bottom of the stairs, always kept closed, was wide open and I could hear Rupert and Adam calling for help. I ran across the kitchen and looked up. At the top of the stairs, on the narrow landing, two worried white faces peered down at me.

I ran up the stairs to them and carried them down, one under each arm. I knew that they could not have opened the stair door, and guessed it must have been Henry. By standing on his back legs, he was able to open most of the doors in the house, which all had old latches instead of door knobs. He had led Pandora and Berkeley into trouble the summer before. One afternoon he had opened the sitting room door, and I had gone in there to find Pandora sitting on the chesterfield chewing her cud, surrounded by sleeping cats. Henry had also opened the pantry door and let Berkeley in to eat her way through half a sack of chicken food. Now he had allowed Rupert and Adam to go exploring upstairs.

I mixed up their milk and they quickly downed the bottles. Then I went upstairs to see what they had been doing. They had obviously found it easy to run up the stairs, but once at the top had found the prospect of going down again too daunting. 'Sheep always move better going uphill,' I had once been told.

I went into the bedrooms. Things were strewn about all over the floor, and books had been pulled out of Katy's bookshelf, but at least they did not appear to have been chewed. And *somebody* had been sitting on my bed, because the covers were rumpled and there was a hollow by my pillow like a hare's form. They were growing quickly now, and getting more adventurous all the time. Soon it would be time for the 'little boys' to join Pandora and Berkeley in the barn at night.

My next task was to make my shepherd's smock for the lambing class the following week. The old smocks were all cut in squares or rectangles and the shaping of the garment came from the gathers made by the actual smocking. There were traditional patterns for the different trades. The old shepherd's smocks were decorated with crooks, rams' horns and hurdles, embroidered on the collars and side panels. I looked through the book and chose a Wiltshire shepherd's wedding smock to copy. The material was thick and difficult to work and the whole thing was immensely time-consuming. I sat up night after night.

At last my smock was finished and looked reasonably like the real thing. Laura was most impressed, but when I told her it was made especially for cleaning out the barn, trimming the sheep's feet and getting generally filthy, she was horrified.

'All that work,' she exclaimed, 'you'll spoil it. It's a shame.'

I put it on and went out to the barn to clean the sheep pen and give my smock an authentic sheepy smell. I did not want it to look too new.

The day of the lambing class was a cold, damp day, with a

fine rain falling. Gerald was at home, as the college term had finished, and he had a few weeks free from History tutoring.

'Are you sure you don't mind looking after Rupert and Adam, and giving them their bottles?'

'No, of course not. So long as I know when they have to be fed and how much to give them.'

'I've left the list pinned up beside the dresser. I warm the bottles in a saucepan with boiling water, but not for long. Try the milk on the back of your hand before you give it to them in case it's too hot. If you can't feel it, it's just right.'

'Yes, yes, I know about that. Don't worry about them. Just go off to the class and have a good day. They'll be perfectly all right.'

'Don't forget to keep the dogs in until the post and papers have been.' There was a box on the gate for the post and papers, but if the dogs were in the garden, Henry would leap up and down against the gate and terrify the Phil Collins look-alike paper man. He refused to get out of his car and if we did not go out to rescue him, he drove away and left us paperless.

'Don't fuss,' said Gerald. 'I'm perfectly capable of looking after them all. If you don't hurry up you'll be late. Don't forget your smock, after all the effort. What time do you think you'll be back?'

'I think the class ends at four, so four-thirty to five. The cats and dogs have all been fed, and everyone outside, it's just Rupert and Adam. I'd better go, then. See you later.'

The lambing course was to be held on a farm near Wetherbury. The directions ended down a series of obscure and unmarked lanes. I got lost several times and was finally directed by a milkman. I wondered what the other people on the course would be like and imagined them to be young agricultural students with brawny arms, quite capable of 'throwing' Berkeley and in charge of large flocks. Pandora and Berkeley had grown enormous over the winter and Pandora's fleece was now about eight inches long, making her look even larger. I still had not mastered the art of 'throwing' them myself, that is sitting them back on their haunches and getting them *under control*. Every time I tried to throw Berkeley I ended up on the ground while she stood over me looking very pleased with herself. At the moment I trimmed their feet by lifting one foot at a time, like shoeing a cart-horse.

The other people at the class turned out to be very like myself: rather eccentric ladies with a few sheep, although unlike me their ewes produced offspring for the freezer. There was also a young married couple with a smallholding and a new flock of twenty-five ewes, all bought tupped the autumn before. I was, however, the only person there with ewes who were not pregnant, and half of my flock made up of wethers.

One woman sat and smoked cigars and tried to persuade the rest of us that the only sheep to have were Portlands. She said that Portlands produced very sweet joints, which was of no interest to me. Personally I thought Portlands rather a non-event. They are small, rather primitive-type sheep with a con-genital hereditary disorder known as 'screwtail'. This in fact sounds more interesting than it is. It conjures up a picture of a sheep with a corkscrew piglet-like tail, but it is simply that the bones of the tail are fused together.

Portlands were not for me, nor did I care for her blue haze of cigar smoke drifting continually over the table. I like sheep to be large and woolly, and I like cigars to be smoked by men.

The vet who was taking the class was Will. The morning was taken up with the theoretical side of lambing: presentations, difficulties, what to do and when to call the vet. As far as I was concerned, that was as soon as any difficulty presented itself. Will had a lovely sense of humour and the morning passed quickly and pleasantly, interrupted by a break for coffee.

After lunch we were to have the practical demonstration of lambing.

'Come outside and meet Agnes,' said Will.

We fetched our wellies and protective clothing from our cars and followed Will to one of the barns. It was still raining and there was an icy wind round the farmyard, but my smock was windproof, and over my thick handspun jersey from one of Ian's Cheviots, I felt reasonably warm.

'Agnes' was a large polythene box on a stand with a plastic pelvis inside to represent a ewe. The whole thing was then filled up with warm water and the idea was to practise delivering lambs through a hole in the side; first in the normal presentation of head and front feet first, and then in abnormal presentations. Will picked up a sack from the floor and took out two dead lambs. They were stiff and one had dried blood around its nose and mouth. There was a cracking sound as he tried to bend the legs into the required position. The dead lamb was then put into a bucket of hot water to make it more supple.

I turned away feeling faint and went outside and leaned against the barn wall. As I was not going to breed from my sheep I wondered why I had come. Will put his head round the door.

'Lizzy, are you all right?' he asked.

'I'm sorry Will, I can't do it.'

'Well, you'll just have to give me a ring.'

I left the others to struggle bravely with the inner workings of Agnes and her still-born offspring and wandered off to look at the farm. There were two hundred and fifty ewes there and most had lambed already. They were in large open-sided sheds and barns, and there was a variety of breeds: a few Jacobs with their tiny black and white spotted lambs; sturdy black-faced Suffolks; Wensleydales with long silky fleeces; roman-nosed Cheviots and long-necked Bluefaced Leicesters looking very like llamas. There were also some French sheep which I had not seen before and which looked singularly unattractive. Their faces were bright orange pink and almost hairless.

It had been an interesting and informative day, but as I drove home along the narrow lanes I felt saddened by the thought of all the sheep endlessly producing lambs until they were no longer useful, and then driven into those hideous trucks and sent off to slaughter. Poor sheep, pushed around always, for one reason or another. All their pain and all their effort simply to feed people and line their pockets — line their pockets with the wool of dead ewes. I wondered then, not for the first time, why it was that I could not just accept things the way other

people did; why stray cats and sad lost dogs and helpless sheep hurt me.

I was glad when I turned the corner of our lane and saw the little house ahead among the fields. When I opened the door Tom and Katy were sitting at the kitchen table with their homework books spread out round them, and Gerald was in the middle of making a pot of tea. Rupert and Adam came running up, pushing their noses against my leg, flicking their tails and insisting that they were hungry.

'Hi, Mum, how did you get on?' asked Tom.

'Hello, Mother, did you have a good day?' said Katy.

'Here you are, I've just made some tea,' and Gerald handed me a mug. 'What sort of day did you have? And don't take any notice of those two greedy little things. I gave them some milk half an hour ago.'

'I'm glad to be home,' I said, sitting by the Aga and warming my hands round the mug of tea, while Rupert and Adam tried to climb on my knee and the dogs sniffed noisily at my shoes. 'It wasn't at all what I had expected. We were supposed to practise with dead lambs, pulling them out of a polythene box called Agnes, which represented the ewe.'

'How horrible,' said Katy. 'Did you do it?'

'No. I wandered off round the farm and looked at the sheep and left the others to it. I don't know what Will thought. He must think I'm stupid. It was silly of me to go.'

'It doesn't matter,' said Gerald. 'Yours aren't going to lamb anyway, so don't worry about it.'

'What were the other people like?' asked Katy.

'Quite nice, except for one dreadful woman who talked too much and smoked cigars. How have you all been getting on? Have the little boys been all right? Were they good?'

'They've been fine,' said Gerald, 'no trouble at all. They were sitting together in their box before you came in, nearly asleep. They just think that they can get round you for more food. Meg phoned this afternoon' — Meg was my sister — 'and Mrs Pembridge. She wondered if you'd go and spin at an open farm weekend she's having in May.'

'Oh, that's nice. I'll give her a ring later.' I picked up Adam, who was now getting quite large for sitting on knees. At first he had sat in the middle of my skirt, not much bigger than a kitten. Now he sprawled across my knee, his front legs dangling. He pushed insistently at my neck, asking for food. I stroked his ears and he became quiet.

'Someone give Rupert a cuddle, or he'll feel left out.'

Tom picked him up. 'Come here, Rupert mate, you come and sit with me.'

We all sat round the Aga, cuddling the lambs, drinking more tea. Eventually I got up and went to mix their milk, and then out to the garden to take Pandora and Berkeley to the barn while Tom went to the hens to shut them in for the night. Pandora and Berkeley stood in their pen, munching happily at their pile of hay. I stroked their soft noses, felt their warm breath on my hand. At least they would be spared the fate of other sheep, of endless lambings. They chewed busily, tufts of hay sticking out of the corners of their mouths.

'Goodnight, Pandora, goodnight, Berkeley,' I said to them as always.

Easter was cold that year with an icy wind, as Easter often seems to be. We went for a walk across the fields towards the wood. The fields were separated by deep ditches and their banks were covered with primroses. I had seen the ditches cleared in November and the banks burnt to blackness, and I supposed this was why the primroses were so prolific. The rootstocks below ground were safe from flames and the choking grass was kept in check. There were so many of them, that lovely pale yellow with the sweet scent. Between the primroses were thick green bluebell leaves. Where the banks were yellow now, they would later be blue.

The wood itself was strangely empty. The trees were tall and thin and growing too close to each other and the ground was covered with a thick layer of dry brown leaves. They seemed to be nearly all oak leaves, although the trees at the edge of the wood were mainly hawthorn, with here and there some thin pine trees, their long bare trunks like telegraph poles, pushing up through the other trees towards the sky.

I love trees but I do not like woods very much. I love elms beside a field or willows and alders leaning over a stream, and I think Paradise must be an apple orchard where it is forever May, the trees painted pink with blossom. But woods always give me an uneasy feeling. They seem to be full of hidden eyes and the branches of the trees seem to stretch forward as if to take hold of anything that passes by. I suppose it is probably the result of reading too many fairy stories as a child, where the wood was always full of bears and witches. The dogs, however, loved the wood and went crashing about through the sticks and dry leaves, their noses to the ground.

I had refused to wear a coat, as I felt that April should be warm enough to go without one, but although I was wearing my thick handspun jersey, I was frozen, and thankful when we were home again with our bunches of primroses.

The following week brought the day of the sheep disorders class. I set out with some misgivings, but it proved to be a very useful and much more pleasant day. As before the morning was taken up with theory and the afternoon was for practical work. We learned the importance of regular worming of sheep, as a heavy worm infestation can quickly kill a lamb. We were told about the revolting blow flies that lay their eggs on a sheep's back or in wet and dirty wool round their tails. The maggots, when they hatch, eat into the sheep's flesh, literally eating it alive. The sheep become very distressed and can die in a few days. The blow flies look like bluebottles, but are bright green and most active in hot, thundery weather. We were told about fluke and pulpy kidney, blackleg, tetanus, braxy and lamb dys- entery — there seemed no end to their ailments. Many of them seemed to be symptomless, ending in sudden death. I began to feel very worried about my little flock, and decided to give them all another worm dose as soon as I was home.

Someone in the class asked how long sheep would live, as I had asked David.

'A sheep's natural lifespan is longer than that of the average cat or dog,' we were told. 'I know of a splendid ram living on Farnham Common, which is twenty-three and still going strong.'

In the afternoon we inspected some penned sheep, looked at their teeth and trimmed their feet. I struggled with some heavy ewes, but was shown the correct way to turn them over. Perhaps I would get the better of Berkeley after all.

## CHAPTER FOUR

Rupert and Adam now spent their days in the meadow with Pandora and Berkeley, although I still gave them a bottle of milk each, morning and evening. I watched them all one afternoon, sitting together near the apple tree, all chewing their cud, their jaws moving rhythmically up and down. They were a real little flock now, doing things together. My little rams were now nearly eight weeks old and grazing properly with the big sheep.

Pandora and Berkeley were sitting together on the bank near the hedge and Rupert and Adam sat at a little distance with their backs turned to the wind. The grass in the meadow was almost flattened and the poplars and wild cherry trees in the hedge were being tossed by the wind, which sent showers of white blossom across the grass. It was the last day of April, but as cold as November.

Suddenly one of the chickens ran flapping and squawking from the hen house and the sheep all leaped to their feet. Pandora and Berkeley looked slightly dazed as if they had been woken from sleep. I often wondered if they got indigestion from being disturbed in the middle of cudding. They seemed to lapse into a kind of trance, sitting with half-closed eyes, motionless except for the busy jaws.

Adam looked round enquiringly, his little pink ears sticking out on each side of his head, ready to catch the sound of the back door opening or footsteps on the gravel. He gave a few hopeful bleats. He was always on the look-out for a biscuit or a piece of bread and honey. Rupert stretched himself upwards, arching his neck, then sat down again, folding his legs under him in the same place that he had been sitting before their disturbance.

Adam sat down again and resumed his cudding, but Pandora and Berkeley turned and began walking up the field, pushing against each other and then turning to butt their heads together. But they did not seem in the mood for a real battle and after one or two half-hearted efforts they both put their heads down to the ground and began grazing.

Rupert and Adam, although both pure white sheep, were still very different in appearance. Rupert was round and quite fat, like a little barrel. Adam was taller and leaner and his face was smooth and covered in thick hair, while Rupert's was almost covered with woolly curls. There was just a smooth oval round his nose and mouth like the sewn-on muzzles of teddy bears. He had also lost his tail. It had been ringed when he was a few days old and had gradually withered away and dropped off, but Adam's tail had been left. It was a fairly short tail, and thick and flat as if it had been ironed. Adam was also growing some horns. Now they were about an inch and a half long and sticking straight up out of his head. He spent a good deal of time rubbing his head against the trunk of the apple tree. I wondered whether the newly growing horns were irritating him, or whether he was practising for future battles, as a cat sharpens her claws before she sets out to hunt.

If April had been a cold month, May brought long hot days, shiny yellow buttercups along the roadside and a mass of pink blossom to cover the old twisted apple tree at the edge of the meadow. It also brought nearer the prospect of shearing Pandora and Berkeley.

The day for the shearing class arrived. I woke early that day and listened to a blackbird singing in the ancient apple tree. The sky was clear, pale green with early morning. Then I heard a cuckoo calling: a magical sound, the end of winter and the beginning of summer.

I went out to the barn and let the sheep out into the garden.

They trotted round the corner of the house, Pandora in the lead, making their way to the meadow. Berkeley nibbled at the hedge as she walked, Adam and Rupert skipping and jumping after her, glad to be alive on such a beautiful day. Gilbert and Polly made their way across the gravel on their flat orange feet to the doorstep for their breakfast, and the hens came tumbling and flapping out of their house, pecking and scratching about in the grass for the corn I threw down for them.

The sky was cloudless without a breath of wind as I drove down the lane. It was going to be a hot day, a perfect shearing day. The classes were being held in the grounds of a National Trust house about ten miles away. The house was surrounded by five hundred acres of parkland, and as I drove through the park along an avenue lined with tall lime trees I saw sheep everywhere. There were plenty of lambs, sturdy and black-faced and a good deal larger than my two at home.

About twenty lambs had formed themselves into a group like a gang of children and were running in wide circles one after the other. Suddenly they stopped and turned, and then began to run in a different direction after another leader. Round and round they went, backwards and forwards, running round the huge oak trees dotting the parkland, jumping now and again over a straw bale, one after the other in a line. They seemed so happy in the sunlight. I also knew that if lambs ran about like that it meant that they were fit and healthy.

I had been told to follow the drive past the house until I came to some farm buildings. The house itself was very impressive: a huge grey stone mansion with turrets and towers and seemingly endless windows. There was a wide sweep of gravel in front of the house and beyond that a carefully laid out garden with low box hedges and wide herbaceous borders. At the side of the house was a great spreading blue-grey cedar tree, at least as old as the house.

I came to the stable block and farm buildings and was welcomed by a tall middle-aged man with fairish hair and blue eyes and a broad smile.

'Hello, I've come for the shearing class. Is this the right place?'

'Yes, I'm Bob. I'm taking the class. We've got the sheep penned up ready round the back of the stables. Have you done any shearing at all?'

'No, not yet, I'm afraid. I've only watched other people so far.'

'Don't worry, come on. You'll be shearing by the end of the day.'

I had my doubts about that but I followed him to the pens where several people were already gathered. We all introduced ourselves and discussed our various flocks. It turned out that all the sheep in the park, which I had admired as I drove in, belonged to Bob, the shearer. He rented the grazing from the National Trust and had nearly two thousand ewes. In comparison to my two it seemed an enormous flock that would surely demand attention twenty-four hours of every day.

Bob had a partner, Andy, and was also helped by his son. Andy was there this morning and hustled the first ewe out of one of the pens, dragging her to the shearing board. Bob parted the thick fleece. It was so white next to the skin compared with the greyish overall colour of the sheep.

'See this line just above the skin? That's where the lanolin is rising. When you see that the sheep is ready to be clipped. If you try and do them before the rise, they are more difficult. It's called the yolk, because it's yellow, produced by the glands just under the skin. That's what gives the fleece its soft, greasy feel. It's the same lanolin that goes into soaps and creams to make your hands soft. Check round the tail of the sheep. If it's very dirty and soiled it needs to be dagged a few days before — clipping away the soiled wool with some hand shears. Right, Andy, if you start the machine, I'll show the ladies how it's done.'

Andy pulled a starting cord on the small petrol engine standing on a platform next to the board, and it whirred into life. Two long leads trailed from it, with clippers at the end. Bob turned the ewe so that her back rested against his legs and her head was turned across his left knee.

'Grip the sheep between your knees, fairly tightly, then she shouldn't struggle too much. Start down the neck and brisket, holding the skin away with one hand. Keep the skin taut all the time, or the sheep will get nicked.'

He made some long sweeping cuts down the ewe's neck and then across her right shoulder to the spine, working down her right side, then turned her across his leg, pushing the fleece under her as he did so.

'Now clip down the spine on the left side, keeping the strokes even. Avoid double cuts as that spoils the fleece. Finish off round the tail and inside the back leg. Make sure you don't cut the pizzle on a ram or the ewe's udder.'

The fleece fell away and lay in a soft white mass, the side next to the skin uppermost. Bob pushed the ewe to her feet. She stood still for a few seconds, then jumped away, surprised at her new lightness.

'Spread the fleece with the flesh side down, fold in the sides to the centre, then roll up from the tail end. Pull the neck wool and twist it, then roll round the fleece to secure it, and tuck it in. Herdwick and Rough Fell fleeces are rolled with the flesh side inside, but all other breeds are done like this.' He held up a perfectly rolled fleece. He had made it all look so easy. Now we had to try our hands at it.

I watched two of the other women making their first attempts at shearing. They both managed to finish their ewes, but the poor sheep were covered with cuts. Bob produced a tin of thick yellow paste and daubed them. They ran off, spotted like leopards.

Then it was my turn. Bob helped me to get the ewe into the right position and then handed me the clippers. They were surprisingly heavy.

'Now start here, that's right.' He guided my hand. 'Make longer strokes. Keep the skin pulled towards you with your left hand.'

I struggled with the ewe and the clippers, but was terrified of cutting the poor creature. Progress was slow. Bob was wonderfully patient with us all, let loose on his unsuspecting sheep. It was hot, back-aching work. By half-past twelve we were all thankful to have a break.

We had taken lunch with us, so we sat under a large oak tree and ate our sandwiches. Bob told us about his work. This was the busiest time of the year for him. As a contract shearer with Andy, they toured three counties, visiting farms from early morning to nightfall, and in six weeks sheared twenty thousand sheep. I was beginning to wonder if I should even be able to do two.

'The important thing is to do the sheep as quickly as you can. One woman spent a whole afternoon clipping a sheep with hand shears, and then it died an hour later. She'd kept it on its side too long. Sheep that are not handled very often sometimes die of fright, too. Their heart just gives up when you've got them under the clippers. I always have one or two die on me every year.'

It was all beginning to sound more and more alarming. We went back to work. I tried shearing again, but the sheep seemed very large and the clippers made my hand ache. Eventually we had sheared a small pen of sheep, and they grazed now in a small enclosure near us, their cuts and nicks all covered with yellow blobs.

'It's no good,' I said to Bob, 'I'm just hopeless. I don't think I'll ever be able to shear my own sheep.'

'Where do you live?' he asked.

'Near Castle Monkton. Do you know it? It's a small village near Fordington.'

'Yes. I go to Castle Monkton every summer to shear a small flock. Mrs Hall, she's got thirty Jacobs. Do you know her?'

'No, I haven't met her yet. We're out of the village, in a little hamlet called Monks Green.'

'Well, when I go to Mrs Hall I'll come on and do yours for you. I can't say when it will be. I'll have to phone you up the night before. That's how we work, it depends on the weather. How many sheep have you got to shear?'

'Only two, but I've got two lambs as well, so there'll be four next year. It seems an awful lot of bother for you for just two sheep.'

'That's all right, my dear. Don't you worry about them, we'll get them sheared for you.'

'That's very kind of you. I've been worrying about them for ages. I know I won't be able to do them very well.'

'Give me your telephone number and the address before you go. Now, ladies, would you like a tour of the park and the sheep?'

We piled into the back of his pick-up truck and set off down rough tracks across the parkland. It was divided by fencing and every now and again we stopped at a gate. Bob got out and opened the gate, then drove through. We took it in turns to close the gates, then jump back into the truck. Bob stopped in places and we all got out while he pointed out some of his best ewes and lambs to us. They all looked very healthy. The lambs had grown well and he was obviously very proud of his large flock.

'I've had the grazing here for eight years now. When I first came there were a lot of thistles, and the grass was much rougher. We cut some of the thistles, but the sheep have gradually improved the pasture. Sheep are good for cleaning up grazing. It gets evenly manured as they move across it, and with their close bite they slowly clear the weeds.'

We spent a pleasant hour in the park. It was a peaceful end to a very tiring day. The thought of shearing twenty thousand sheep every summer was incredible, but his tough outdoor life was one that he enjoyed and kept him healthy.

When it was time to go, I thanked Bob for our day's demonstrations and gave him my address and telephone number.

'Don't worry, I won't forget your two,' he said as I drove away.

I arrived home hot and exhausted. My shepherd's smock, smeared in mud and dung, now certainly looked authentic.

* * *

Katy and I sat in the garden drinking coffee, looking at the weekly local paper. It was a hot, still afternoon. The field across the lane from the cottage was sown with oilseed rape, now bright yellow with the flowers, and the scent from them drifted across the garden. The dogs were lying in the house in cool, dark corners, and Gilbert and Polly were sitting under the lilac bush, their heads tucked under their wings. Polly seemed to be fast asleep, but Gilbert had one bright beady eye showing, keeping a watch on everything that was going on.

Katy idly brushed her bare feet through the grass.

'I've got some awful essays to do for Monday,' she sighed. 'History and Geography and some flower drawings for art next week. I don't mind those — art's the only thing I enjoy. There aren't many flowers left in the garden, though — Pandora and Berkeley seem to have eaten most of them. I thought I might walk up the lane and pick some wild ones. Do you want to come?'

'Yes, lovely. When do you want to go? Now? Oh, listen to this. "For sale: three beehives with bees and all equipment." There's a phone number in Castle Monkton. What about getting some bees? I've always wanted to have bees. Grandpa used to keep them years ago, and he never got stung. If you like the bees they don't sting you. That's what he said. Just think of all that lovely honey we'd have.'

'Mother, not bees. You're crazy. We've got enough trouble with that horrible goose without being attacked by bees every time we sit in the garden. Come on, let's go for a walk and get the flowers.'

The lane that ran past the cottage had tall, straggly hedges each side. There were pale pink dog roses twined among the hazel and blackthorn bushes, and in one place cascades of wild honeysuckle. The roadside was lined with flowers — clovers, and vetches, bedstraw, buttercups, prunella and yarrow. Where the lane turned a corner and the road divided, one leading to Castle Monkton and the other going through wide wheat and barley fields past scattered farms to further villages, there was a large clump of beautiful white moon daisies. Katy picked some carefully, choosing her specimens with deliberation, to add to the honeysuckle. I was less fussy and picked some daisies to add to the bunch of red and white clovers, golden buttercups and yellow vetch.

We sat in the grass at the side of the road and picked the petals off a red clover, sucking the ends for the honey taste. No cars passed along the lane to spoil the quiet afternoon.

'Do you remember the holiday we had in Wiltshire,' said Katy, 'and that lovely walk we had over the downs where we found all those orchids?'

'Yes, and Tom had his arm in plaster after falling off his bike. Poor Tom, that was awful at the time, but it seems so long ago now.'

'Well, it was. He was only eight then. Next term I'm going to be in the sixth form — if I pass my exams,' she added. 'And then next year I'll be old enough to drive. I can't wait for that. Or to leave school, I really hate it. Especially the headmaster. He's so stuffy and prim. You know Philip and I are doing the school magazine? He called us into his study and said he thought some of the material was unsuitable. She laughed. 'Just because he didn't like some cartoons Philip had done of the teachers. There was one of Johnson in those awful check trousers he wears, and Miss Edwards in her tweeds and big ugly men's shoes.'

'Oh, I wish I'd seen them. Have you got any of the magazine material at home?'

'No, Philip's got it at the moment. But he's coming over tomorrow afternoon to do some more work on the magazine with me. We'll show you if you like.'

She was quiet for a few minutes, then she spoke again. 'Mother, are you and Father happy? I mean, sometimes I think perhaps you're not, really. Philip's parents always go out together at the weekends, but you and Father never go out.'

I sighed. 'Well, he never wants to go anywhere, except to all those archaeology meetings. Oh, Katy, I don't know. Nothing's perfect. I love living here. I've got everything I want — the house, the animals and you and Tom. I don't know what I'd do without you two. Come on, let's get back. Tom will be home soon and will wonder where we are.'

'You know you've always said you'd like to go and live in Wales or Scotland? Do you still want to?'

'Perhaps one day. But not now. Come on, let's go and have a cup of tea.'

While we sat at the table having supper we had our usual discussion about the day.

'There's an ad in the local paper for some bees,' I said.

'Did you phone about them?' asked Gerald. 'When we moved here you said you wanted to get some bees.'

'Well, no. I thought I should ask you first anyway.'

'That doesn't usually stop you. One of the lecturers at the college keeps bees. I could ask him to come and give us some advice to start us off. Where are they?'

'Only in Castle Monkton. Shall I find the paper?'

Katy groaned. 'Not bees as well as Gilbert.'

'We've got plenty of room here. They wouldn't have to be in the garden. We could keep the hives at the top of the meadow. The bees would probably spend most of their time in the fields anyway. There's all that oilseed rape over the road at the moment, just going to waste. The bees would love it. It would be so nice to have our own honey,' I said.

'I'll phone up,' said Gerald, 'but they've probably gone by now.'

'I do hope so,' said Katy.

The bees were still for sale, so after supper Gerald and I drove to the village. The house was at the end of a lane turning off the main high street. We stopped at the gate. It was a large Victorian house surrounded by a tall privet hedge and an overgrown garden. A smiling woman came to the door and led us to the back of the house where the beehives stood among long grass under a plum tree.

'I bought the bees for my son, last summer,' she said, 'but he's started work now, so he doesn't have so much time. There are bee gloves, and a hat and a smoker, and some spare combs. Have you got bees?'

'No,' said Gerald, 'but my wife's always talked about getting some.'

'My grandfather used to keep them,' I explained, 'but a long time ago.'

'My son looks at them once a week during the summer,' she continued. 'You have to make sure that they're not hatching out lots of queens. That's when they swarm.'

We watched the bees coming out and entering the hive, such busy, industrious workers. They hummed gently round the lupins and columbines near us.

'Well, what do you think?' said Gerald turning to me.

'It would be fun to have them. But how are we going to get them home? We can't just put them in the car.'

'I could have a word with Ted tomorrow. He's got an estate car and he takes his beehives round to different places during the summer, to orchards to help with pollinating.' He turned back to the woman. 'Could I pay for them now, and come and collect them at the weekend with a friend?'

'Yes, of course. I'll give you the rest of the things now to take with you.'

We followed her back to the house and collected the bee hat and long white gloves, spare combs and a curious metal object looking like an over-large oil can. That, she said, was the smoker.

Ted came over the following evening. He was a genial man in his early fifties, with greying curly hair and a beard. He got out of his car, holding a large brown wide-brimmed hat covered with netting, and a pair of long stout gloves. He and Gerald drove away down the lane and returned half an hour later with three beehives in the back of his car, tied round with string.

They carried the beehives one at a time to the top of the meadow and set them down under the oak tree. Katy, Tom and I followed. The three white hives looked nostalgically rural sitting there in the grass, a symbol of summers of long ago, when life was unhurried and people had time for such country pursuits and pleasures. Ted untied the string, but left the bee-hives closed up for the night.

'I'll come over tomorrow afternoon, and we'll open them up and I'll show you what you'll have to do with them. I've been keeping bees for twenty-five years now. So long as you remember the basic rules they're very easy.'

The following afternoon Ted returned with his wife, Mary. She was a short, fair-haired woman who taught in an infant school. She and Ted had never had any children of their own, and I thought it rather sad that she had devoted her life to looking after other people's. But she was full of fun and interested in everything. She was delighted with Rupert and Adam and amazed by all the sheep when they ran up to her to take some biscuits from her hand.

Gerald and I dressed ourselves up, ready to confront the bees. We had one bee hat and I had made another by sewing net curtain material onto a wide-brimmed straw hat.

'Always keep your arms covered,' said Ted, 'and your legs.'

I put on my shepherd's smock, with its long sleeves, over a pair of jeans, then with our hats and gloves we set off to the top of the meadow. Tom and Katy wanted to come and watch, but I told them to wait in the garden. Once we had got the idea of looking after the bees, I would let them help with them too, but to start with I thought it better if they kept at a distance. Katy seemed quite enthusiastic about them now that they had actually arrived.

Tom and Katy stood by the gate into the meadow, but Mary stayed in the house, watching us out of the back window. I saw her shut the window as we walked away, and wondered why. Ted opened the bottom panel on each of the hives. There was a sound of angry buzzing from inside. I waited eagerly for the bees to appear. Suddenly they came out, first one, then three more and then lots of them, crawling onto the landing platform and then taking to the air. They buzzed round the hive in some agitation and flew at our faces. I was thankful that we had our hats, and moved back several paces nearer the hedge.

Ted lifted the cover off one of the hives to reveal a dark, seething mass. He lifted the frames out, one by one. The bees were building them up and furious at having their homes

disturbed. Ted stuffed some paper into the smoker, lit the end, and then gave some puffs into the hive. The buzzing subsided a little.

'The smoke makes them drowsy, so use the smoker when you come to remove the frames and put in new ones. The trouble is, the smoke also makes them angry.'

That was obvious. The buzzing from deep down inside the hive was getting louder. Ted replaced the cover and moved to the next hive. He inspected each hive in turn.

'If you watch them, you'll see some of the bees leaving the landing board and flying off in a straight line, while the others just stay buzzing round the hive. Those are the scouts, going out to look for pollen. They'll come back and report to the hive and then more of them will go out to collect it. With all these fields round here you should have some good honey from them. Don't forget about the spraying, though. If you tell the local farmers you've got bees they should let you know before they spray. You'll need to keep the hives shut for three days afterwards, otherwise the bees will die.'

We stood and watched them, gloating over our latest acquisition. The bees did not seem very friendly and kept making determined attacks at our faces which, luckily, were covered by the netting.

'They'll calm down. It's just moving them that has made them restless,' said Ted reassuringly.

'How many bees do you think there are?' I asked him.

'The average hive has sixty thousand bees in it. Some hives have even more, but when they get overcrowded they start to hatch out more queens and then some of the workers leave with a new queen to find another hive. That's when you get a swarm. You can build up your stock like that. You want to get another empty beehive, so that you'll have somewhere to put them when they do swarm.'

We went back to the house. Mary was still peering worriedly through the kitchen window.

'I never go near the bees when Ted's looking at them,' she said when we went inside. 'They swarmed one day and got into the chicken run and killed half the chickens. Poor things were lying dead all over the place.'

'Mary's not too fond of the bees, I'm afraid,' said Ted.

We had tea round the large pine table and then I took Mary into the sitting room to show her my spinning wheel, while Gerald and Ted pored over the finds from the local archaeology dig. I found some fleece and Mary tried her hand at spinning.

'I did some years ago at teacher training college,' she said, 'and really enjoyed it. I've always meant to take it up again, but never got round to it.'

'You could do some with the children with simple hand spindles. Just a pencil and a piece of plasticine or a slice of potato on the end. I've been to some of the local schools and even the youngest ones can usually do a bit. The boys are always better at it than the girls, though. I'll show you, it's very easy.'

When they left I gave Mary a bag of fleece and she promised to try some spinning with her classes. 'I have enjoyed the afternoon,' she said, 'and I loved meeting your sheep.'

When they had gone we all went back to the meadow to look at our new beehives. The buzzing from inside seemed to have quietened; there was now just a gentle peaceful humming and a small cloud of bees round the top of each hive. We stood near the hedge a few yards away watching them. Suddenly a bee flew straight from the hive towards us, getting into my hair, followed by several more. I shook my head. Tom and Katy backed away hastily. The bees seemed to be getting angry again. I like bees, I kept thinking, but the bees didn't seem to like us.

Next morning was another beautiful cloudless day. We had breakfast in the garden, and then sat on the bench under the kitchen window reading the Sunday papers.

'Shall we go and see what the bees are doing?' I asked Gerald.

'All right, but I think we had better put on the hats and gloves. Just in case, until we get used to them.'

We dressed ourselves up again and marched up to the top of the meadow. Pandora and Berkeley and the lambs were grazing near the apple tree and Pandora looked at us in surprise in our ridiculous outfits. I waved my hands at them to discourage them from following us and they backed away. The scouts were obviously on the look-out for people as well as pollen, and when we were within fifteen feet of the hives, bees came flying out angrily, straight at our faces. Gerald lifted the top off one of the hives, and the bees buzzed and fumed and crawled on his gloves, while some of them flew at the netting on our faces. He soon replaced the top.

'I remember when I was in Nigeria, someone was killed by some bees,' I said. 'They found him dead in a cave, and when they did a post mortem his lungs were full of bees.'

'Bees in Africa are different,' said Gerald.

'They were wild bees and much bigger than these. But you never know. These seem to be distinctly unfriendly.'

'These are only honey bees. They always get a bit excited when their hives are inspected,' said Gerald.

'They seem to be into aerial warfare, not making honey,' I said. 'Perhaps it wasn't a good idea to get them.'

'It's a bit late to think of that now,' he replied.

'But suppose they swarm on the chickens, like Mary was saying, or the sheep? I couldn't bear it if the bees killed one of the sheep.'

'I thought you wanted to have bees.'

'But their one idea seems to be to attack people.'

'Did you know that bee stings are supposed to be good for arthritis? Lots of people with it get themselves stung on purpose.'

'Well, I haven't got arthritis,' I said.

We returned to the garden and no one mentioned the bees for the rest of the day. I went upstairs several times to check on the sheep from the bedroom window. They had stayed in the lower half of the field all day, well away from the hives. Perhaps they knew something that we didn't. There sat the hives at the top of the meadow, like three white time bombs. I was quickly going off the idea of bee-keeping.

Next morning, after the children had been trundled away by the school bus and Gerald had left for the college, I dressed up in the bee outfit and decided that if we were going to keep bees I would just have to get used to them, and the sooner the better. As before they flew towards me angrily as I approached. They settled on my sleeves and the netting over my face, buzzing furiously. Undeterred, I lifted the cover off one of the hives. A great angry sound swelled up inside the hive. I put the top back quickly.

'I think the bees should go,' I said to Gerald when he came home. 'I'm sure they're killer bees up there, not honey bees. No wonder that poor boy wanted to get rid of them. I'm just surprised he kept them as long as he did.'

'When Ted and I went to collect them, the woman said that someone had phoned after us, who seemed desperate to have the bees. Apparently he had a pollinating contract with some fruit farms, and took the bees round to the different orchards. She said he had lost several hives last winter and urgently needed more. She might have taken his telephone number. I could give her a ring, I suppose, and see. If not we'll just have to advertise them in the paper.'

Yes, the woman remembered us of course, and had taken the man's phone number. She had it somewhere if Gerald would hold on. He scribbled it down on the back of an envelope.

'Well, that's a bit of luck,' he said. 'I'd better phone him up and see if he still wants them.'

An hour later a large estate car turned into the drive. A tall red-haired man got out, wearing corduroy trousers and an open-neck checked shirt with the sleeves rolled up to his elbows. Gerald found a bee hat and some gloves and together they went to the field. I followed, intrigued by this stranger who was prepared to face our killer bees without any protective clothing.

'I've been with bees all my life,' he said to Gerald as they walked up the field. 'My father used to keep them and his father before him. I've got twenty hives at the moment, but I urgently need more for the contracts I've got. I've got my name down at the local police station, so they always give me a call if there's a swarm in the area. I've started off several hives this year like that. I went to one last week in a local school. The bees had settled on a bench in the school playground.'

'How do you catch a swarm?' I asked.

'Easy. Just take a cardboard box along, and knock the bees into that. Then take them home and put them in a spare hive.'

'We were told about a swarm that killed some chickens,' I went on.

'There was a swarm near us a few weeks ago that got on a horse and stung it badly. It was in a terrible state and quite hysterical. The vet had to pump it full of antihistamines and tranquillisers. Bees and animals don't mix,' he said. 'Bees dislike animal smells. It makes them agitated.'

The hives were carried down to his car one at a time and stowed in the back. He waved cheerfully as he drove away, several loose bees buzzing about in the car.

That evening I thought about the poor horse swarmed on by bees. It must have been terrified. I thought then how easily it might have been one of my sheep. 'Bees and animals don't mix,' the red-haired stranger had said. So that was the end of our bee-keeping attempts.

# CHAPTER FIVE

One morning I had a telephone call from David. He said he was going to Fordington to look at a ram and wondered if he could call in for a cup of coffee on the way back.

I was sitting on the doorstep reading the paper when he arrived. The dogs ran down to the gate, barking. I followed them and opened the gate so that David could drive in.

'Did you find it all right?' I asked as he got out of the car. 'You didn't get lost?'

'Not a lot. I was all right until I got to that turning about a mile down the road — the one without a signpost. There was an old man on a bicycle and when I asked him the way to Monks Green, he said he'd never heard of it. So I went the other way. Then I came back to Castle Monkton and started again. I passed the old chap a second time. He must have come past here.'

'Henry was barking at someone on a bicycle a little while ago. I expect that was him.'

David laughed. 'Silly old fool. Never mind, let's have that coffee, then you can show me the sheep.'

He followed me up the steps and into the house.

'Did you go to the shearing classes?' he asked as I made some coffee.

'Yes, but I was hopeless. There were six of us at the class and by the end the sheep that we had been shearing were all spotted with yellow where they'd been cut and daubed with ointment. It was awful. That was the worst part of it. I was so afraid of cutting the sheep.'

'They heal up quickly. You have to start on something, otherwise you never learn.'

'Anyway, the chap who was taking the class said he goes to a small flock in Castle Monkton, so he'll come and shear mine afterwards.'

'Who was taking the class? Was it Bob Holden?'

'Yes, do you know him?'

'He and Andy come and shear mine. He's a good man. He goes to lots of small flocks in between the big ones. He'll fit everyone in. When he comes to me I'll ask him if he's clipped two ewes belonging to a very strange vegetarian lady who keeps her sheep as pets.' He laughed. 'How's that lamb?'

'Rupert's wonderful. He's grown quite a lot and he's so friendly. Pandora's always been a bit wary of strangers, but Rupert will talk to anyone. I got another lamb the week after from a lamb's orphanage at Bennington. He's not a bit like Rupert, though. He was getting very aggressive at one time, butting the chairs and the dogs, but he's calmed down now.'

'You can never tell with wethers, especially if they're bottle-fed. A lot depends on the breed. Ryelands are soft. I take my old rams to shows and the kids climb on their backs. But some rams need a stick to them. Wiltshire Horns are the worst. I saw a Wiltshire ram floor three large men at a sale once. The breeds with horns are always more aggressive. The horns are weapons and they know it. What breed is he?'

'He's a Finnish Dorset cross.'

'Dorset Down or Dorset Horn?'

'Dorset Horn, I presumed. He's got a pink nose and he's getting some horns.'

'Well, just watch him. You have to let them know who's boss. Come on, you can show me your flock.'

'Does four count as a flock?'

'Of course.'

I put some biscuits into my pocket. The sheep were all at the top of the meadow but when I called them they came running down happily, swinging their tails and skipping through the clover and the long grass. The grass had grown considerably this second year and reached nearly to the top of Rupert's and Adam's backs. David pressed his hand along their spines.

'They're all fat,' he announced. 'None of them would grade.'

'But they're not going to market. Do you think Rupert looks well?'

'Yes, very. For a little runt he's not doing badly.'

We walked about in the meadow through the long grass and clover flowers.

'You want to get this cut,' said David, 'you'd get some hay off it. The sheep don't like it too long anyway. You'll find they'll make short patches in it and keep going back to those.'

'Yes, they have. There are little islands of short grass dotted about and they keep nibbling at those and leaving the rest.'

'In Kent, they say that the sheep like the grass that has grown the night before.'

A few evenings later Bob Holden telephoned. He said he would be going to shear Mrs Hall's sheep the next day and would come on and do Pandora and Berkeley afterwards. I gave him directions to Monks Green from the village, remembering the unsignposted turning that had confused David.

I worried all day about the shearing. I always felt it was a sheep's misfortune to grow wool, and much as I liked the soft bundles of fleece to spin, I was always glad when the sheep had returned to their woolly winter state. Shorn bare, they looked sad and thin. I remembered that Bob had told me that sheep sometimes died of fright when they were being sheared. At least Pandora and Berkeley were used to being handled. When the school bus stopped at the gate, they were still in their beautiful winter coats, sitting near the apple tree chewing their cud.

'Have they been to shear Pandora?' asked Katy as they came in through the open door.

'No, not yet. It just depends how they've been getting on with the other flocks. They may not be here until quite late.'

'Oh, good,' said Tom, 'we can watch. Can I go up on my bike to Alex and tell him? He'd like to see them sheared, too.'

'Yes, of course. Don't be long. Do you want your tea now or when you come back?'

'When I come back, thanks.' He dumped his bag of school books on the table, went to the barn for his bike and disappeared along the lane. He and Alex were soon back. We all sat on the doorstep drinking mugs of tea. Then I heard the sound of a car coming along the lane. Bob's red truck stopped at the gate. The dogs rushed down barking and sending the gravel flying with their feet.

'Quick, boys, can you shut the dogs inside?' They dragged the hounds away, protesting, and shut them into the sitting room.

They drove in and stopped in front of the barn. Bob and Andy and Bob's son, John, got out of the truck.

'Hello, it is good of you to come just for two of them. Have you had a very busy day? Would you like a cup of tea? Or a beer?'

'Cup of tea would be much appreciated,' answered Bob. 'Where do you want them clipped?'

'Wherever it's easiest for you. What about on the lawn at the bottom of the steps?'

'That looks all right to me. Right, Andy, let's get the gear set up.' Andy backed the truck nearer the house and they lifted out the shearing machine and set it up at the bottom of the steps while I made them some tea. Then I went to the meadow to fetch Pandora and Berkeley. They were standing by the gate with the lambs, peering over it with interest having heard the commotion from the dogs. Visitors usually meant extra biscuits and Berkeley was licking her black lips in anticipation. I opened the gate, took hold of Berkeley's collar and led her round to the front of the house. The others followed. Katy, Tom and Alex were sitting on the doorstep waiting for the shearing to begin.

I led Berkeley up to the steps and Andy took hold of her collar, then with a quick, effortless movement had her on her

back and resting against his legs. Bob started the machine and the clippers began peeling away the thick brown fleece. It spread out round her in a large soft pile. As a lamb she had been completely black, and as her fleece had grown, the tips of it had faded in the sun, so that she had turned into a golden-brown sheep; now, with the wool being stripped away, she was completely black again. Andy turned her across his knee, sheared down her left side, then pushed her to her feet. It had taken him three minutes, and there were no ugly cuts or scratches. She stood still for a minute, looking surprised, and then gazed at us all in turn.

Pandora had been watching from the corner of the house and now disappeared to the back lawn. I ran after her and brought her back to the steps for her turn. Her fleece had changed from black and white spots as a lamb to brown and white patches, shaggy like an Afghan rug. But as her wool, too, was stripped away, the black and white spots came back. Her tail without its wool was long and stringy. She was soon finished and I refastened her collar. She bleated at us, looking so changed — like a dalmatian with horns. Her fleece lay on the grass, the side that had been next to her skin uppermost. It was amazingly soft, and glistened in the sun from the oil in it, like silken cobwebs.

'This is a good fleece,' said Bob, rolling it up, 'I should think it weighs about eight pounds. That's heavy for a Jacob. Did you say you brought her up on a bottle? You've done well with her. She's a good ewe.'

Rupert and Adam trotted up and began sniffing at the rolled-up wool.

Bob laughed. 'You've got two lambs as well. They're not from these ewes, are they? Their udders looked dry.'

He was a very observant shepherd.

'No, they're bottle lambs as well. Two little wethers.'

Bob pointed to Rupert. 'What breed is that one? It's not one of those Ryelands, is it?'

'Yes. He came from David Roberts at Coney Green near Wetherbury.'

'We're going to David next week. Those blooming sheep of his — they've got wool everywhere. The ewes even have wool on their udders.'

We all laughed. Katy, Tom and Alex were enjoying this.

'I could tell you some stories,' he went on. 'One woman we went to bought three sheep at a market, then put them in with a ram — found out they were all wethers. Forgot to look underneath them first. Another woman was in a real panic because she thought all her sheep's top teeth had dropped out. Seems she didn't know they don't have top teeth anyway. Well, you live and learn, but some folk don't seem to learn an awful lot.'

They began packing away the machine, and loaded it into the back of the truck. I offered them another cup of tea.

'No, thank you kindly. We'd best be going. We've got forty to clip in the next village and then a few odd ones on the way home.'

'Thank you very much for doing them. Could you come and shear them for me next year? There'll be four of them then, including the woolly one.'

He smiled. 'I expect so. We'll see you next year, about the same time.'

They drove away down the lane, waving their arms out of the windows.

I found some biscuits for the sheep and we took them back to the meadow. Pandora stood by the gate, bleating forlornly. Rupert and Adam sniffed at her bare sides.

'Poor Pandora, she looks so strange without her wool,' I said. 'I expect she feels cold, too.'

Katy ran her hand over Berkeley's wide back.

'She feels just like bus seats,' she said.

After supper Gerald went to inspect the newly shorn sheep.

'I'm surprised how much the grass has grown up this year,' he said, as we walked about in the meadow. 'They don't seem to be eating it very fast.'

'They'll never eat all this. It's too long for them now anyway.

We could get it cut, and then we'd have some hay for the winter.'

'Yes, that's an idea. I might go up to the farm sometime and see if they could do it for us.' The farm to which he referred was our nearest neighbour, four fields away.

A few days later a tractor appeared at the gate with a hay cutter attached to the back. Getting through the farm gate at the end of the drive was easy, but the gate into the meadow, being only three feet wide, presented more of a problem. The post to which the gate fastened was a fencing stake at the end of the wire. Tom and Katy were home for half term and Tom had come out into the garden at the sound of the tractor. Together, with the help of the driver, we pulled out the post and pulled it, with the wire, back towards the hedge. Tom and I took the sheep to the barn, and then went back to the field to watch the mowing.

The tractor went round the edge of the field, leaving wide bands of grass lying in its wake. A skylark was singing high above us. The smell of the mown grass drifted sweetly on the air. As the tractor went round and round the field in ever-decreasing circles I saw that the skylark was now fluttering in great agitation over the field, flying after the tractor and then returning to hover a few feet above the grass still uncut.

'Oh, my God, Tom! Look at that skylark. She must have a nest in the grass. Come on, we've got to find it or the babies will be mown to pieces.'

We ran into the middle of the field and began hunting frantically. I found the first baby just on the edge of the last band that had been cut. It was not hurt, and tried to scuttle away. I picked it up and held my skirt at the hem, putting the baby bird into it. I called to Tom, and he ran across to join me. We soon found another baby skylark nearby. The mother bird was now getting frantic. She kept fluttering above us and then dropping down into the grass a good distance away, then rising again to repeat the performance. We hunted through the long grass stems.

'I've found another,' said Tom triumphantly, carefully picking

it up and putting it into my skirt with the others. The mower
came round again. The square of grass left to cut was rapidly
getting smaller. Tom ran across to the tractor and signalled to
the driver. He stopped and waited while we carried on search-
ing. There was only a narrow strip of grass left uncut now. We
hunted through it but found nothing.

'Perhaps there aren't any more,' I said to Tom, 'but we must
make sure.' I was afraid of finding one of the babies mangled
up by the mower, but we searched among the piles of grass
that had already been cut. Then I saw something small and
brown fluttering about a few feet away. Tom picked it up and
put it into my skirt with the other three. It was quite unhurt.
They nestled together — soft brown shapes, already with tiny
wings properly feathered, but still too small to fly. The mother
bird soared up into the sky and began singing above us as if
she knew that we had saved her babies.

The mower came round again and then down the last strip
of grass, and back to the gateway. The driver stopped and got
out. Tom and I walked up the field and carefully put the little
baby skylarks down in the middle. I looked up and saw the
mother bird watching us. Then we went back to the gate. Katy
had appeared at the gateway.

'Mother, what were you and Tom doing, running about in
the field like that?'

'There were some baby skylarks in the grass. We picked them
up to save them from the mower. Look, there's the mother.' We
saw her drop down into the grass where we had left the babies.
'I hope they'll be all right,' I said anxiously, 'they were so
beautiful.'

The tractor driver seemed amused. He was laughing and
shaking his head. There was no room for sentiment in farming.
'She'll find them all right, don't you worry,' he said.

When he had gone we pushed the gatepost back into the
ground and stood by the apple tree looking at the bands of
mown grass lying all over the field. Up above us a skylark was
singing and soaring, pouring out her sweet song. 'The bird of

Heaven,' Blake had called the skylark, and I had held one in my hand.

The hot dry weather continued. Every morning I went and raked and turned the hay. It was very time-consuming, working across two acres, but very satisfying. The skylark soared and sang above me, crickets were chirping in the hedge at the edge of the field and greenfinches sang 'chee-ree' from the wild cherry trees. There was no human sound at all. The sheep wandered about, grazing along the strips between the mounds of hay. I found several mouse nests — carefully made domes of grass full of squirming brown babies — and worked round them, trying to disturb them as little as possible. In one nest the babies were nearly fully grown and they scampered away and scattered into the grass.

The cats dozed in the sweet-smelling hay near the apple tree, watching me through half-closed eyes, idly washing themselves. Barrington stretched out in the sun, warming her old bones and poor battered body. When we had found the cats, left behind at the house by the previous owners, I had thought she was a mangy old tom. Her fur was ragged, her backbone sticking up in a ridge. We had started feeding them all and gradually they had filled out, their fur becoming glossy and sleek. Then Barrington had surprised us all by having some kittens. Now

those kittens were fully grown cats and they dozed lazily near her, waiting for supper time.

We spent the weekend making the hay into large mounds and tying it round with twine. Tom and Katy helped, propping the bundles on end against each other, like very primitive corn stooks. By the end of the day the field was covered with little green pyramids.

Dark clouds began to gather on the horizon along the line of hills that we could see from the top of the meadow — the East Anglian Heights. They piled up into threatening mounds. I thought I heard the sound of distant thunder.

'Oh, no,' I said to Gerald. 'I'm sure there's going to be a storm tonight, just when the hay is ready to go in. What are we going to do?'

'We'd better start getting as much of it in as we can. We'll stack it in the barn in the far corner, away from the sheep, or Berkeley will help herself, and when the winter comes there won't be much left.'

We were all tired and aching after our hard day, but we began carrying the mounds to the barn, two at a time. The barn filled up. Gerald stacked the bundles carefully in rows and eventually we had half the field cleared. But by then it was getting dark and the air was beginning to feel damp.

'The dew's falling — we'll have to leave the rest till tomorrow and hope that the storm misses us,' he said. The sheep were already in their pen and had been very interested in the comings and goings. Gilbert and Polly stood in the barn doorway, so I shooed them into their house and shut them in, then went back to the field to close the henhouse. As I walked round the house a few large, heavy drops of rain splashed onto the path as if in warning, and then stopped. The rumble of thunder came nearer.

When we went to bed there was still no rain, but the thunder grumbled on in the distance. In the morning the sun shone across the meadow in a golden haze, the skylark was singing high above, and the green pyramids of hay stood dry and green, waiting to be collected. I let all the animals out, and Katy and

I made some toast and coffee and piled it onto a large tray with some yoghourt. We took our breakfast into the meadow and sat in the sun. It was like being on holiday.

*　*　*

The following week we were sitting round the pine table having lunch. My sister Meg was visiting us. She had married, and divorced some years ago, a rather eccentric musician who now lived in France. Her children were away, spending their summer holiday with him in his cottage, south of Paris.

'Happy birthday,' she said, raising her glass of wine to me. 'What does it feel like to be forty?' She was several years younger than I.

'Happy birthday, Mother,' said Tom and Katy together.

Gerald smiled and raised his glass. He already knew. 'Happy birthday,' he said.

'Thank you, everyone,' I answered. 'It feels pretty good at the moment. I think I'm going to like it. I'm much happier now than when I was twenty. I certainly wouldn't want to go back.'

'Here's to fame and fortune,' said Meg.

'Wait till I'm rich and famous,' I said, and they all laughed. It was something of a family joke. 'Wait till you see the sheep on television. They're going to be famous as well.'

'What are you going to do that's different so you can remember this birthday?' Meg asked.

'I shall sleep in the barn with the sheep tonight,' I answered, 'that will be different.'

Meg laughed. 'Oh, God, you're crazy, Liz,' she said.

Gerald looked unamused. 'That's a stupid idea,' he said.

'But she's only joking, Gerald,' said Meg. 'She's just pulling your leg.'

'No. I think it's a good idea. Yes, that's what I'm going to do.'

'What fun,' said Tom, 'we could all sleep in the barn.'

'No thanks,' said Katy, 'there might be rats.'

77

'Let's have some more wine, Dad,' said Tom, holding out his glass.

'Not too much for you, young man,' said Gerald, but he refilled all our glasses.

Just then the telephone rang and I got up to answer it. 'Hi, Sis, Happy birthday,' said a man's voice.

'Rodney! It's lovely to hear you. How are you? and how's Melissa?'

'We're fine. Are you having a good day? We miss you lots. Melissa sends her love. I may be over next month. I might have to see some people in London about our new wells. I'll be down to see you if I do.'

'How's the job going?' Rodney was an exploration geologist in Texas.

'It's great at the moment. I've got my own helicopter now to visit the sites. We've got a new site at Graham, that's about a hundred miles west of Dallas. I've been up there all week, just got back last night. But tell me what you're doing.'

'Meg's here at the moment. We're just having lunch with lots of wine. I sold a piece about Berkeley to a magazine. I'll send you a copy when it's out.' Berkeley had been named after an oil company, Berkeley Exploration, tipped by Rodney for a successful future. 'I'm still doing the shawls for the shop in Chelsea. And the sheep got sheared last week, and poor Pandora looks awful — quite unrecognisable. I've got an idea for a book about the sheep. I've been doing some odd scribbles.'

'That's great. You sound terrific. It's so good to talk to you. You sound so English.'

'I can't believe you're so far away. I do miss you. I wish you'd come back to England.'

'We'll be back one day, I promise. I'll come and buy a Norfolk farmhouse.'

'What's the time over there?'

'Seven. We just got up. How are the kids? How's Gerald, and Meg?'

'They're all well. Do you want a quick word with Meg?'

'OK. Have a great day, won't you? Take care and I'll see you soon. Give my love to the kids.'

'I will. Thanks for phoning, miss you lots, love you lots, here's Meg.'

I gave the phone to Meg.

'How's Uncle Rodney?' asked Katy, as I sat down at the table again.

'He sends his love to you and Tom. He said he might have to come to London next month to see about some new wells, so he'll come and see us if he does.'

'Oh, great,' said Tom. 'How about some more wine?'

'You've had quite enough for one day, young man,' said Gerald.

'I do miss Rodney,' I said with a sigh. 'I wish he wasn't so far away.'

'Cheer up, Mother, it's your birthday,' said Katy. 'He won't stay in America for ever, I'm sure. He'll be back one day, you'll see.'

'Rodney sounds all right,' said Meg as she returned to the table. 'It seems strange to think of him eight thousand miles away. It's just like talking to him when he was in Bracknell.'

'Work's going well for him, anyway. Come on, eat up, there's lots of food. Let's go for a walk afterwards up the lane.' I refilled Meg's and Katy's glasses and my own. 'We could take the sheep with us.'

'No, Mother. I know it's your birthday, but we can't take all of them as well as the dogs,' said Katy.

'Meg's here, she can take some leads.'

'Thanks very much,' said Meg. 'Well, I'm not taking any of those horrible hounds.' Meg was not fond of dogs. 'I suppose the lambs would be all right as they don't bite.'

We set off later, a strangely assorted group. Gerald had Henry and Berkeley on leads, Katy had Sophie, Tom took Wolf, I had Pandora and Adam, and Meg took little Rupert.

'I'm really not sure about this,' she said. 'I never thought I'd be walking down the road with a sheep on a lead.'

The sheep trotted along obediently, much better behaved

than the dogs who strained and tugged and choked at their leads. Berkeley stopped to nibble at some flowers in passing, so we all stopped, and the other sheep began eating by the side of the road. Katy, Meg and I sat down in the grass and watched them.

'Do you remember our day trips to Wales last year?' I said to them.

'How could I forget them,' replied Meg, 'especially the one where you went climbing over those cliffs at Tewkesbury looking for woad, and nearly broke your neck.'

'I didn't tell you, but the week after, I found a nursery at Fordington that sells woad plants.'

We fell about in the grass laughing.

'Gerald said there'd be a nursery that sold it,' said Meg. 'He was right after all.'

'Still, it was fun going to look for it.'

'Yes it was,' she agreed, 'but you're utterly mad, you know. How does Gerald put up with you?'

Later, at bedtime, Gerald saw me coming downstairs dressed in jeans and a thick jersey.

'You're surely not serious?' he asked.

'Yes. I'm going to sleep in the barn to make this birthday different. Being forty is supposed to be a memorable occasion.' I went out to join the sheep. Pandora and Berkeley were still chewing their cud, but Adam and Rupert were lying with their heads down and eyes shut and appeared to be fast asleep. I pulled the heavy barn doors shut behind me and then went into their pen with them. Adam and Rupert raised their heads.

The warm darkness of the barn was filled with the scent of the hay we had gathered and the steady breathing of the sheep. I lay down against Adam. He put his head down again and in what seemed like only a few seconds he was back to sleep. I was sure he was asleep, because his breathing became slower and deeper and he kept twitching as if he were dreaming. There were strange rustling noises from the corners of the barn. I wondered if there were rats in here as Katy had suggested. Gilbert and Polly, in the little house near the sheep pen, were very quiet, and I imagined them both sitting in their straw with their heads tucked into their wings.

It was warm and comfortable in the straw and I went to sleep and dreamed that I was standing on a hillside covered with heather and cotton grass, surrounded by sheep, and looking out over a wide bay with sparkling silver sea.

# CHAPTER SIX

By the following summer Adam had turned into the proverbial cuckoo — big, bold and greedy. He was taller than Pandora, and at least as heavy as, if not heavier than Berkeley. His horns had not grown very long, but they curved forwards round his ears and he knew how to use them to their best advantage: flicking his head sideways with a deft movement that always caught me unawares and left my legs covered in small round bruises, the size of a ten pence piece.

'Beware of the wether' on the gate would not have come amiss, but might have looked rather ridiculous. Our Phil Collins look-alike paper man, who already thought we were a little odd, would probably have thought that I was complaining about the torrential downpours that filled the lane in winter, and shaken his head at my spelling.

By contrast Rupert was a model of good behaviour. He was small and docile and easy to manage. I could turn him easily to trim his feet, but had a struggle with the others, although I was learning.

Bob and Andy came to shear them again as they had promised. Afterwards they all stood in the field near the gate, complaining loudly and staring at each other. If I had been surprised by the difference in Pandora and Berkeley after their first shearing, Rupert was the biggest surprise. I had never seen his face without all the woolly curls, which almost hid his eyes. Adam gained large pink rolls of fat on his neck, like old men who have lunched too well on expense accounts.

David, casting his eye over some newly shorn ewes, had said, 'That's how I like to see them — you can tell what a sheep's really like.' I, however, could not wait for their wool to start growing again. Rupert's and Adam's fleeces were beautifully soft and the side that had been next to their skin was as white as the wild cherry blossom.

We had divided the meadow into two paddocks, and with four grown sheep this year, the grass had not grown up sufficiently to have it tractor mown. Gerald and I had cut some at the top of the field by scythe, but it was a back-breaking task. The old farmer nearby had given us some advice on scything:

'The best thing to do with a scythe is hang it in an apple tree,' he laughed, 'and leave it there.'

The obvious answer to the over-abundance of grass was more sheep. I was turning it over in my mind.

Katy and I decided to go to the Royal Show at Stoneleigh, so we left early one morning about half-past six. It was a clear, bright morning and the roads were very quiet. It was a good feeling to be out at that time while so many people were still asleep, and we were looking forward to the day. The Royal Show was the place to go and see sheep: nearly every breed would be represented. I was interested in seeing some of the mountain breeds, especially the Herdwicks. Their fleeces ranged from brown to slate grey, purple grey and almost white. The lambs were born black, but changed to grey-brown with white faces by shearing time, and then their fleeces became paler every year, so that a very old Herdwick might be completely white. I was hoping that I might be able to meet some Herdwick breeders to buy a fleece or even get a bottle lamb the following spring.

We arrived at the showground in Warwickshire by half-past eight. The queues of cars were already building up as we inched along the last mile and a half and finally drove into the large grass field roped round as a car park. I bought a programme at the gate and we studied the map of the showground, then made in the direction of the sheep lines. The sheep were all penned under large, open stands. We wandered past the pens, looking at rows of well-trimmed sheep, some of the pens pinned with rosettes from the previous day's successes.

We saw David talking to a large bearded man whom Katy later christened Neptune. He waved and called out and came up to us. David loved the shows — the atmosphere, the friendly competition, and the chance to meet up with old friends. He was smiling broadly.

'Hello,' he said, 'is this the lovely Katy? You've come just in time for breakfast. Come along, back to my van, and I'll cook you something.'

David took his sheep round to the shows in a large van, which on arrival was swept out when the sheep had been penned, then fitted with straw bales along each side, a small gas cooker, boxes of food and bottles of whisky.

'Right, drink first, while I get the food cooked.' He poured out three glasses of whisky, handing Katy and me one each. 'Will a fried egg sandwich do?' he asked. 'It's no good offering you two bacon and eggs.'

'Can I do anything useful?' I asked.

'No, you sit down and have your drink. I'm glad you've brought Katy. She brightens the place up. We had a great time last night, you should have been here — had a barbecue with some of the boys.'

Three men appeared and stood on the van's ramp.

'Come on in,' said David, 'help yourselves.' He indicated the bottle on one of the bales. A sandy-haired man sat down next to me, the other two sat one each side of Katy. More people appeared. There was a great deal of laughter and friendly banter.

'Poor old Jim, have you seen his ram? It's gone lame on him, just when he was hoping to win the championship.'

'My ewes are scouring badly this morning. I've been pouring stuff down their throats.'

'You want to get yourself some decent sheep.'

'Anyone seen Ray this morning?'

'I shouldn't think he can stand up after last night.'

'Where do you come from?' asked the man next to me. He had a pleasing Scottish accent.

'North Essex. About ten miles from the Suffolk border.'

'Anywhere near Wetherbury? There's a big Suffolk breeder there, John Watkins. He's got some of the best rams in the country.'

'I go to Wetherbury to do my shopping. I've heard of John Watkins, everyone has round there, but I don't know him personally.'

'Do you keep sheep?'

'Yes,' I said, 'but only a few.'

'How many have you got?'

'Well, not many.'

'Come on, lass, how many?'

'Just four at the moment.'

'That doesn't matter. What breed are they?'

I laughed. 'They're all different. One's a Jacob, one's a black Cheviot, one's a Ryeland, and the other's a Finn Dorset.'

'How do you get a black Cheviot?'

'Well, she's a cross really — half Jacob. She's enormous and looks like a pregnant grizzly bear.'

'All your sheep are fat,' said David, handing me the fried egg sandwich, 'but she feeds them bread and honey,' he said to the Scotsman.

'Do you breed from them?' he asked.

'No, I just keep them for the wool. I spin. What sheep have you got?'

'Mostly Suffolks, but I've got twenty Lincolns.'

'Lincolns? Do you have any fleeces for sale?' Lincoln Longwools have beautiful silky fleeces that spin into lustrous cobwebs of wool. I had been wanting to get hold of a Lincoln fleece for some time.

'I could let you have a fleece. I haven't got any here, but I'll post you one if you like when I get home next week.' He took a pencil and a scrap of paper from his pocket. 'They're big fleeces, you know, weigh about twenty pounds. Give me your address and I won't forget.' He scribbled it down and put the paper back in his pocket.

I glanced across at Katy. She was laughing at something one of the men next to her was saying, but in the general noise and commotion I couldn't catch what it was. Anyway, she looked happy.

'What does your husband do? Is he a farmer?' asked the Scotsman.

'No. He's a History lecturer. We've got a cottage and a couple of acres. The sheep are my project. I just have them for fun, I'm afraid. I've brought them up on bottles. Where do you live?'

'Near Boston, hence the Lincolns. Not that far from you, really, give or take a hundred miles,' he said laughing. 'Do you go to the Lincoln Show?'

'I haven't been yet. This is the first time I've been to the Royal.'

'You should. It's a good show. I go every year, so does David. It's usually the same crowd at all the shows.'

'Come on, girls,' said David, 'I'm going to show you my sheep.'

'Make sure that's all,' said someone and they all laughed.

We wandered off to the sheep pens. David's Ryelands looked immaculate. He had three pens of them, three ewe lambs in one, a pair of ram lambs, and two rams. We leaned over the hurdles admiring them.

'I must say I do like Ryelands,' I said. 'They're so easy to look after. I was thinking about getting another some time.'

'Why don't you have a ewe this time? I've got some good ewe lambs for sale if you want one.'

'Could you bring me one?'

'Yes. Next week if you like. Has Jock been trying to sell you a Lincoln? They're big sheep. Come on, I'll show you his pen.'

The Lincolns had great long fleeces hanging almost to the ground, in long, silken curls. Curls of wool hung over their faces, hiding their eyes, like Old English sheepdogs. We looked at some black Welsh Mountains, the ewes small and hornless,

the rams with splendid black horns curling round their ears;
we saw badger-faced sheep, small white mountain sheep with
black-and-tan striped faces; Beaulah Speckle Face; Swaledales,
Lonks, Derbyshire Gritstone and Devon Longwools. They were
all there, the breeds of sheep that so far I had only seen as
photographs in books.

'How many breeds of sheep are there?' I asked David as we
walked along the pens, past every combination of black faces,
white faces and coloured fleeces imaginable.

'Over fifty British breeds,' he answered. 'And there are quite
a lot of continental breeds here, too.'

'Where are the Herdwicks? I do want to see those.'

'Over here in the next bay. Arthur's the chap you want to
see about Herdwicks. He's in the ring at the moment. We'll
find him later when the judging's finished.'

We came to the Herdwicks. They had wonderful, almost
mauve-coloured wool, looking like great thick rugs thrown over
them, and smooth white faces with gentle-looking eyes. It was
the first time I had seen any in real life, although I had read
about them: how they lived on the fells where no other sheep
could survive, in an area of England with the highest rainfall;
of their wonderful homing instincts; how they were supposed
to be descended from sheep that had swum ashore from Viking
ships wrecked on the rocky Cumbrian coast. They were wonderful. I knew that I had to have a Herdwick to add to my little
flock.

'I've got to get ready to go in the ring soon,' said David.
'Come and watch the judging. There's also a very good display
by the National Sheep Association in their tent. And the British
Wool Marketing Board have a stand: there's plenty to see. It
would take the whole week to see everything here. Look, I'll
have to go. See you both back at the van at lunchtime, if
not before? And we'll have a chat with Arthur about those
Herdwicks.'

'Thanks, David, and thanks for breakfast.'

'Just go back to the van and help yourselves to anything. See
you later,' and he disappeared into the crowd.

'He's fun,' said Katy, after he had gone. 'They're all a good laugh. I'm glad I came. I was afraid it was going to be boring.'

'Where shall we go first? More sheep, cattle, pigs, craft stalls?'

'I don't mind, Mother, wherever you like.'

We passed the judging rings and stopped to watch for a while. Some magnificent Jacob rams were being paraded and inspected. They lined up and we watched the judge examining each one in turn — running his hand along its back and down each leg, looking at its teeth, inspecting its hindquarters.

The craft marquees were a crush of people. We pushed through the crowds in the hot, airless tents. Katy bought herself some blue and green enamelled earrings, and I bought some home-made fudge and a T-shirt with a pig and 'This is the boar you're looking for' written on the front, for Tom.

The day grew hotter and there seemed to be people every- where. We took our shoes off and walked on the grass at the side of the wide, gritted paths. We visited the Rare Breed Survival Trust stand, and I bought lots of sheep postcards to stick on the kitchen wall, and a poster of a beautiful Herdwick ram from the British Wool Marketing Board.

By lunch time we were both hot and tired and we made our way wearily back to David's van. It was brimming over with people. More whisky was handed round and we sat on the straw bales drinking and eating bread and cheese.

By the end of the day Katy and I were exhausted. But it had been a good day. I had never seen so many different breeds of sheep, and I had the promise of two fleeces to arrive in the post: the Lincoln and a Herdwick from David's friend Arthur. He had given me his address and telephone number and said that if I wanted a Herdwick lamb in the spring I could have one.

David made us a cup of tea before we left and said he would bring me the Ryeland ewe lamb the following week.

* * *

The fleeces arrived in large, lumpy parcels. I unwrapped them quickly and gloated over them. I had booked the Guildhall at Finchingfield, a few miles away, for a week in September. Katy and I were going to hold an exhibition there of spinning, weaving and painting, and now I should have a good variety of fleeces to use. Katy had been very busy doing drawings and watercolours, and her boyfriend, Philip, who was also doing 'A' level art at her school and was hoping to go to Art College, was going to show some paintings with us.

David arrived with the ewe lamb in the back of his car. She was small and neat and seemed very friendly for a lamb that had not been bottle reared. She had one small clip out of the end of each ear.

'That's the way I mark them,' he explained, 'working round the ear depending on the number. One ear is for tens, the other single numbers. End of the ear is three, so she is number thirty-three.'

Meg had a tortoise called Number Forty-six, but the lamb was much too pretty to be called only by a number.

'I thought I might call her Ariadne or Portia,' I said to David as he lifted her out and stood her on the drive.

'Ariadne? That's awful,' he said.

'Right, Portia it is, then.'

She opened her mouth and bleated at us, a funny staccato bleat in a small high voice. It was very distinctive. All the sheep had different voices and I could tell which one of them was calling without having to see them. Portia's voice was different again. There would be no mistaking her.

We took her to the meadow where the four other sheep were leaning over the gate, having heard the car. Rupert, once so small, now looked large compared to her, but they both had the same engaging woolly faces, the same quiet temperament. Portia stood in the middle of them, looking lost and forlorn while they sniffed at her. She bleated again and they pushed and jostled her.

'Poor little thing,' I said. 'It's horrid for her being put in with strange sheep.'

'They'll soon settle down,' said David. 'How about some coffee?'

We watched them through the kitchen window as we drank our coffee. Eventually they wandered away from the gate and began grazing. Portia moved away from the others and went towards the far hedge to graze on her own.

I went out to them later, after David had left, and they all came running up to meet me, with Portia running after them. I held out some biscuits for them which they quickly gobbled up, and Portia took a piece from my hand. She seemed remarkably unafraid of humans, and I hoped that she would soon settle in and feel at home.

At the weekend Katy, Philip and I went to Finchingfield to see the caretaker and look round the Guildhall. I liked Philip very much. He was a tall, good-looking boy, with a mass of long, dark, curly hair and brown eyes. He always wore unusual clothes — colourful waistcoats and Indian shirts, canvas boots and leg warmers — and was great fun to be with. He was also very talented.

There was an art exhibition currently being held in the Guild-hall, a wonderful fifteenth-century building. The ground floor had been made into almshouses and the top storey was used for exhibitions and various village meetings. We climbed the wooden staircase of great thick oak boards and walked into the long, high-ceilinged room, its walls now hung round with local views. There were several people in the room, looking at the paintings or talking to a smiling, plump, middle-aged woman sitting at a small table in the centre of the room.

Katy and Philip walked round the room looking at the paintings, but I was much more interested in the room itself. A huge oak beam ran across the centre above the leaded windows, and above that the ceiling, heavily beamed, sloped inwards. There were great oak beams round the walls, and the sloping floor was made of old floorboards two feet wide. The windows on one side of the room looked out onto the village street below, running steeply downhill to a narrow bridge and the village pond where several ducks and geese were swimming — a scene made famous by many a painter on postcards and chocolate box lids. From the other windows the view was the church with its splendid tower and a fine blue and gold clock, and a slightly overgrown churchyard.

It was a wonderful room. I love old houses — they seem to have a peace and a sense of security about them — and I thought that the week sitting in this lovely room would be very enjoyable.

When we got home we sat round the pine kitchen table and discussed the posters that Philip was doing, and made a detailed list of all our exhibits. I was going to type it out and make photocopies so that we could hand them out to the visitors.

'We'll put some posters up at school,' said Philip, 'and my mum says she'll put some round the village. She's going to ask all the shops and the pubs to put one up. I'll go into Fordington next week on my bike and take some posters.'

'Good. I'll take some to Finchingfield and the surrounding villages. The cards I ordered will be ready on Monday, so we can send those to people as well. I'll let you have some as soon as I've got them. I think it's going to be a great success, and you've both done some lovely paintings.'

'It will be great if we sell some,' said Philip.

'It's a shame it's in school time,' said Katy, 'because you'll have to be there on your own most of the time, but we can come on after school and we'll be able to stay there all the weekend.'

'I don't mind being there. It was booked for the whole of August, but there should still be visitors about in the second week of September. And we've got both the weekends, so that's good.'

'Well, you'll be able to sit and spin lots of wool, anyway,' said Katy.

We set our things out on Friday evening. I had taken my smock, some hand shears, and wool tokens, used in the Middle Ages to seal the bags of wool ready for sale to the merchants. I also took my nineteenth-century shepherd's crook of which I was very proud but never used, and two sheep bells. These were both eighteenth-century bells, and one had been found in the field at the back of the house — proof that once before there had been sheep at Monks Green. We had listed these at the beginning of our catalogue, marked 'not for sale.' I also had a chart of sample wools that I had dyed with plants, producing eighty different shades, and some sheep posters. I had made jerseys and waistcoats and rugs, and Katy had been busy knitting leg warmers, hats and purses from my handspun wool. We carried the boxes up the stairs with the bags of fleeces and the spinning wheel.

We spent several happy hours putting out all the exhibits, and hanging the paintings. We put numbered labels on them all to correspond with our numbering in the catalogue. Philip had done a wonderful pen and ink drawing of a local water mill. Watermills have always fascinated me, and I would love to live in one beside a gently flowing river.

'That's really beautiful, Philip. Can I buy it and put a 'sold' sticker on it?'

'Yes.' He grinned broadly. 'My first sale.'

We were there fifteen minutes early in the morning, but already a little crowd of people was waiting outside the Guild-hall. We were kept busy all day, with friends, relations and strangers. Gerald brought Tom and Alex in the morning, and in the afternoon Meg arrived. Philip's parents came, Laura came, we had visitors from France, Scandinavia and several from America. There was a small kitchen tucked under the stairs where we could make tea and coffee and have something to eat, but we hardly had any time for refreshments.

When we turned the huge old key in the lock of the Guildhall door in the evening we were all tired and ready to go home. Philip and Alex had supper with us and we opened a bottle of wine to celebrate our success.

'It all looked very nice,' said Gerald, 'you've set it out very well.'

'My mum and dad are going tomorrow,' said Alex, 'and taking my gran.'

Katy and Philip were bubbling with excitement. They had both sold some paintings.

'Everyone wanted to buy my smock,' I said, 'but that's definitely not for sale. I took an order for one this afternoon, though, from an American woman. She wants it just the same as mine, but made in silk, so she can wear it to cocktail parties. It was nice to have the order, but now I'm rather regretting it. It took such ages to make. At least the silk will be easier to sew than that canvas.'

'I had an order to do a painting of someone's house,' said Philip.

'Well done,' said Gerald. He raised his glass. 'Here's to a successful week.'

It was a *very* successful week. We sold nearly everything and met some interesting people, one from as far away as New Zealand. I had orders for wool and rugs, and enough orders for jerseys and leg warmers to keep me and Katy busy for the next few months.

I took my spinning wheel into the garden and sat near the apple tree in the warm, still autumn air. The pink blossom of summer had gone and now large red-green apples hung from the ancient branches and iridescent starlings chuckled and whistled from the top of the tree, their plumage glinting in the sunshine. I watched the swallows gathering on the telegraph

wires and thought how quickly another year had almost slipped away.

I looked at the sheep wandering about in the meadow, four large woolly beasts grazing near the hedge, and little Portia, at a distance from the others, nibbling the newly fallen leaves under the oak tree. She was still always slightly apart from the rest of the flock, but she settled in the barn with them at night and had already learnt to run to me when I called her name.

The sheep had all learnt their own individual names as well as any dog, and if I was walking about in the meadow with them and spoke to one of them by name, that one would stop grazing and put his or her head up, while the others carried on eating. Portia had learnt more quickly than the others: she was really quite a remarkable little creature.

## CHAPTER SEVEN

The next four-legged creature to join the household was not another sheep but an aged cat called Ben. I had a call one morning from the girl who ran the local cat sanctuary, asking if I could give a home to an old cat. She explained that he had belonged to an elderly woman who could no longer live on her own and had gone to live in sheltered accommodation.

'I feel so sorry for both of them,' she said. 'The woman has always lived on her own and had Ben from a kitten. He's ten now, and it seems awful that she can't take him with her. I do think it's wrong to separate elderly people from their pets. She must miss him so much, and the poor old cat is really unhappy. All they had in the world was each other. It's such a shame.'

'I'll come and see him. But do you think he'll be happy here with us and all the other animals?'

'I've asked several other people already, but nobody wants him. I'd keep him myself, although I've got nine in the house now, but my Tommy hates him, and keeps attacking him. Poor old cat, he's so friendly, but he seems so sad.'

I put a cat basket in the car and went to fetch him. He was a big black and white cat, with huge sad eyes, and he just sat and stared at us without moving. I bent down and stroked him.

'Hello, Ben,' I said.

He opened his mouth and mewed, showing Dracula teeth. I picked him up and put him into the basket. He sat quietly in the bottom, unresisting.

When I got home I took him into the bathroom and arranged a blanket for him to lie on, then went to find him some milk and food. I took the saucers back and put them down next to him. He was sitting on the blanket where I had left him, and did not seem interested in the food. He just sat and stared at me with his huge, sad eyes.

'Poor old Ben,' I said, stroking him gently. 'Have some milk. Come on, Ben. You'll be all right. You'll soon get used to everybody.' I continued stroking him, but he made no move, either towards the food or away from me. After a while I left him, thinking he might prefer to be on his own to eat.

I went back to him later, but he was still sitting on the blanket and the food was untouched. I picked him up, and he lay heavily in my arms, sad, silent and old.

In the evening I carried him into the kitchen and sat with him on my knee, stroking him gently and talking to him, but he seemed shut away inside a shell, as if he had lost the will to live.

After five days, I was getting really worried about him. 'I don't know what to do about Ben,' I said to Gerald one evening as I sat with the old cat on my knee. 'He still hasn't eaten anything. All he will have is milk.'

'Well, you will keep getting all these animals,' he said rather crossly. 'You can't save them all.'

I looked down at the black head resting against my arm. Perhaps he should have been put to sleep when his owner could no longer keep him, I thought. It was not fair to an old animal to try and rehome him. I did not believe in life at any price. There should be quality of life as well, and Ben didn't want to have a new life with other people. I put him back on his blanket last thing at night, and went to bed feeling sad and guilty.

Next morning I went in to him with fresh food and milk, but now I had given up hope that he would take any. He was sitting in the corner on his blanket, but as I opened the door and said, 'Hello, Ben,' as I always did, he got up and came up to me and then started walking round me and rubbing against my legs. Then he began to purr, quietly at first, and then a deep singing sound that throbbed through the whole of his body as I bent and stroked him. Then he turned his attention to the food I had put down for him and ate all of it, and emptied the saucer of milk. When he had finished he came back to me and started rubbing round my legs again. He had suddenly decided that he wanted to live with us after all.

I picked him up and hugged him to me.

'Dear old Ben, silly old Ben,' I said softly.

He rubbed his chin along my arm and continued purring.

After we had all had breakfast I took him into the garden and sat on the lawn, while he padded about and sniffed in the flower beds. The other cats watched him from a discreet distance. He looked at them now and again and then carried on with the important business of exploring his new surroundings. He came up to me several times and walked over my skirt, then went on with his inspection.

When he had completed his tour of the garden I took him inside again and he sat down in front of the Aga and began washing himself. That evening I put his saucer of food down in the lobby where all the other cats were being fed, and he ate it all, scarcely taking any notice of them. I shut him in the bathroom with his blanket again last thing at night.

Next morning I gave him his breakfast near the rest of the cats and when he had finished he followed Barrington out of the cat door. She walked half-way across the lawn, then turned round and waited for him to catch up with her. I watched them walking across the grass together and then disappearing through the hedge.

I saw them later, sitting on the bank under the apple tree in the sun. Ben was licking the top of Barrington's head and they had obviously made friends. Ben was here to stay.

From that day he was a changed animal. He curled up on the bench in the lobby at night next to Barrington; he rolled about on the lawn in the sun; he followed us about and climbed on our knees. He played games with fallen leaves, scattering them and darting about, waving his tail. One day I saw him catch a mouse behind the barn. He carried it proudly round to

the back door and dropped it on the step. For an old cat of ten and a half he was pretty sprightly. It was wonderful to see him so happy. Just a few weeks earlier I had felt that he should have been put to sleep; now I could hardly believe that it was the same cat.

Adam, too, had changed, but not for the better. He was becoming extremely ill-tempered, and every time I went into the meadow to walk about with the sheep he would put his ears back, step back a few paces slowly and deliberately, his eyes blazing with anger, and then hurl himself at me, butting me hard, twisting his head from side to side, to get the maximum effect from his horns. I shouted at him, I smacked his nose, but it made no difference.

'Take a stick to him,' said David, when I told him what a problem Adam was becoming.

'But he's only a wether, why is he getting so naughty?'

'He's been spoilt, that's his trouble. Give him a good whack on the nose. He won't like that.'

I kept a stick beside the gate and took it with me every time I went into the meadow. I hated hitting his soft pink nose like that, but he backed off a little.

Rupert was quite the opposite. He was so docile and good tempered. If I sat down in the grass he and Portia would often come trotting up and then sit down next to me and start chewing their cud. Rupert loved everybody.

I had a Dutch friend called Gerda, who lived in Castle Monkton. Her husband, Ralph, was an elderly English writer and they had a beautiful old house on the edge of the village, half hidden behind a tall brick wall. Inside was an enchanted garden of mossy paths, stone figures, giant ferns and cool, grey-leaved scented plants; asters and verbenas and cascades of roses. Behind the house was an orchard, and they also had a meadow with a little larch wood on its farthest boundary. I loved those trees in the spring, with their beautiful pale green leaves bursting into life again, transforming the bare, brown branches of winter, dotted with knobbly fircones.

Gerda had a few sheep and a small, cantankerous Jacob ram,

which she called 'Little Yeacoub'. Little Yeacoub was a fiend in sheep's clothing. He spent a good deal of his time running at the apple trees and battering his head against them. He charged the door of the garden shed and splintered it to fire-wood. Gerda armed herself with a large stick every time she went near him, and I was beginning to wonder if Adam was going to become as bad.

In the end Gerda decided she could stand no more. She gave Little Yeacoub to a friend, and he was last seen travelling up the A1 in the back of a mini-clubman on his way to Yorkshire. I have often wondered since what became of him.

Gerda loved her sheep and it was a great sadness to her that she had to get rid of her ram. 'But it is so peaceful now, without Little Yeacoub,' she said, as we sat in the orchard, watching the sunlight make dappled shadows on the grass. 'The other sheep are so gentle. It is better without him.' They grazed near us and Rupert sat on the grass beside us, chewing his cud.

'Oh, sweetheart,' she said. 'he is so lovely, this little one. I would like to have one the same.' Rupert looked at us with his smiling face, basking in the sunlight and our admiration. He loved outings and I sometimes took him with me when I went to see Gerda. He stood in the back of the car, his nose level with my head, looking out through the windscreen at the road ahead.

'He is very quiet. Even the Ryeland rams are docile. I think it is because they don't have horns. They certainly don't behave like Little Yeacoub. I wouldn't want to have a Jacob ram, or even a Jacob wether. Adam's becoming quite a problem now. I'm not sure what I'm going to do about him. I've started taking a stick into the field with me, but sometimes it just makes him more angry.'

Gerda stroked the top of Rupert's woolly head.

'Ah, little one,' she said, 'you are so gentle. His wool is good for spinning?' she asked. Gerda had been spinning for years and made wonderful jerseys for her family, knitting them all on a circular needle and making intricate patterns round the yokes from naturally coloured grey, brown and black wool.

'Yes, Ryeland wool is the best there is.'

'Perhaps your friend has a lamb I could have. I think I would like a little ewe. I like it when they have lambs. The sheep are always such good mothers — I love to see them.'

'I'll ask David, if you like. I'm sure he's still got some ewe lambs for sale. The Ryelands are so easy to look after, and small enough to turn easily to trim their feet.'

Ralph came across the grass to join us. He was a darling old man, with wispy white hair and faded blue eyes. He smiled at us sitting there in the grass with the sheep.

'I see that Rupert has come to tea again,' he said. 'I hope you've got some of his favourite biscuits, Gerda.'

Gerda got up laughing and smoothed her skirt.

'I am just coming to put the kettle on and then we will have tea in the garden.'

David was highly amused to hear of Rupert's afternoon outings. He still had a few ewe lambs left, now five months old, so I gave him Gerda's telephone number and he promised to ring her about one.

The following week, Gerda and I wandered about among the herbs and lilies in her garden, then sat on a little stone bench in the sun, waiting for David and the lamb to arrive.

'How is Gerald?' she asked.

'Oh, he's busy with the College and his archaeology. He spends his weekends going off on digs.'

'You are not happy with Gerald?'

'No, not really. Sometimes I wonder why I married him. We never go out together — we never have, only when the children were small. Then we had family outings to the seaside or museums. But now, we don't seem to have anything in common any more.'

She put her hand on mine. 'I am sorry, sweetheart. I did not think you were really happy. It is sad.'

'You and Ralph seem so happy together.'

'Yes, we are. I have had a wonderful life with Ralph. We have had such fun together. And we are good friends.'

'I can't say I wish I'd never married him, because I wouldn't have Katy and Tom. They are the best thing that's ever happened to me. But when they leave home and Gerald and I are on our own, I don't know what it will be like. I'm dreading it.'

'Perhaps life will change. We never know what is going to happen in the future,' she said.

'I think that's just as well,' I answered. 'If we could see some of the awful things lying in wait for us, we'd never want to go on.'

The door in the wall that opened out onto the pavement swung open, and David appeared, in his check cap and large wellies, looking slightly apprehensive and then smiling broadly when he saw us.

'I wasn't sure if I'd found the right place,' he said. 'I drove straight past the first time.'

'Gerda, this is David.' She held out her hand.

'Hello, I am Gerda,' she said. 'I am glad to see you. You have brought the lamb for me?'

We followed him through the doorway and saw a little woolly face peering out of the back window of the car. David opened the back door and lifted her out and carried her into the garden. Gerda led the way to the orchard.

'Oh, she is lovely. She is like a little toy. Thank you. I shall call her Zoë.'

The lamb stood in the long grass of the orchard and Gerda's other sheep came up to inspect her and sniff at her.

'I wormed her before I brought her,' said David. 'You've got some good lambs on your ewes. You should breed from the Ryeland.'

'Yes, I want to,' said Gerda. 'I love to see the lambs.'

'That's what I like to hear,' said David grinning and winking at me. 'Shame to keep ewes and not breed from them.'

Gerda made some coffee and we sat in the conservatory, with Ralph. There was a lovely smell from the scented geraniums and stephanotis, and a large grape vine ran up one wall and covered the ceiling, shading us from the heat outside. Giant orange-flowered cactus and enormous *Begonia rex* plants stood in pots on the black-and-white tiled floor.

* * *

103

A few evenings later, Gerald was out at one of his meetings and Katy and I were sitting at the kitchen table. Tom had already gone to bed and Katy was struggling with her physics homework. We were startled by a loud knocking on the door. The dogs, who had been lying on the rug near us, got up and went to the door and sniffed at it, but did not bark. The knocking was repeated.

Katy went to the window and looked out.

'There's a large white dog on the doorstep,' she said.

I joined her at the window. It was no large white dog, it was Adam, banging on the door with his hoof while Pandora ate the pansies from the terracotta pot beside the door. The others were ranged under the window in a line, making a feast of the Michaelmas daisies.

I opened the door and they pushed in, tapping their hooves over the tiles, nosing around to see if there was anything to eat. Something must have disturbed them and woken them in the barn, so they had decided to break out of their pen and have a midnight feast. I found the biscuit tin and they jostled and pushed, licking their lips, their warm breath and soft noses on my hands as they nibbled at their favourite snack. I led them back to the barn and shut them in again.

Our hens had been joined by a handsome grey and white barred cockerel, who had been named Boris. He was a very friendly bird, and strutted and clucked around with his wives all day, scratching about for beetles or worms, which he always saved for the hens. As soon as he found something to eat, he would make low clucking noises, bobbing his head up and down, and the hens would come running immediately to eat the delicacy.

In the afternoons he led his wives up to the front door and stood on the top step crowing loudly, while they waited around him. He was always rewarded by some corn, and it became a daily ritual. The only trouble we ever had with Boris was occasional fights with Gilbert. Most of the time they kept at a distance from each other, always aware of where the other was, but passing by with cold, indifferent looks. But now and again there would be a great commotion from Polly, and looking out of the window we would see her bobbing up and down and squawking and getting very agitated. And there were Boris and Gilbert at each other's throats, Boris with a beakful of Gilbert's long neck, and Gilbert scattering grey and white feathers everywhere.

Wolf was always at the door immediately. He knew what Polly's squawks meant and it was the only time he was allowed to chase anything. He wanted to make the most of it. As soon as the door was opened he would rush round the house, skidding and half falling over as he took the corners at speed on his three legs. Gilbert and Boris scattered in opposite directions, and would then stand, one each end of the lawn, shake themselves, and stretch their wings. Wolf sat in the middle, his big pink tongue hanging out, looking from one to the other, hoping, no doubt, that they would start fighting again.

But he was always disappointed: such outbursts were followed by weeks of calm. Katy, however, had started taking Wolf into the garden with her to ward off Gilbert, and he made a very willing bodyguard, loping about, eyeing Gilbert and keeping him under the lilac bush.

As well as Boris we had acquired a few bantam hens. There were three jet black ones with greenish feet, rather like little moorhens, a fawn speckled one, and a buff-coloured hen, rather larger and fatter than the others, which Tom had christened Parsley. The bantam hens, however, would have nothing to do with the hen-house. As it was getting dark, we could hear them, flapping and crashing about as they got up onto the lower branches of the lilac bush, and then gradually climbed higher until they were all sitting in its topmost branches. In the mornings they took off from their perches, flying onto the lawn and landing in a flurry of feathers and squawks, bumping their beaks on the grass and looking most undignified.

The big brown hens always walked into the field, and then went up to their house and inside when it was egg-laying time. Afterwards they would stand in the hen-house doorway, announcing to all the world that they had just laid an egg. Not so the bantams. They sneaked off quietly to little corners of the garden, making nests under the hedge or behind the barn, and leaving them as quietly as they had gone to them. We spent a good deal of time hunting for eggs. It was a race between us and the dogs. Sometimes we won, sometimes they did.

Tom came running in excitedly one Saturday morning as I was clearing away the breakfast things.

'Parsley's got a nest in the barn, and there are some baby chicks in it. I went to get my bike and she was just standing in the doorway with them. You must come and see.'

I ran across the drive with Tom, and there in the barn doorway, in the sun, stood Parsley, her wings drooping slightly, her feathers fluffed out, clucking and fussing, while round her scuttled seven little balls of fluff.

I bent down to look at them closer.

'Tom, aren't they wonderful? What amazing little things.'

Three of them were jet black, two were greyish and the other two yellow. We picked them up and they sat on our hands, cheeping.

'Fancy Parsley hatching them out like that, without us knowing,' said Tom. 'The nest is just over here, behind Gilbert's house.' He pointed to a flattened circle of hay in which lay broken pieces of egg shell.

I wondered what would happen when the cats saw all these enticing little morsels. Perhaps we should make a pen for them all, to keep them out of harm's way until they were older. Parsley strutted out onto the gravel drive, calling her little brood after her, and they ran about, cheeping excitedly, keeping close to her all the time. Fiona, the black long-haired cat who had taken Adam's fancy when he was a lamb, appeared from under the lavender bush and began creeping forward slowly, inching her way towards the chicks, flattened to the ground and swishing her tail. Parsley rushed forward with her wings outstretched, her feathers fluffed so that she looked twice the size. Fiona turned and streaked away and disappeared behind the lilac bush.

'I think Parsley's going to be able to look after them all right,' said Tom. 'I think they'll be safe from the cats.'

Parsley walked about the garden all day, scratching and pecking at the grass roots, calling her chicks to stay close to her. They ran about in tiny circles near her feet, and cheaped and pecked at the grass. The cats all watched from a safe distance. A feline face seemed to be lurking under every bush or plant, but they kept well away from Parsley.

Gilbert was very interested in the baby chicks. He padded after them all on his big orange feet, making quiet little noises in his throat, putting his long neck out and turning his head to look at them sideways with his beady eyes. He seemed to take a tender paternal interest in them, and followed Parsley and her brood all day, looking at us inquiringly if we were near, as if to ask us where they had all suddenly come from and what on earth these tiny things could be. I did not think that Gilbert had anything to do with their appearance. That was obviously thanks to Boris.

About an hour before dusk, Parsley and her babies made their way back to the barn, and she settled herself back on the nest with them all hidden under her wings or her body.

There are millions of chickens in the world, all hatched from eggs, but it seemed miraculous that such beautiful little creatures could grow and develop from a blob of yellow and white fluid. We all spent hours watching them every day.

Parsley was a diligent mother. The chicks became more adventurous and scratched vigorously about for beetles, encouraged by their doting mother. Their wings grew tiny feathers, and gradually the soft down was replaced by stubs of feathers, first on their backs, and then all over. The little black chicks grew black feathers, and the other four became grey and white mottled, like Boris. It soon became obvious that these four were also cockerels, and they began to have sparring matches, tiny as they still were, facing up to each other with neck feathers bristling and heads outstretched.

One day, when the chicks were about six weeks old, Gerda brought me a tiny yellow two-day-old chick. She explained that a friend of hers had been trying to hatch some peahen eggs. They are notoriously difficult, and although three hatched out, two of the chicks died the same day. The solitary chick was very unhappy and cheeped loudly for its companions. When the chick was still alive three days later in its little incubator, she had bought a day-old chick from a farm to keep it company, but then next morning the peachick was dead.

So Gerda brought me the tiny yellow ball of fluff. thinking that maybe Parsley would take it under her wing. But Parsley was not interested in some strange chick. She was too busy looking after her own growing family, and gave it a few good pecks on the head.

I took it into the house and put it in a hay-filled cardboard box next to the Aga. I put some chick crumbs on a saucer and the tiny chick cheeped and pecked excitedly.

'What's this?' asked Gerald when he came home that evening.

I told him the story of the peachicks.

'It's a Rhode Island Red,' I added. 'They're very good layers.' I really had no idea what it was, but I thought the idea of a potentially useful hen might placate him.

The tiny chick grew with amazing speed. By the time it was three weeks old, white feathers had appeared on its wings and the yellow down was changing to white stubby quills on its back. A week later, though six weeks younger than Parsley's little brood, it was about the same size. It ran about the kitchen floor and scratched about on the lawn, seemingly quite happy in its solitary state. It ran up to me when I called it and took its chick crumbs from my hand.

Gerald eyed it suspiciously.

'That is certainly not a Rhode Island Red,' he said. 'And look at the speed it's growing. I think it's a bloody cockerel.' I was beginning to think so too, but I said nothing, simply called it Oliver.

Oliver had the largest feet I had ever seen on any chicken, great yellow toes on sturdy yellow legs. He had snow-white feathers and began to grow a large red comb and drooping tail feathers. He was quite happy to spend the day wandering

around the garden, often after the dogs, and as soon as it was dark he would find his way back to the house and perch on the arm of the oak settle next to the Aga for the night.

He was so tame. He would follow the sheep up the meadow, and sometimes, if I looked out of the bedroom window to check on them, I would see a blob of white by the top hedge under the oak tree. If I went out to the garden and called 'Oliver', there would be a great flapping and squawking and he would run with wings outstretched from the top of the meadow back to the garden. I always gave him some corn on my hand when he came, and in the mornings, when Gilbert and Polly and the bantams were having their breakfast on the doorstep and Oliver was supposed to join them, he refused to peck corn from the path, but always took it out of my hand.

Sometimes in the evening I took him into the sitting room with me and he would settle himself on my shoulder and sit there all evening while the rest of us watched television.

In a few months he became nearly as big and heavy as Gilbert, but without his long neck. It was obvious then that what we had was a cob cockerel, normally kept as quick maturing birds to be fattened for Christmas. I have seen these cob cockerels in their fattening pens, at a few months old, grown so large and heavy that they can no longer stand up, their legs and feet swollen and distorted.

Christmas came and went. I had dire warnings from everyone who saw him. 'You won't be able to keep him. They go off their legs.'

Oliver must have walked several miles every day, following the dogs round the garden or the sheep round the meadow. His thick yellow legs remained strong and sturdy. The little bantam cockerels were forever scrapping and fighting with each other, but Oliver was a confirmed pacifist. Perhaps he even thought of himself as a dog or a sheep, but he never made any attempt to fight, either with Boris or Gilbert or the fierce little birds that Parsley had raised.

# CHAPTER EIGHT

Spring came round again. Wild violet flowers appeared under the hedge and pale green elm seeds drifted on the wind. The cats, after spending most of the winter inside lying lazily in front of the fire, began to make excursions along the hedgerows and up to the wood. The sheep nibbled at the fresh young blackberry shoots and new elder leaves in the hedge bordering their meadow, and Oliver and the other chickens clucked and scratched about in the flower beds, looking for suitable dust-bathing spots.

One Saturday we all went to an open farm weekend. It was a calm, still day, of blue sky and catkinned hedges, blackthorn blossom and soft grey pussy willows.

The farm was reported in the local press as having rare breeds of animals and demonstrations of traditional crafts. There was a wide cobbled yard and several large timber and thatched barns along one side. A blacksmith was working in the first barn hammering a shoe over blazing coals to fit to an enormous cart-horse, standing patiently near him, surrounded by visitors. Tom and Katy watched as the hot, hissing metal was fixed to the hoof.

In a corner of the same barn a thin, plain woman was sitting at a spinning wheel, with a pile of fleece at her feet, explaining to a group of onlookers how she spun dog hair and mixed it in with fleece to make 'exciting yarn'. I have spun dog hair, but in my opinion it makes very inferior yarn compared to sheep fleece, and besides that, the overpowering smell of dog while one is spinning it is quite disgusting.

I had been contacted during the winter by an American woman, living in London for two years, who had a small bag of dog combings which she wanted spinning. Having once spun up a dustbin bagful of Old English Sheep Dog combings, which made four and a half pounds of knitting yarn when finished and had delighted the dogs' owners (until, I suspected, they saw how much it had cost them), I had vowed never to do dog hair again. I thought I could smell that awful bag of combings long after I had posted the finished skeins. But she was very insistent.

They missed their dog so much, she said, especially her husband, and the friend who was looking after it for them until they returned home to the States had sent her a bag of dog combings by air mail. There wasn't very much of it, she said, and it was a lovely pale grey, and she desperately wanted to make her husband a scarf for Christmas.

In the end I relented, and the little parcel arrived in the post a few days later. It was a pretty colour, and I spun a few yards as a sample. It felt very coarse and rough to me, so I sent her the sample, thinking that she would reject the idea of having the rest of it spun. She telephoned me as soon as she received it. She was delighted. It was wonderful, she said, just like their dog, and her husband would be thrilled with it. So I spun the rest of it, and she sent the cheque with a Christmas card and a special note of thanks. I have often wondered what the poor man thought of his present, and whether it brought his neck out in a rash.

So I turned away from this woman and her spinning and went in search of the animals. We came first to the fowls. There were large cages of peacocks, and of Indian pheasants; strange looking ducks and fussy little bantams with feathered legs. There were hens that laid green eggs and enormous pale-gold chickens as large as Oliver.

Then we came to the sheep. They were in a long open-sided barn divided up into pens, and in each one was a ewe with one or two lambs. The lambs were all quite young, some of them obviously only a few hours old. They were, of course, quite enchanting. There was a variety of breeds: Jacobs with their little spotted lambs; some small soft-woolled Shetland sheep, each with a single lamb; two Southdown ewes, looking like scaled-down Ryelands with their wool-covered faces and legs; and a large dark-faced Oxford ewe and her lamb.

We stopped next at a pen containing a Dorset Horn ewe with her pink-nosed lamb, looking so like Adam when we had first collected him from the orphanage. The ewe, too, had the distinctive pink nose of the Dorsets, and a pair of curving horns curling round her ears. The lamb pushed under her to suckle and the ewe stamped her foot at us, the natural sheep's act of defiance to guard her baby. Several women with noisy children pulling at their hands were also looking at the Dorset Horn ewe and her lamb.

'Look at the ram, with its horns,' one of them said. I wondered how they could be so unobservant. I felt like telling her that if it had been a ram, it would have had the most enormous pair of horns she was ever likely to see on a sheep, curling twice or even three times in great circles either side of its face. Katy and I just looked at each other.

'Funny looking ram,' said Katy in a very loud voice as we walked away. 'Some people are stupid.'

I went back to the sheep again while Gerald, Tom, and Katy were looking at the Shetland ponies. They drew me like a magnet — the smell of them, their gentle faces with the pale eyes, and the lambs. Sheep had got into my blood like a drug, I was hooked on them. I knew that whatever happened I could never give up my sheep for anyone. I could not imagine life now without those wonderful wool-covered creatures.

A few days later I had a telephone call from a friend of Gerda's in Castle Monkton. It was Mrs Hall, the owner of the flock of Jacob sheep which Bob Holden clipped before coming to shear my little charges.

'Gerda Lewis gave me your name,' she said. 'I have a two-day-old lamb to bottle-feed and I wondered if you would be interested in having it?'

'I'd love to have it. What breed is it? Is it a ewe or a ram?' As if I cared. I'd have taken a three-legged lamb. Anything.

'It's a pure-bred Jacob ewe lamb, but the mother is refusing to feed her. She has triplets, and this one is in fact the strongest of the three, but the ewe keeps pushing her away. She won't have anything to do with her.'

So it was another little Jacob triplet, as Pandora had been. I could hardly wait to go and fetch her.

As I drove into the farmyard a cheerful, smiling woman appeared from one of the barns. She was wearing a fawn jersey and trousers, tucked into wellingtons, with a dark green padded nylon waistcoat and a red and green patterned headscarf. She led me into the barns to look at the sheep. There was a fine drizzling rain falling, but the ewes were all standing in clean straw, out of the wind and the rain, and looked well cared for. The Jacob ewes all had two horns, curving elegantly over the backs of their heads behind their ears, not sticking straight up in menacing fashion as Pandora's horns did. All the sheep turned their heads and stared at us with inquisitive faces.

A shaggy brown and white ewe was penned into a loose-box with three tiny lambs. Two of the lambs were standing near their mother, but the third was away from the others in a corner on her own. She went up to the mother ewe and tried to suckle from her, but the old ewe put her head down and grunted, butting the lamb away and pushing her frail little body against the wall. She pushed her repeatedly, knocking the lamb to the ground.

'You see, she just doesn't seem to like the lamb. She won't let her near her,' said Mrs Hall, going into the stable and picking up the unhappy lamb. She was tiny, even smaller than Pandora had been. She handed her to me.

'She's lovely,' I said. 'Poor little thing, being pushed about by her mother like that. It's such a shame.' She had the typical black ears and black eye patches, and tight curls of black and white wool on her back.

'She's nicely marked,' continued Mrs Hall. 'You see the black dots on her knees? You could call her Dotty.'

'I shall call her Tallulah,' I said, wrapping her in a piece of blanket I had taken with me, so that only her head was showing.

Mrs Hall laughed. 'That's very grand. I'm sure she will be well loved and have a happy life with you.'

'Thank you, she's so beautiful. Come and see her, won't you?'

'Yes, I will, when she's older.'

I got into the car and put the tiny lamb on my knee. She kept very still, curled up under the steering wheel, while I drove home through the village and down the lane.

When Tom and Katy came home from school there was another straw-filled box beside the Aga. They peered into it. Tallulah was fast asleep, curled round in the straw, her front legs folded under her, the back ones stretched straight forward, so that her head was lying across them.

'She's so small,' said Katy, 'and she's really pretty. Where did you get her from?'

'A friend of Gerda's who lives in the village phoned me up this morning and asked if I wanted her, so of course I said yes. She's one of triplets like Pandora was, but the old mother ewe wouldn't have anything to do with her, and kept knocking her over. I was afraid she was going to kill her.'

The lamb stirred and stretched herself, and opened her eyes. I picked her up, and she pushed her nose into my neck.

'Let me hold her,' said Katy. 'She seems hungry.'

'It's time for her to have some more milk. I'll mix it up while you've got her.'

Tallulah sucked at the bottle, dribbles of milk bubbling round the corners of her mouth. Her little neck was cardboard thin, and as she drank her head seemed to wobble a bit, as if the tiny neck was not strong enough to support her head. But she soon finished the milk. I sat on the settle with her and she curled herself on my knee in the same way as a cat, then put her head down across her legs, and after about ten minutes she was asleep again.

For the first two days she seemed to sleep most of the time. The other lambs had sniffed around the room a little, or shown some interest in the cats, but she was the youngest of the lambs I had brought up. Pandora had been four days old when I first had her, Rupert had been a week old and Adam had been ten days old.

After three days she suddenly seemed to come alive. Her neck filled out and became much stronger, so that her head stopped wobbling every time she had her milk. She started skipping about the kitchen on her shiny pointed hooves, dancing after the cats, jumping up in the air and playing silly games with the dogs. She would tiptoe up to them, put her head down as if she was going to sniff them, then suddenly take a jump backwards, leaping high in the air as she did so. Then she would repeat the performance, sometimes over and over again, as if she were making fun of them. Henry particularly found this most disconcerting. He lay in his basket, head down, wagging his tail a little and looking as if he felt very foolish. Sophie would not take much of Tallulah's games, and bared her teeth, curling up her lips in anger. Tallulah just jumped away as if she were laughing.

In the morning, when the dogs were let out into the garden, she ran down the steps after them and started nibbling at the primrose flowers under the kitchen window. The little mouth kept moving, chewing the petals round and round, and then spitting them out again.

One morning the dogs had been called in again and I opened the front door to go out to the barn to the others, taking Tallulah with me. She skipped down the front steps just as the Phil Collins look-alike stopped at the gate with our newspaper. He was half-way out of the car when he saw her and beat a hasty retreat. I picked her up and went down to the gate, by which time he was out of the car again, waving the paper.

'Oh, it's a lamb,' he said, smiling with relief, 'I thought it was a dog, that's why I got back in the car.'

He drove away and I put Tallulah down on the grass. Katy opened her bedroom window and leaned out.

'That gave him a fright,' she laughed. 'Did he think she was some kind of weird spaniel?'

The following week the telephone rang as I was in the middle of feeding the cats and dogs.

'Is that Mrs Kingstone?' asked a man's voice.

'Yes, speaking,' I answered.

'This is Milton Zoo. We have a very young llama that needs bottle-feeding and I wondered if you would be interested in having it?'

'A llama? Yes, I'd certainly like to have it. When can I come and fetch it? How much do you want for it?

There was a pause on the other end, then the voice started laughing. 'April Fool!' said Philip.

*     *     *

In due course two small black horns appeared on the top of Tallulah's head. Pandora's horns had grown through sticking straight up out of her head, but Tallulah's were pointing backwards. So she was only going to have two horns, the same as her mother.

She was the most energetic little creature. She never seemed to tire of jumping and skipping or running after cats and chickens. I took her into the meadow to meet the rest of the flock. They looked at her with disapproval. Pandora and Berkeley put

their heads down, but I waved my hand at them, and they backed away. They lost interest after a while and wandered back to their grass. I walked along beside the hedge and Tallulah followed like a little dog, dancing through the clover in her black ballet shoes.

She soon got used to spending her day with the rest of the flock, while sleeping in her box in the kitchen at night. In the morning, after she had finished her bottle of milk, I took her to the gate by the apple tree and she trotted in and started eating the pink petals that had fallen from the apple blossom. She always stayed under the tree for about half an hour nibbling up the petals. None of the other sheep had ever shown any interest in them, but Tallulah seemed to find them delicious.

The days grew longer and hotter. The meadow became dotted with clover flowers and moon daisies and bright blue speedwells. Clouds of tawny speckled skipper butterflies danced over the flowers and cuckoos called all day long. Fat green caterpillars spun silken threads and dangled from the poplar and willow trees. Tiny brown caterpillars launched themselves into space from the oak trees, and our swallows came back to nest in the barn again.

Tallulah gradually became part of the flock and was weaned from her bottle, joining the rest of the sheep in the barn at night. Berkeley had always been fond of disappearing, pushing or eating her way through the hedge, wriggling her fat black shape under the wire netting. Her expeditions still continued from time to time. At the start there had only been her and Pandora to chase home. Now there were more of them: Rupert and Adam and even little Tallulah, as well as Pandora. The only one who never joined in the great escapes was Portia. She would stay behind and stand in the middle of the meadow, crying loudly and forlornly for the others to come back. It was very useful, as I always knew as soon as there had been a break-out, thanks to Portia.

'You're a sneaky little grass, Portia,' said Tom.

I came home one evening after giving a spinning demonstration in the village, and as I got out of the car I heard the familiar sounds of Portia calling for help.

'They've been shouting for some time,' said Katy, 'ever since it got dark. I think they're cold.'

A week after shearing, cold they might be, but that was not why Portia was shouting, as I knew only too well. I went to the meadow. There was Portia standing forlornly in the middle and complaining loudly. The others had gone.

'Where are you?' I shouted. 'What are you all doing?'

There were answering bleats from half-way up the field behind the hedge.

Katy and I went round to the next-door field, wading through long wet grass, past enormous mounds of evil-smelling elephant dung that had been left in the corner. Informed sources assured me that it was beet slurry mixed with lime, but I was keeping an open mind on that. Katy was of the opinion that the mounds emanated from the hippo house at the nearest zoo.

'Adam! Pandora!' I called. 'Come along!'

I heard the jingling of their bells on their collars and then they appeared, white and blotched shapes in the moonlight, running down the edge of the field with happy shouts of recognition, swinging their tails, jumping past the elephant dung and into the road.

'How could you do that to me? You're naughty sheep,' I scolded them.

They looked at me reproachfully. I had gone out and left them. They had heard the car. And why had I been so long in coming to find them?

They ran round to the gate and into the garden where Portia was now on the lawn, shouting louder than ever. I took them to their pen in the barn. My day would begin tomorrow with filling up holes in the hedge. Not exactly what I had planned.

Katy and I went inside again and made a cup of coffee. I picked up the newspaper and turned to the crossword.

'Can you hear sheep in the flower garden?' was the first clue.

Yes, was the answer, frequently. Adam and Pandora eating the roses, Rupert getting high on wormwood (supposed to

induce hallucinations), Berkeley reducing the clumps of chives
to the level of a bowling green, and all of them generally making
beasts of themselves among the Michaelmas daisies.

## CHAPTER NINE

Rupert trotted obediently up the path beside me on his collar and lead. We were met at the door by the headmistress of the junior school. She held out her hand.

'Hello, I'm Monica. You must be Elizabeth, and is this Rupert?'

At the mention of his name he pricked his ears and looked up at her.

'Isn't he sweet? The children are all so excited about his visit. It's very good of you to come and bring him with you.'

'I'm afraid he's not really house-trained, but I've brought a pile of newspapers to put on the floor, and he's brought his breakfast with him.'

'Don't worry. All the floors have washable tiles, and we've got a bucket and a mop. Can I help you carry anything?'

'If you could just hold his lead, I'll fetch the things from the car.'

I collected the bag of fleece, posters, booklets, and some skeins of wool, and Rupert's bag of sheep nuts and carrots with his bowl. Monica led the way through the glass doors to a wide hall, opening into the general assembly area, off which were the classrooms. The school was arranged on an open plan, so that each classroom led off the hall without doors. A sea of eager little faces was peering from each room as we made for our first class.

The children crowded round and patted Rupert while I

spread out some newspapers and found him some food. I spread the fleece out in one corner of the room and pinned a poster to the wall showing different breeds of sheep.

The infants' class was more interested in fussing Rupert than spinning, but with the help of two teachers, I pushed blobs of plasticine onto their pencils, tied them with a length of wool, and then showed them how to pull out the fleece to make a thread, spinning their pencils as they did so. Rupert nosed around, inspecting the bookshelves and some natural history exhibits. He sniffed at a bird's nest, but was particularly interested in a jar of wild flowers, which I managed to reach in time to prevent the flowers being added to his breakfast.

The children pulled and fingered the fleece, surprised at how soft and oily it felt. One freckle-faced little boy twirled his pencil and, with a bit of help from me, managed to draw out a length of wool. He beamed at the rest of the class, then wound it carefully onto the pencil, ready to begin again. After several attempts, he spun a piece on his own, at which he was delighted. Two small girls had joined forces, and between them were spinning some wool, one turning the pencil while the other pulled on the fleece.

It was surprising how quickly some of them mastered the improvised spindles. None of them was older than five, but three of the small boys were making good progress, and soon demanded more lumps of fleece. Others fared less well.

'Miss, my wool's broken.'

'Please, Miss, I can't do it.'

'Will you help me? Will you do it for me, please, Miss?'

'Miss, Miss, look at Rupert. He's knocked all those books over.'

'Go away, Rupert, you can't eat my wool.'

And so it went on, twenty small children, all talking at once, all demanding attention. They wanted to know how old Rupert was, whether I had any other sheep, what Rupert did all day, what the other sheep were called. The questions were endless, but they were all happy and laughing, enjoying the novelty of a sheep disrupting their lessons.

Rupert pee-ed on the newspapers, which sent them all into a fit of giggles.

'Mr Frost will be cross with you, Rupert' — Mr Frost was the school caretaker — 'but don't worry, we won't tell him,' said one small girl, clasping her arm round Rupert's neck.

I picked up the wet papers and stuffed them into a large dustbin bag, while one of the teachers produced the mop and bucket. Then the bell rang for playtime and twenty little volunteers pushed forward, begging to take Rupert for a walk round the school field. Monica chose two of the girls, and they walked out proudly holding the lead, one each side of him, while I was taken to the staffroom for a cup of coffee.

The next class of children, being older, managed the spinning with less difficulty. Rupert wandered around and then out into the hall and across to one of the other classrooms to disrupt a maths lesson.

By lunchtime there were bits of wool strewn about everywhere and the children were despatched to the cloakrooms to wash their grease-covered hands and faces. I took Rupert outside and tied his lead to a post near the front door which I could see through one of the hall windows while we had lunch. I sat at a table with some of the children. I was surprised how school lunches had changed since I was at school — no watery cabbage and lumpy mashed potatoes. Each child had a plate of salad — grated cheese and grated raw carrot, tomato and lettuce and deep-fried potato rissoles. The children ate their food with enjoyment. There was very little wasted. When I was at school the kitchen had a large black bucket labelled 'Pigs Will', and by the end of lunchtime it was full to overflowing. The bucket always intrigued us. 'Pigs will what?' we always wanted to know, but never found out.

As soon as lunch was finished and the tables cleared, there was a mad scramble of children to go outside and find Rupert. I untied his lead and two more children were detailed to take him for a walk, this time two of the boys. We sat in the staffroom with a cup of coffee, watching a little procession making a tour of the school field — Rupert and the boys in the lead, while the other children followed in an orderly fashion, like a king and his train of courtiers.

The afternoon spinning lessons progressed well. Rupert, by now feeling very much at home, wandered between the classrooms. There were constant calls of 'Rupert' from every direction and he trotted about being cuddled and patted, going back and forth across the hall from one room to another.

At the end of the afternoon the children crowded round the school entrance to watch Rupert climb back into the car and go home.

'Thank you so much for taking all that time and trouble for our children, Elizabeth,' said Monica. 'It has been very much appreciated and I'm sure the children have all had a wonderful day. These experiences mean so much to them. It's something they never forget.'

I could not speak for Rupert, but the day had been unforgettable for me, too. The children stood by the school gate waving and blowing kisses as we drove away.

'Goodbye, Rupert,' they called. 'Come back and see us again.'

When we arrived home I took Rupert to the gate into the meadow beside the apple tree. The others were grazing near the oak tree and came running down the field towards us, Pandora in the lead, Berkeley thundering after her, and Adam, Portia and Tallulah close behind. They reached the gate and stood breathless and excited, licking their lips for biscuits. I held the biscuits out for them and they pushed and jostled each other, Adam butting at the others.

They sniffed at Rupert and pushed him a bit, then began to walk back across the grass towards the hedge. Rupert started pulling hungrily at the clover. He had to make up for lost eating time.

The following week a large brown envelope arrived in the post, together with an air mail letter which I knew immediately was from Rodney in Texas. I always looked forward eagerly to these blue striped-edged envelopes, and put it aside while I opened the other one, to sit and linger over it with a cup of coffee.

There was a letter from Monica thanking me for taking Rupert to the school, and two dozen letters from the children, along with some drawings of Rupert — eating a mountain of food labelled hay, oats and carrots; looking out of a car window; several of him standing in the school field next to the climbing frame; and a very graphic drawing by a boy of eight and a half, of Rupert pee-ing on the floor. The children's letters were a delight to read.

Dear Mrs Kingstone
Thank-you for bringing rurpurt he is very nice, and he had very thick wool as well. At home I done a lot of spinning and I liked rurpurt very much and he was very funny.
by Carla

Dear Mrs E Kingstone
Thank you for brining rupet the sheep. how is he? and how are you? I hope all of your sheep are all rite. I find spining very intresting I like the bit twisting and turning about I had never touched a sheep befor
Thank you agen<br>yours sent-sereley<br>Tanya XXXXXX

Dear mrs kingstone
thank you for bringing Rupert over to our school he was lovely. I hope your other sheep are well and I hope you are well. Has Rupert got his proper winter coat yet? Our sheep on the wall don't seem to be doing any-thing interesting except standing there goodbye Jane

To mrs kingstone Thank you for bringing Rupert to school. I enjoyed spinning. And I liked Rupert a lot. I would like to see him again. And I liked his wooly coat. He is very warm.
love from Louis XXXXXX

Dear mrs kingstone I hope Rupet is being good I hope the rest of the sheep are being good. I hope you are very well we all was glad that you bort rupet is a nice flufy sheep we liked rupet he is nice to strok from stephen

The letters were wonderful. The children must have taken so

much time and trouble to write them, and they all had drawings
of sheep at the bottom of the pages. But my favourite letter was
from a little girl called Toni. At the bottom of the page she had
drawn a round, cuddly-looking sheep with blue eyes, and she
had written:

Dear Mrs Kingstone
I hope Rupert is all rite from being in school Our flor is not so
dirty eny more becos Mr frost clend the flor and we did not tell
on Rupert thank you
                         from Toni

Rupert's visit to the school had obviously been a success. I
made myself a cup of coffee and then opened the letter from
Rodney.

It was a long, interesting letter. They had been to San
Antonio in New Mexico for a weekend and visited a large craft
market selling Navajo Indian rugs and weavings. They had also
bought a pair of goats, but Rodney said that the goats spent all
their time bleating pathetically, or invading their vegetable plot.
He had bought the goats hoping they would clear some of the
scrub land on their twenty acres. But the goats apparently had
other ideas and preferred to eat the melons, courgettes and
aubergines which they had carefully planted. It sounded a

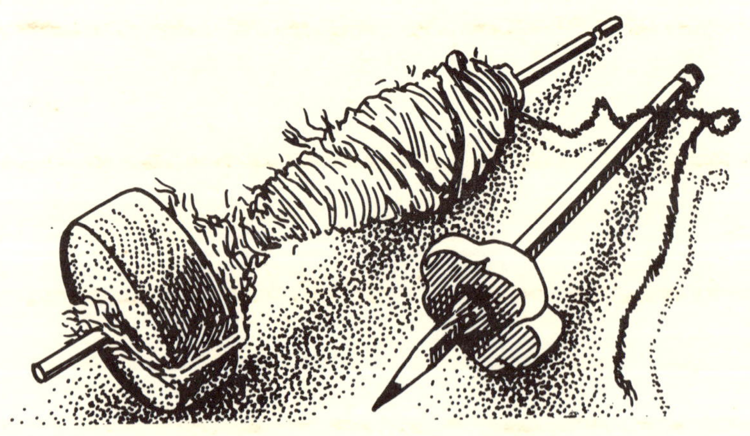

familiar story, remembering Berkeley's penchant for roses, raspberry canes and strawberry plants.

'There are lots of beautiful wildflowers here,' he wrote, 'you would really love them. I hope one day you can come out in the spring and enjoy them with us. About this time of year the roadsides and fields in this area turn a gorgeous bright red with thousands of Indian Paintbrush wild flowers — a small plant abut six to eight inches high packed in their thousands, sometimes covering acres and acres of land. They are really beautiful.'

Rodney and Melissa wanted Katy and Tom to go out and stay with them that summer during their school holiday, and wondered if Gerald and I would be agreeable. By then Katy would have taken her 'A' levels and they thought it would be a good relaxation for her after all her hard work, and if we would let them go he would send both their tickets.

Katy and Tom were full of excitement. They danced about the kitchen, throwing their school books in the air.

'Hey, great!' shouted Tom, 'America! That's brilliant! I hope Dad will let us go.'

When Gerald came in that evening he was hardly through the door before they were both talking to him at once. All through supper we talked about nothing but the impending trip to Texas.

'I must say, it's very generous of Rodney and a wonderful opportunity for you both. We'll have to get passports and visas and check on your vaccinations,' he said. 'You haven't got long to gct cvcrything ready — only two months.'

'Seems ages,' said Tom, 'I wish we were going tomorrow.'

The next few weeks passed very quickly. Katy spent hours revising for her exams — reading her English literature books long into the night, drawing endless still life pictures of the contents of the pantry or the tool shelves in the barn. Her bedroom floor was littered with wool and material and lumps of fleece for her textile project. We filled in the passport forms and I drove to Peterborough to collect the passports so that we could send them to the American Embassy as soon as possible to obtain the visas necessary for their visit. That was likely to be the longest delay, Rodney had warned us, perhaps six weeks, and as the date printed on their tickets drew nearer we waited every morning for the postman to arrive, fretting anxiously for the passports and visas.

Eventually they arrived with a week to spare. And then it was time to pack the cases, to drive to Gatwick Airport and send Katy and Tom on their ten-hour flight half-way across the world.

We left Monks Green in the first light of dawn — a pale yellow-green sky, with a mist in the valley and the wood pigeons cooing in the willow tree behind the barn. We drove through the neatly-hedged fields of North Essex to join the M11, and then towards the grey horizon of endless buildings and cooling towers that clustered round the Dartford tunnel, obliterating trees and fields, like another world.

Then across the pale, rolling hills of Kent and into the bustle of the airport. When we had first talked about Katy and Tom going to America it had seemed far away in the future, but now suddenly I realised that they were going and I had a terrible panic-feeling that I might never see them again.

'Take care, my darlings,' I said, hugging them both, and then they were gone, mingling with the other passengers and out of sight down the covered walkway to the departure lounge.

Gerald and I went to the rooftop restaurant and stood by the rail in silence, like strangers, watching the luggage being loaded into the huge red and white plane below us. The passengers boarded under cover, but I waved frantically, hoping that maybe Katy and Tom would see us from one of the portholes.

Eventually the engines started and the plane inched forward and turned towards the runway, creeping along the tarmac like a great red and white dragon, the victims it had swallowed hidden from view. It stood at the end of the main runway, waiting for a signal to surge forward and vanish into the sky.

Then the plane began to move and race down the runway. I turned away in fear. I could not watch the great red and white beast with its precious cargo — the two people I loved more than anything else in the world — being carried away beyond the clouds.

'They're safely up,' said Gerald, 'you can look now.'

I turned back and saw that already, in a few seconds, the plane was high, climbing steeply, and then banking to make a half-circle towards us.

'Goodbye, goodbye,' I said, waving at the fast disappearing plane, soon no more than a speck high in the sky as it headed north-westwards in a straight line towards the Pole.

'Please, God, take care of them,' I whispered as the speck became a blur, and I strained my eyes at the spot where it had disappeared.

'Come and have a drink,' said Gerald walking to a table nearby. 'Do you want anything to eat?'

'No, thanks. I'm not hungry.'

'You should have something,' he said.

'Gerald, I couldn't eat a thing.'

I sat down at the table and Gerald went to get the drinks. I wondered numbly what I should do without Katy and Tom. Now, after nearly twenty years, Gerald and I were on our own again and I thought of the long empty years stretching ahead, of life without Katy and Tom. This time they would be coming back, but next time they would not. Soon they would leave for ever. They had their whole lives before them, but mine seemed to be slipping away with very little to show for it.

Gerald returned to the table and we sat in uneasy silence, sipping our drinks. The tears welled in my eyes and ran down my face. I thought of Katy and Tom, shut in the red and white dragon, somewhere above the clouds, somewhere far away on the edge of the world. I did not want to go home. I wanted to stay there, sitting in the rooftop restaurant until I could be sure that they had reached America safely. But it would be midnight before I should hear from them, and at last we got up and left the table, to drive back to the little cottage in the middle of the fields.

When we arrived home I went to the meadow to sit under the oak tree with the sheep. Rupert and Portia were already sitting down in the shade, chewing their cud, while the other four grazed nearby. I sat down next to Rupert and leaned against his back. It was a hot, still afternoon, the silence broke only by the steady chomping of the sheeps' jaws and the occasional buzz of a heavy bumble bee drifting past, its fat brown and orange velvet body skimming the clover blossoms.

Below me was the house with its mossy tiled roof, and away in the distance, through a heat-haze of grey-green trees, was the line of dark blue hills. Peaceful rural England. I thought of the first time I had sat under this oak tree and how in a few years life had changed so much. Katy and Tom were then just schoolchildren; now Katy was eighteen. Then sheep-keeping had been nothing more than a dream. Now the sheep were beginning to take over my life.

I went back to the garden where Gerald was lying asleep on the lawn in the sun, stretched out on a rug in a pair of fawn-coloured shorts and his socks and shoes. I went into the house to make a cup of tea and start cooking for supper.

It seemed a long evening. Gerald sat with his archaeology books and I fiddled about with some wool and my spinning wheel, but found it hard to concentrate. In the end I gave up and sat down to watch a television play that was only remotely interesting. But it was an excuse to leave Gerald sitting in the kitchen, and as I knitted at the same time I could pretend to myself that I was not altogether idle.

Just before midnight the telephone rang. Tom and Katy chatted happily on the other end, tired after their long journey, but full of excitement. With the difference in time it was still only late afternoon there. They were already surprised at the space everywhere, the wide sun-bleached streets, and the heat.

'When we stepped out of the plane it was like walking into an oven,' said Katy.

They sent lots of postcards, of Dallas and the American countryside and wild flowers, and of the Gulf of Mexico where Rodney and Melissa took them for a weekend.

The six weeks without them at home were quiet and uneventful. I spun up several fleeces and spent an afternoon in the lane digging for roots of bedstraw. The clouds of white flowers were all along the roadside, and the roots when boiled with the wool gave a beautiful pink dye. Bedstraw is a close relation of Madder, grown on the continent as a dye plant to produce the colours Rose Madder, Madder Red and Madder Brown. The roots were long and stringy and seemed always to be tangled up with blackberry roots. I put them into a sack and carried them back to the cottage, some to save for use in the winter when other dye plants were scarce.

Gerald busied himself with his books and his Roman coin collection. I spent a morning in the barn playing at shepherds — giving all the sheep a worm dose and trimming up their feet. I had recently bought myself a pair of proper hoof trimmers, seeing them on a stand at one of the agricultural shows. Up until now I had always used my best cutting-out scissors which were very sharp and did the job perfectly well. I could never bring myself to use a sharp knife to cut the overgrown edges of the hoof as I had seen other shepherds do. The hoof trim-mers looked rather like a pair of secateurs but with straight, not curved blades. I turned the sheep over one at a time and inspected their feet. The new hoof trimmers were much easier to use than my scissors and they were soon all attended to and taken back to the meadow.

The week before Tom and Katy were due back from Amer-ica, Gerald took himself off for a fortnight to Dorset, to live in an Iron Age settlement with other amateur archaeologists. It was supposed to be a holiday with all the excitement of discover-ing the ruins of Peru, or the ancient civilisation of Greece. But I believe it rained most of the time and their enthusiasm was severely dampened, along with their food and clothing.

Left on my own in the house, there was a wonderful peace. The days were golden and warm, with a first hint of the smell of autumn in the air. Every morning the meadow was covered with silken spiders' webs glistening with dew, like patches of lace spread out to dry. The leaves in the hedge along the meadow were turning yellow, and clusters of pale toadstools appeared in the long grass under the hedge and in little fairy rings on the lawn. Starlings sang and whistled from the top of the apple tree or the willows behind the barn, their feathers shining blue-green in the sunlight.

The hens scratched happily in the flower beds, or had dust baths in the still dry earth near the apple tree. Dorset may have been suffering torrential downpours, but the sun shone on Monks Green. Gilbert and Polly padded about, crushing the pale toadstools on the lawn with their big orange feet.

I tidied and polished the house, and made cakes ready for Katy and Tom's return. I telephoned Gatwick Airport to check their flight number and arrival time. They were due in at 8.0 a.m. I planned to leave home at four-thirty in the morning, but I was so excited at the thought of them coming back that I did not feel like sleeping at all, and was tempted to drive straight down to Gatwick that night. In the end I went to bed for a few hours, after setting two alarm clocks and asking the operator to give me an early morning telephone call.

There were still stars in the western sky as I left in the morning, but the sky in the east was streaked green and prim-rose. The sheep had seemed surprised to be let out of the barn while it was still dark. I had opened the hen-house door and the door to Gilbert and Polly's house, and hoped the fox would not decide to make an early morning visit.

The roads were quiet and it was not long before I reached the motorway and then the Dartford tunnel and into Kent. I reached the airport and parked the car, then went to the rooftop restaurant to wait for their plane. It was a hazy morning, with shafts of sunlight breaking through the thin mist. I watched several planes take off, and another one land, which I presumed were running the shuttle service to the Midlands. Then, exactly at eight o'clock, I saw a huge plane approaching the main runway, its grey shape looming out of the mist, headlights shining like great torches. It seemed to hang motionless in the air, suspended over the runway by invisible powers. Then suddenly it was down and rushing forward along the grey tarmac, while the tannoy announced the arrival of the flight from Los Angeles and Dallas Fort Worth.

I watched the plane slow to walking pace and taxi off the main runway to a halt in one of the unloading bays. As the passengers had boarded undercover, now they disembarked hidden from view of the rooftop. I rushed down the stairs and into the arrival lounge to join the group of people already there, waiting for relatives and friends to pass through customs. We did not have to wait long. After about ten minutes the first passengers appeared, some smiling, some looking tired after their flight, and many of them obviously American.

Then I saw Katy and Tom, walking side by side; they looked older and more grown-up, they were tanned golden brown by the Texas sun, and Tom had grown much taller in just six weeks. We hugged each other.

'Hello, my darlings, I'm so pleased to see you. Are you both exhausted? You look so well, and Tom's grown so tall.'

'It's good to see you, Mother,' said Katy. 'Have you been all right? I did miss you, but America was wonderful.'

Tom, now head and shoulders above me, put his arm round me as we walked across to collect the baggage.

'How've you been, old Mother?' he said fondly, then added, 'You're shrinking.'

'No I'm not,' I laughed, 'you're just getting taller. Do you both want breakfast or coffee or anything now?'

'We had breakfast on the plane,' said Katy. 'Let's stop for elevenses on the way home.'

We collected their cases and went to the multi-storey car park. In my haste to see them again I had forgotten to look at the level number on the wall. We searched up and down the rows of cars.

'Well?' said Tom.

'It must be here somewhere,' I said. 'I parked next to a red Rover.'

'Well, that's probably gone by now,' said Katy. 'I can't see the car anywhere. Let's try the next level.'

We trailed down the stairs with the cases, Tom and Katy laughing and shaking their heads. There was the car, and the red Rover.

'Don't worry abut it, Mum,' said Tom, 'must be old age.'

'England looks so grey,' said Katy as we drove along the M23, through the softly muted shades of the autumn downs. 'All the roads in America look white from the sun, and I've never seen the sky look so blue.'

'And the roads are so much wider,' said Tom. 'They have six lanes out there. This would be nothing. But they all drive much slower. There's a fifty-mile speed limit on the roads, even out in the country where there's no traffic. Uncle Rodney says he's always getting speeding tickets.'

'It's just all so different,' said Katy, 'things I never really noticed before, like the houses. Out in the country they have individual houses but in the towns all the buildings look like glass towers. No rows of semi-detached houses — they couldn't understand what they were when I tried to explain. And no one ever walks anywhere. They go everywhere by car and just stop outside each shop, do their shopping and then drive to the next shop, even if it's not far away. Auntie Melissa and I walked round town one morning and everyone kept offering us a lift.'

'The water sports centres were good,' said Tom. 'There are lots of them called "Wet' N' Wild". I went water skiing — I've got some photos to prove it. I fell off quite a bit to start with but it was good fun. And we went fishing in the Gulf of Mexico.'

'We went down there for a weekend,' said Katy. 'It was really beautiful. Miles of silver sand. The road ran along by the beach and on the other side were swamps full of little alligators. I'll never forget walking along the sand there as the sun was setting and all the oil refineries on the skyline.

'The worst part about America is that they are so racist, in Dallas anyway. The black people and the Mexicans get all the worst jobs and people are so rude to them. There are a lot of illegal immigrants among the Mexicans — they swim the Rio Grande to get into Texas from Mexico, so the Americans call all the Mexicans "wet backs". There are lots of Mexican restaurants in Dallas, and we went to a big craft centre that had some beautiful silver and turquoise jewellery from Mexico.'

'What about that wedding we went to?' said Tom.

'Oh, Mother, you wouldn't believe it,' said Katy laughing. 'It was awful. They were drinking champagne out of plastic glasses.'

'And two hunks of about nineteen kept chatting Katy up,' said Tom, laughing as well. 'She was getting really cross, I could see. And they kept on phoning up for days afterwards.'

'Oh, they were dreadful,' said Katy, 'and the size and shape of a pair of gorillas.'

'Whose wedding was it?'

'Someone from Uncle Rodney's office,' said Tom. 'He didn't want to go, but he said it would be rude if he didn't, so Katy and I went too. It was a good laugh, though, wasn't it, Katy? And there was lots of booze.'

'Yes, it was fun in spite of the gorillas.'

'Can you look in my purse, Katy, and find a fifty pence piece?' I said as we approached the Dartford tunnel. We joined the queue for the automatic barrier. I wound down the car window and threw the fifty pence out into the bin — at least it was meant to go into the bin. I had managed the operation perfectly well on the way to the airport and on countless other occasions. But I missed. The fifty pence fell onto the concrete beside the bin and I had to get out of the car to retrieve it while cars behind hooted indignantly at the delay. Tom and Katy fell about laughing.

'You are an old fool, Mother. First you lose the car in the airport car park, then you throw your fifty pence into the road, instead of the bin like everyone else.'

'Sorry, it must be the excitement. I think we should stop and have some elevenses as soon as we find a turn-off.'

We left the M11 at the Harlow junction and came out into the middle of the town near the market. It was still not ten o'clock and there were plenty of parking spaces along the kerbs. We walked through the market and found a coffee shop, and had large cream doughnuts with our coffee while I was trying to keep in my mind a mental picture of where we had left the car. I did not want to mislay it a second time that morning.

We walked back along the pavement at the side of the market

and happened to pass a pet shop. There in the window were four kittens. They were very small, black and white with blue eyes. Katy stood looking at them.

'Oh, they're so lovely. And so little. Look at that one, it's got a tadpole tail and hairy knees. I wish I could have one. I love kittens. I wonder who's going to buy them. Poor little things.'

What stroke of fate had made us stop in Harlow? I wondered, and why did we have to walk right past this pet shop? With eight cats at home, we did not need a kitten.

'But we've got lots of cats already,' I said.

'I know,' said Katy, 'but the kittens are so sweet.' She lingered by the window as Tom and I started to walk away. I stopped and went back.

'All right, if you really want one, I'll get you one. Come on, let's go in and look at them, but I don't know what Father is going to say.' I had a fairly good idea. It was bad enough having cats arriving on the doorstep, or being wished on one by friends, but actually *buying* a cat was a different matter altogether.

The kittens were two pounds each.

'Two pounds?' said Tom. 'That's a bit steep. I could easily ask around when we get home, and find you one for nothing.'

But we had gone into the pet shop to purchase a kitten. Katy chose the one with the tadpole tail and the hairy knees, which had caught her attention outside. He was put in a cardboard box and she carried him delightedly back to the car. She took him out of the box and sat him on her knee. He was a very appealing kitten. Tom stroked his head.

'You're not bad for a cat, mate,' he said. 'What are you going to call him, Sis?'

'I don't know,' said Katy, 'a name to remind me of America. One of the places we went to, perhaps, but not Dallas.'

'Where did you go on the Gulf of Mexico?' I asked.

'Well, Port Arthur. I could call him Arthur, I suppose, but I don't like that much. I know. There was a town called Lufkin which we drove through on the way down, an oil town beside a lake. What about Lufkin?'

'Lufkin's fun, and different. Yes, I like that.'

Lufkin curled himself up on Katy's knee and slept all the way back to Monks Green.

*CHAPTER TEN*

A few months later, Katy left home for good. She had decided to push her dreams of doing art to the back of her mind and train to become a nurse. She had written to Schools of Nursing in different parts of the country, and the first to reply and offer her an interview, and subsequently a place, was Oxford. She departed to one of the most beautiful cities in England and left Tom and me in charge of Lufkin's welfare. He was quickly growing into a bold, adventurous kitten, exploring every corner of the house, playing games with the dogs and pretending to chase the chickens, who ran flapping and squawking in panic every time he jumped out from behind a bush.

'It's not the same without Katy,' said Tom sadly one evening, as he sat at the kitchen table with his homework books spread out round him. It was now his turn to spend long hours studying for 'O' levels.

'I know,' I said. 'I wonder how she's going to like nursing. It will be a lot of hard work, and upsetting, too, at times.'

'She'll do it,' said Tom. 'She's made up her mind, so she will.'

Gerald was in the sitting room looking at a string of beads he had ordered by post, which had arrived that morning. He held them out – exquisitely beautiful blue-grey ceramic, still glazed.

'These are at least four thousand years old,' he said. 'They're from Mesopotamia.'

'But where did they come from?' I asked. 'Did someone just find them in the sand?'

'No, of course not,' he said. 'They're from a grave.'

'But that's horrible, robbing graves.'

'It's not quite like that,' he said.

'But you wouldn't go and dig up a grave that was fifty years old, or a hundred years old, so what's the difference? It doesn't matter how old the grave is.'

'Archaeology is finding out about the past.' He held out the beads, but I couldn't bring myself to touch them, beautiful though they were. He hung them up on an old nail at the side of the inglenook fireplace.

'I'm sure it will bring bad luck,' I said.

'Don't be so silly,' said Gerald. 'You do have some ridiculous ideas.'

'I would hate to think that someone might dig me up one day.'

'Then you'd better be cremated.' He turned away angrily and left the room.

I looked at the beads hanging beside the fireplace, catching the light from the flames: smooth, slightly square and irregular, but all of an even size. I had an uneasy feeling. Our happy tranquil country life was fast disintegrating and I wondered how it would end.

I set my spinning wheel near the fire and found the bag of wool on which I had been working. For the last few months I had been receiving through the post a steady supply of fleeces to spin into skeins, sent from all over the country. I'd had wool from Scotland and Wales and the Isle of Man, as well as most counties of England, and had started to correspond on a regular basis with a lovely woman on the Isle of Man, who sent the most amusing accounts of her life there and her own flock of sheep. Her letters always made me laugh and were a welcome start to the day. She had sent me some fleeces to spin for her, and also two Manx Loaghtan fleeces for my own use. They were very soft and a beautiful golden brown. Loaghtan is Manx Gaelic for a particular shade of brown, from which the breed takes its name. The lambs are almost black when born, but the sun has a bleaching effect on the fleece and gradually lightens it. When first sheared the adult sheep look quite dark, but quickly resume their gold-brown colour in the summer sun.

'The Loaghtan sheep can be wild,' wrote Sheila, 'and though small, it can take a couple of men to hold them down for shearing. I have done a few with the help of a friend, and as they all have horns, you are all right until you get them half sheared, then, putting their heads back, they tend to stick the forward-facing horns up your bum!

'Shearing has to be well-timed, otherwise they rub the coats off and the wool is lost. In my opinion they are a wild sheep that has been tamed, but the instinct to be up and away is still there. A friend of mine who keeps two of them says they are easy to handle, but then told me that they had taken off over the Ayres, which is a stretch of Manx National Trust land at the north of the island, and it was over a week before she got them back, and only then by appealing on the Manx local radio for news of them.'

The rams, it seemed, were particularly wild. She told me of a Loaghtan ram with a local flock, which had escaped his field down an almost sheer cliff face and haunted the countryside for over three months at tupping time, causing plenty of half-breed lambs in the spring. The ram was finally trapped with some difficulty on her farm late one Sunday night, and nearly ran four grown men into the ground in the process. Sheila said that it was a tall, thin beast, which had been living off its balls for all of the three months and little else, and looked like it, but was still a devil to catch.

Temperament in sheep obviously varied a great deal. Quite a contrast to David's docile Ryeland rams, especially the old one he took to the shows, which allowed children to sit on its back and was very partial to a tot of whisky.

I took the wool from its bag and began turning my spinning wheel. I was half-way through a bag of musk ox wool that I had been sent by a man in Surrey, who had been on an expedition to Greenland and had picked up the wool, naturally shed by the musk oxen and lying about everywhere. It was a pale coffee colour and wonderfully soft, and the resulting skeins were like mohair. It was very easy to spin and I had really enjoyed working with it and having the opportunity to handle something so rare.

Encouraged by David, I had approached the local Adult Education Centre and had been asked to give some evening classes on spinning and natural dyeing. I was not sure how the classes would work out, but thought that they could prove to be a lot of fun, exchanging ideas with like-minded people and brewing up dyes on the school gas rings, as the classes were held in the local comprehensive school in Castle Monkton.

The day of the first class arrived and I collected up all the things I would need for the introductory lesson: bags of fleece to show the difference in the breeds — long coarse wool from Scottish Blackface; silky cobwebby strands from a Lincoln Longwool; fine short wool from the down breeds of Suffolk, Dorset and Ryeland.

I had some hand spindles, pretty pottery ones which Gerda had made for me especially for the classes, little bags of wool to use with them, a poster of British sheep breeds, notebook and drawing pins. I also took back copies of *The Guardian*, a mop, dustpan and brush, a dish and a bag of sheep nuts. Because Rupert was going to the class with me.

Rupert always enjoyed outings, and as the classes were to be all about sheep and wool, I thought it would be fun for everyone to see a sheep at close quarters; with his superior fine fleece he would be a very good example of wool on the hoof.

I folded down the back seats of the car and loaded in the wool, then went to fetch Rupert from the barn. I attached the lead to his collar and led him to the car. All the sheep wore collars and bells — little Indian bells which I bought in a craft shop in Norwich. The bells tinkled as they grazed, a lovely sound coming in through the open cottage windows and also an indication of their whereabouts or of anything that had alarmed them. All the old flocks of sheep wore bells, so that the shepherds could tell whether the sheep were grazing peacefully, or whether they were in danger and fleeing in panic, perhaps from a marauding dog.

I have also been told that the sound of the sheep bells is comforting to the sheep, since being flock animals they like to hear the other bells around them and know that they are not alone.

Rupert stood behind me, leaning his chin on the back of my seat and looking out through the windscreen at the road ahead. Gerda was also going to the classes, although she had no need to learn anything, but more as moral support for me. She had promised to arrive early to help with Rupert. She was already there and we unloaded the sacks of fleece.

The lessons were to be in the art room, up three flights of stairs. We trundled up, the fifteen pounds of Lincoln cobwebs getting heavier on every floor. Then we went back for Rupert who was now complaining loudly because he had been LEFT BEHIND. He trotted happily across the playground, but viewed the stairs with suspicion. I rattled a bowl of sheep nuts and began walking up. Rupert darted after me, pulling Gerda with him on the end of the lead.

I spread the fleeces out on a work bench, pinned up the poster on a cork notice board, gave Rupert his bowl of nuts and spread pages of *The Guardian* around him. Rupert is wonderful, but not really house-trained. When I had first had Pandora I had tried house-training her, but in the end had given up. I was told by Will, the vet, that animals born in a nest, such as dogs, rabbits, cats or pigs, are easily trained, but animals born in the open field are not. Animals such as sheep, gazelle or buffalo wander across the pasture, manuring it as they go, and their defence from danger is to flee. On the whole the animals born in a nest are the predators, and those born in the open field are the prey, so even distribution of their droppings makes them less likely to be singled out for attack.

The class arrived. They were friendly, cheerful and eager to learn. One woman had brought a basket with mugs, a jar of coffee, milk, sugar and an electric kettle, so that we could have a break at half-time, without going down to the hall and getting coffee in plastic cups from the machine. Everyone voted this a very good idea, so we organised a rota for providing coffee for the rest of the classes.

One or two people had sheep of their own, but they were all surprised to see how tame and friendly Rupert was.

'Isn't he sweet!' said one. 'Does he go everywhere with you?'

'I love his woolly pyjamas,' said someone else. With his woolly legs, Rupert did look as if he had fluffy trousers on. I wondered what David would say to the idea of his flock being dressed in woolly pyjamas.

Rupert nosed around. He inspected some paint pots on a low shelf, sniffed at everyone's shoes, went to his bowl to see if there was any more supper left and then came and stood quietly next to me, his head level with my knee.

The spinning progressed quite well. Someone was worried about lumps in her wool. The first time it is not easy; just producing a continuous thread is difficult.

'A lot of shop wool has lumps in it now,' I said encouragingly, 'it looks more interesting like that.'

The room and Rupert warmed up. The line of unwashed fleeces along one side of the art room exuded a strong sheepy smell — not unpleasant, a smell that I love, but perhaps not to everyone's taste. I thought I would open a few windows before the room began to smell too much like a farmyard. The art room windows had mysterious catches that resisted any attempts to open them. I stood on the window sill and wrestled, but to no avail. I gave up in the end, as I had visions of hurtling through the glass to the playground below. I wondered if there would be complaints from the school tomorrow. They might think I had taken a herd of elephants upstairs.

The rest of the class did not appear to mind. After all, that was what it was all about — sheep, wool, getting one's hands covered with grease.

'The lanolin is very good for your hands, it keeps them soft,' I said as their hands got blacker. They chatted happily together. We had our coffee break and talked about spinning nettles, different breeds of sheep and quick ways of making rugs from

washed unspun wool twisted into ropes, which I intended to show them in a later lesson.

The time passed very quickly and soon it was time to clear up. They departed with their spindles and bags of wool to practise during the week. Two girls took a black and white Jacob fleece to share between them, and someone else, seduced by Rupert and his beautiful wool, took a whole fleece from one of his friends or relations.

Gerda and I trailed down the stairs again with all the sacks and Rupert. We piled it into the car, Rupert jumping in after the sacks, eager to be home. I found a bag of wool was missing, so I left him in the car and went back to the art room.

When I returned Rupert had jumped over to the front and was standing on my seat peering over the steering wheel into the darkness, looking for me. He gave a low bleat of greeting as I opened the door. I shooed him into the back again and got into the car to drive home. He had pee-ed on the seat.

We were soon home and I led Rupert to the barn where the others, their light still on, were munching contentedly. They looked up as we went in, wisps of hay sticking out of the sides of their mouths. I opened the gate to their pen, and Rupert went in to join them. He stood in the middle of them, while they sniffed at him and gave low bleats of recognition. He put his nose up and looked as if he had an important announcement to make.

'Goodnight,' I said to them, switching off their light. Muffled bleats came out of the darkness in answer.

Gerald was out that evening, but Tom was sitting at the kitchen table with his homework.

'Hi, Mum,' he said as I went in, 'how did the classes go?'

'It was quite fun. The other people were really nice. Rupert was good, but I expect the art room smells of sheep.'

Tom laughed. 'I bet it does. I'm glad I'm not doing art. I shall keep out of Miss Pringle's way for the next few days, just in case. What are you getting that bucket of water for?'

'Oh, well, just to clean the car up a bit. Rupert pee-ed on

my seat,' I added as I went out with the hot soapy water and a sponge.

'Occupational hazard,' he said. 'I'll make you some coffee. I've had enough of physics for one night.'

I scrubbed at the seat, then carried out the bags of fleece and newspapers, and left the car windows slightly open — enough for fresh air, not enough for overnight rain. I sat down exhausted beside the Aga with the cup of coffee that Tom had made me and wrote up Rupert's outing in my flock movement book.

*　*　*

It was a long, cold winter, and although I did not know it at the time, it was to be our last at Monks Green. Gerald and I drifted farther apart. We had several discussions about what we were going to do with the rest of our lives, which started off amicably enough but always ended in arguments.

We had days of continuous rain that pleased nobody except the geese. The ditch in the front boundary of the garden filled up to road level and then spread out across the lane, blocking the road a few yards down from our gateway for half a mile. Tom and Alex waded in to inspect the flood and pronounced it three feet deep in the centre. Cars came down the lane as far as our gate, then turned in the gateway and retreated back the way they had come.

The water spilled over the drive, making a pond on the gravel. Gilbert and Polly squawked and bobbed about in the water, dipping their beaks in it, then preening their feathers, splashing about all day. The hens huddled inside their house, and the bantams stood wet and bedraggled under the lilac bush. The sheep sheltered along the hedge or under the apple tree, eating mountains of hay and refusing to graze in the middle of the field in the rain. Adam became increasingly ill-tempered, and every evening when I took them into the barn he made a concerted effort to knock me over, sometimes succeeding.

The summer seemed far away — those long, hot days when

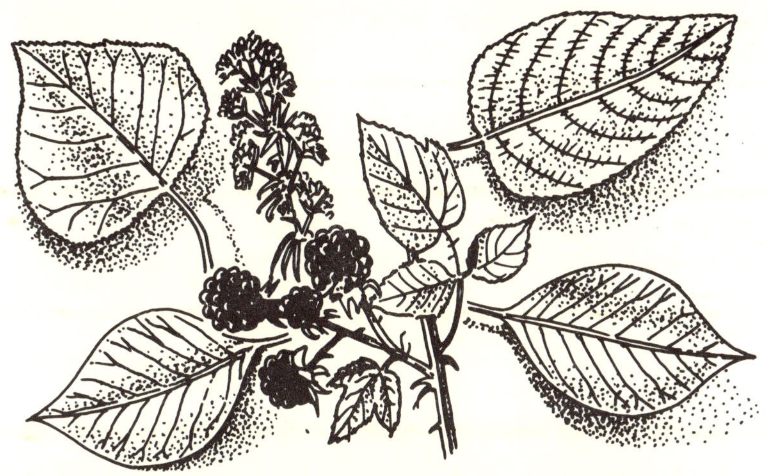

I had picked flowers in the lane or dug up bedstraw roots to dye my wool. Now the stored and dried roots proved very useful and I took them to the evening classes to boil up on the art room stoves. The rest of the class enjoyed the wool dyeing, and the roots gave us some lovely shades of pink and red. I collected poplar twigs from the lawn, which, had blown down during the autumn, and they produced a bright orange dye. Someone brought in some blackberries from her freezer for dyeing, and Gerda collected fir cones from the wood at the back of her orchard. The evening classes were a pleasant weekly diversion in the otherwise bleak days.

One Saturday Gerald was up early and drove away as soon as it was light. He was spending his day on an excursion to Kent to look at some archaeological remains with the rest of the group to which he belonged.

After breakfast, Tom and I went out into the icy January day and across to the barn. There was sleet on the wind. The sheep, out in the field, were huddling along the hedge, nibbling at the tufts of grass by the trees, in spite of their thick coats sheltering from the wind as much as possible.

A pile of logs delivered the afternoon before had been dumped in an untidy heap near the barn. I found the axe and began splitting the larger ones. Tom came up with the wheelbarrow to load them and push them across to the house.

'Come on, Mum, let me do that,' he said. 'I don't want you chopping logs.'

'It's all right, I can manage. Anyway, it'll keep me warm. We'll take it in turns.'

We hacked at the logs and filled the barrow, pushing it back and forth across the drive, piling logs inside against the inglenook fireplace. We soon warmed up and I found it a satisfying occupation, splitting the logs and seeing the pile of them grow inside, knowing that we would have a good log fire to sit by that evening.

The dogs ran about sniffing and getting in the way.

'You'll get your head chopped off, Henry, if you don't watch out,' said Tom, swinging the axe above his head.

Sophie scurried about, her short stumpy tail wagging continuously so that it wagged most of her body as well. Wolf sat down and watched from a distance, his big pink tongue hanging out of the side of his huge mouth.

Gilbert and Polly padded round the corner of the house on their flat, rubbery feet, picking their way across the stones. Gilbert stretched his neck forward and made some scolding noises and then stood, with his head slightly on one side, watching the proceedings with his bright beady eyes. Polly squawked a few times, bouncing up and down every time she opened her beak.

Alex appeared at the gate and the dogs bounded down to greet him. He came up grinning as Tom piled up the barrow.

'Hi, mate,' said Tom, 'have you come to give us a hand?'

'Hello, Alex,' I said, sitting on a large log having a rest from my exertions. 'Isn't it cold! I hope it won't snow tonight.'

'I'll chop some for you now,' he said picking up the axe. 'Where's Gerald?'

'He's gone off for the day to dig up old bones,' I said, laughing. 'Let's have a cup of coffee first. Come on, boys, we'll finish these afterwards.'

'All right,' agreed Tom, 'I could do with a rest. We've got

enough inside now. The side of the fireplace is piled right up. We'll stack the rest behind the barn later.'

We went across the drive, followed by the dogs. The little house was warm and cosy after the bitter cold outside. Tom and Alex sat by the Aga, and we held our hands round the coffee mugs to warm them as we drank. The cats stirred lazily, stretched out on the rug, safe from the cold with nothing to do but dream of mice until supper time.

Gerald came home after I had gone to bed. I heard the car pull into the drive and the dogs barking downstairs. I turned over and pretended to be asleep.

*CHAPTER ELEVEN*

Gerald spent the morning quietly packing books into boxes, folding and packing clothes. As the boxes were filled he carried them out to his car. He took down some of the pictures, carried out his case of Roman coins. Still the blue-grey beads hung by the fireplace, the four-thousand-year-old beads from a Middle Eastern grave.

I could not believe he was really going; that after nearly twenty years he could walk about the house so calmly, packing up his things. I thought, perhaps in a minute he would stop what he was doing and take me out to lunch in a pub, that we would have a long talk and everything would be all right.

But that had never been his way. Gerald disliked pubs. He had always said they were a waste of money. And why go out to eat when we could eat at home? In all the years we had been married, outings had been Sundays with his mother or cultural visits to museums for the children, which bored them literally to tears, so that now as teenagers they refused to go anywhere near museums, and ancient ruined monuments were to be avoided like the plague, the germs of which probably still lurked hidden in crevices of the stones.

At last he took the beads from the nail on the fireplace — the blue beads of ill omen — and wrapped them up in newspaper.

'I'll be going, then ...' He moved towards the door. 'I'll phone during the week.'

I stood at the kitchen window and watched him drive away

152

up the lane. Life begins at forty, so they say, but this did not seem like the beginning of a new life, the start of a new adventure. I felt sad and confused, my mind numbed. I thought how from childhood we are always taught to fit in with other people: taught to be part of a family, part of a team, part of a school. But I thought now how much better it would be if first we were taught to look after ourselves, how to be alone.

Tom put his arm round my shoulder.

'I'll look after you, Mum,' he said.

Gerald came back the following Saturday to see Tom. He parked the car in the gateway. I watched him walk up the drive: I felt that I was looking at a complete stranger. I did not understand how, after all those years together, I could look at him now as if I had never seen him before. It was as if part of my mind had been switched off. I made some coffee and he and Tom went into the sitting room. I went out to the barn to clean out the sheep pen. Later I heard him drive away again.

Tom came and stood in the doorway.

'Are you all right?' he asked.

'Yes. Are you? How was your father? What did he have to say?'

'Not a lot, really. He's got a flat for the moment. He's left the address and a phone number. He was just very quiet, and not very happy.'

'I'm sorry, Tom. I'm sorry about everything.'

'Come on, Mother, don't cry.'

'I don't know what we're all going to do now. Katy's unhappy, everyone's unhappy.'

'Come and have some coffee, then I'll help you finish the barn.'

In the following weeks Gerald phoned up several times. The conversations became progressively acrimonious. He wanted the house sold — 'his' house, he called it, 'his' furniture. Everything belonged to him, he said. I was entitled to nothing.

'If it wasn't for me we wouldn't even be here,' I shouted. 'You'd be stuck in some boring modern house somewhere, that would only be worth half as much as this. Half of this house is mine.'

He put the phone down.

I had other strange telephone calls. Often the phone would ring but there would be no voice on the other end of the line. Once there was silence for some seconds and then one word, half-whispered — 'Goodbye'. One anonymous caller said, 'You'll have to get rid of your sheep. They'll all have to go to the abattoir.' I put the phone down hastily.

I was determined that whatever happened I would keep the sheep. Somehow. Even if it meant I had to move to a different part of the country. I bought some property magazines and wrote to various estate agents asking for their lists of property for sale.

One evening, when I had taken the sheep into the barn, I was scraping the mud from between Pandora's hooves, lifting each foot in turn as she munched at her hay, when Adam, who had been eating in the opposite corner of the pen, suddenly charged across at me and knocked me to the floor. As I struggled to get up he knocked me to the ground again.

I managed to get out of their pen. Adam stood in the middle of the straw, his ears back, his nostrils flaring. It was ridiculous to be afraid of a sheep, but I had to admit I was now afraid of Adam. I remembered how tiny and angelic he had been that morning when Tom and I had first brought him home. Now he had grown into a large, heavy animal, weighing twice as much as I did.

I went back to the house feeling shaken and upset.

'Mum, what's the matter? Whatever's happened?' asked Tom as I went inside.

'It's Adam. I just don't know what to do about him any more.'

'Has he hurt you?'

'He knocked me over in the barn just now. He's made a large red bruise on my leg. I just don't seem to be able to cope with him any more. I can't go and sit in the field now with them all like I used to. It sounds silly, but he frightens me.'

'He wants a good kick,' said Tom.

'I've tried taking a stick with me, but it seems to make him worse.'

'Don't cry, Mum. Come on, I'll get you a cup of tea. I know how sweet he was when he was little and I know you love him, but I think he should go.'

'It seems so awful. It seems wrong to kill him because he's become difficult.'

'Mum, people kill sheep every day — thousands of them. He's had a good life. Nothing lives for ever.'

'I know.'

I had mentioned it on occasions to Will but only in passing, ashamed to admit my inability to cope with Adam. I phoned him at the surgery.

'Hello, Lizzy, how's the flock?'

'Fine, that is . . . well . . .' I hesitated. 'It's Adam,' I said finally. 'I'm worried about him.'

'Is he ill? What exactly is the matter?'

'No, he's not ill. It's just that he's becoming a problem. He's so aggressive. I know it sounds stupid, but sometimes I'm afraid of him. I always take a stick with me now when I go into the field with them all. But if he's in a bad mood it only seems to make him worse. He's very unpredictable. Sometimes he's all right.'

'Rams can be very dangerous, you know. Every year two or three people are killed by rams. A lot depends on the breed. Some are more aggressive than others.'

'I thought wethers were not supposed to be aggressive. I thought it was only the rams.'

'Well again, it depends. If they're not castrated properly, say done with a ring and one of the testicles is missed, you have what is called a rig. And they can get very nasty. We did him, didn't we?'

'Yes, when he was about eight weeks old.'

'Bottle-feeding lambs is always asking for trouble. You get the weak, sickly lambs that for one reason or another have been rejected by the ewe or lost their mother so that they get off to a bad start. And then making too much fuss of them can cause problems as well. Sheep quickly become humanised and forget they're sheep. Farmers don't like bottle lambs in a flock. They have no fear or respect for man or dog and can be a damned nuisance. Sometimes they refuse to join a flock when they are weaned. I know of one bottle-fed lamb that would have nothing to do with the rest of the flock when he was older, but was quite happy to live in a field of horses.'

'The others are no trouble at all. Rupert, the other wether, couldn't be better-tempered. He's so docile and plodding. I can't imagine him going for anyone. I've taken him to schools and he spent the day wandering round the class rooms, and I took him to the evening classes I taught as well. I wouldn't dare take Adam.'

'But they're not the same breed, are they?'

'No. Adam is half Dorset Horn, and Rupert's a Ryeland. Oh, Will, I just don't know what to do.'

'Look, I've got a call out your way this afternoon. I'll come in if I have time and we'll sort something out.'

Will called in later and we sat having a cup of coffee.

'Sometimes I think I'll have to get rid of him,' I said, 'especially now that I'm going to be on my own. I couldn't bear him to go to market or anything. Could you put him to sleep for me?'

'Yes, if you want me to.'

'How would you do it? Like the dogs?'

'If sheep are put to sleep with an injection it has to be done into a jugular vein — in the neck.' He spoke slowly, choosing his words carefully. 'It's not always easy or pleasant to hold them still while it's done. The other way is with a humane killer.'

'You mean shoot him?'

'Yes, through the head.'

'If he was your sheep, which way would you choose?'

He paused. 'Most owners don't like the idea of shooting because it's messy, but that's what I think is the best and quickest way. He wouldn't know anything about it.'

'Oh, Will,' I sobbed, 'what am I going to do? I can't bear to get rid of him, but I can't manage him any more.'

He put his hand on my shoulder.

'He's had a good life and a much longer one than he would have had anywhere else. He could perhaps kill you one day. You have to think of that. But only you can decide.'

'I know. I'm sorry. Everything seems so difficult now. Life is just full of problems.'

'Poor Lizzy,' he said gently. 'You have to decide yourself, but if and when you want me to put him to sleep, I'll do it for you.'

'Would you do it here? I don't want him to go away.'

'Of course.'

'And I want him shot. But not yet. Not yet.'

After Will had gone I sat by the Aga, and cried. Wolf came up to me, pushing his big yellow nose under my hands, whining, worried because he knew I was unhappy.

Over the next few weeks I thought about the problem more and more. I tried to push it to the back of my mind, but I knew that in the end I should have to get rid of Adam. I had to face up to it. I was only putting off the inevitable.

At last I phoned Will, and he arranged to come out the following Monday. I went to the farm and they promised to bring an excavator to dig a hole in the field for me.

On Friday evening Tom and I were just sitting down to supper when a car turned into the drive. It was Katy, home for a surprise weekend. We both ran out to meet her and there were hugs all round and exclamations of delight.

We all had so much to talk about. It was wonderful to have her and Tom there together and we all sat up late into the night by the fire, talking and drinking wine. Katy looked well in spite of the long hours she worked and all the study she had to do. Some of the work she found very upsetting. She was at present on the children's ward and had some heart-rending stories of dying babies she had nursed, and children with leukaemia and other incurable diseases. One in particular had

upset her — a boy of fifteen who had just died. He was the
same age as Tom, and she and Tom were very close.

I was just getting breakfast the next morning when the large
yellow digger appeared at the gate. I went out and went with
the farmer into the field. We decided on a place near the oak
tree and he began digging the hole. When I went back inside
Katy was downstairs looking worried.

'Mother, what's going on? Why is Jim digging a hole in the
field?'

'It's for Adam. Will's going to come and shoot him on
Monday.'

'Oh, Mother,' she put her arms round me. 'Whyever didn't
you tell me?'

Later that morning a van stopped at the gate and a woman
came to the door, holding a large bunch of flowers wrapped in
cellophane and ribbons.

The card read, 'Happy Mother's Day, lots of love, Katy.'

'I didn't think I was going to be able to come back for the
weekend, so I ordered the flowers on Thursday. Anyway, happy
Mother's Day for tomorrow,' she said, laughing.

'Katy, thank you. You are an angel. I don't know what I'd
do without you and Tom.'

'Don't worry,' she said, 'you've always got us.'

When I'd had my cats and dogs put to sleep through illness
and old age, I had always stayed with them, held them in my
arms while they were given their last injection. I felt it was the
last thing I could do for them: to desert them then, leave them
alone with strangers to die, was unthinkable. And I felt that I
should stand beside Adam while Will shot him, but I didn't
know how I was going to face seeing his brains blown out.

When Will drove in that afternoon I had put Adam into the
barn in their pen, while the other sheep were out grazing in
the field. I carried a bowl of sheep nuts across to the barn.

'I don't think I can watch,' I said to Will. 'I feel I should stay
with him, but . . .'

'You leave him to me,' he said. 'Go inside.'

I put the bowl down in the straw.

'If you could do it while he's eating, he wouldn't know then, would he? There's a sheet here, could you put it over his head afterwards?'

'Go inside, Lizzy,' he said gently, taking my arm and steering me towards the door.

I ran across the gravel and round to the back of the house, and sat on the bench under the kitchen window, covering my face with my hands. Suddenly I knew I couldn't go through with it. I couldn't let Will shoot him. I got up and ran to the corner of the house to stop him.

Then I heard the shot. I went back to the bench, and sobbed. How could I have done it? Would I ever stop feeling guilty? This awful day would stay in my mind for ever.

At last I got up and went towards the barn. Will was just coming out, pushing the wheelbarrow. He had wrapped Adam in the sheet and somehow managed to lift him into the barrow on his own. He pushed the barrow across the drive and into the field, and then up to the oak tree. He put Adam into the hole that Jim had dug and threw some earth on top of him. I turned away. I always hated that moment when the cold clay fell onto the bodies.

'Have you got a spade?' he asked.

I went and fetched one from the barn and Will filled in the hole while I stood and watched him, with the tears running down my face.

We went back towards the garden and the other sheep came nosing up.

'They must know what's happened,' I said, 'they must know what I've done.'

'No, they don't,' he said. 'You did the right thing. You've got to put it out of your mind.'

'Would you like a drink?' I asked when we went inside. 'I'm sorry, but I really could do with one.'

'I'll just have some coffee, Lizzy. I've got to do evening surgery. I can't go in smelling of whisky. But you have one.'

So we sat by the Aga and I cried into my whisky while Will drank his coffee.

I was still crying when Tom came home. We went out to the garden together and took some primrose plants to put on the mound of clay under the oak tree.

'You've done the right thing, Mum,' he said. 'And he had a happy life.'

## CHAPTER TWELVE

That dreadful winter seemed to drag on interminably. But at last new leaves began to appear on the hawthorn hedge and the elder trees. The birds began singing again. Then it was Tom's sixteenth birthday. He had been agitating for some time for a motor bike as soon as he was old enough to hold a licence. I was totally opposed to the idea. Some of Tom's friends already owned one, and some of them had also had accidents. Boys on motor bikes were so vulnerable: there was nothing to protect them as they would have in a car. The thought of Tom riding around on a motor bike, perhaps being in some awful crash and being killed or maimed, made me feel physically sick.

But he argued that while he would much rather have a car, at sixteen he was not old enough to drive one and a motor bike would give him some independence. Gerald was quite happy to buy him one for his birthday. And, I thought bitterly, Gerald would have none of the worry, watching Tom set out, and then waiting and praying for him to return safely. It was easy for him to play the generous parent without having the responsibility.

In the end I agreed. It was so important to Tom, and I had no right to stop him growing up. In two years' time he would be old enough to fight, and be killed, in a war. From the time that he was born, that thought had always been at the back of my mind. It is the sadness that every mother of a son must feel, mixed with the pride in her son: that one day he will be a man and may have to fight for his country.

Tom's birthday was on Saturday, and Gerald arrived soon after breakfast. They drove away together and Gerald returned later in the car on his own, followed by Tom dressed in black motor cycle clothes and crash helmet, and riding a gleaming red and black machine. He took off his helmet.

'Well, Mum, what do you think? Isn't it brilliant?'

It was indeed a beautiful bike, and his face shone with excitement.

'Yes, it is. It really is lovely.'

'I was really scared to start with, when I set off along the main road and all the cars kept passing me. But I can practise up and down the lane till I get used to it. Oh, it's fantastic! Just what I wanted. I must go and show Alex. I'll be back soon.'

I watched the black shape disappearing down the road and round the corner, and smiled. He was so delighted with it. It was lovely to see him so happy. It had been a long, miserable winter for Tom as well as for me.

'He's really thrilled,' I said to Gerald as we stood in the drive. 'I just hope he'll be careful.'

Gradually my fears lessened. Tom's bike had a very distinctive sound and I could always hear him coming down the road before he came into view. Sometimes he was followed by two or three other boys on bikes and they would spend happy afternoons washing and polishing their machines on the drive in the sun. The acquisition of a motor bike had opened up another dimension to his life.

I thought of Adam often, and reproached myself bitterly for having him shot. But I thought about Gerda and her 'Little Yeacoub'. As it had been for her when she had given him away to a friend, life without Adam was easier for me. I could go and sit in the field with the sheep without fear of being butted or trampled. The others were all so gentle. They ran up to me and nosed for biscuits, or just stood still while I rubbed their soft ears and stroked their noses.

Gradually the days became warmer, and while I wondered what was to become of us all and where we would all be living

by next winter, my gentle, peaceable sheep were a great comfort to me.

Gerald had contacted the estate agent's office in Fordington, and they sent a valuer out to look at our cottage. He drove up one afternoon in a flashy white Ford Escort with the current year's letter on the number plate, wearing a smooth blue suit and well polished shoes.

'Lovely spot you've got here,' he said, getting out of the car and admiring the view across the fields. No doubt he would write that as 'peaceful, rural location'.

I showed him round the house and he scribbled notes on a clipboard, taking great interest in the 'old oak', the inglenook fireplaces, and the walk-in pantry. That in itself was the size of a study in a modern house. I took him round the garden and to the barn. Gilbert padded after us, honking now and again. The young man seemed slightly disconcerted.

'It's all right, he likes men,' I said, 'he only bites women,' but he did not seem to be very reassured and kept looking nervously over his shoulder at the geese.

Then we went to the field. As we walked through the gate by the apple tree, the sheep put their heads up and then began running happily down to meet us, jumping through the clover, Pandora and Tallulah in the lead. They crowded round us, nosing at the stranger. Berkeley nibbled at the papers on his clipboard and he held them up hastily, out of reach, their edges soggy and chewed.

He paced up and down the field while the sheep followed him. The grass and the clover were quite long, and by the time he had finished the bottoms of his trousers were wet, and the shoes had lost their shine and acquired some sheep droppings to their soles. And someone had left a muddy trotter mark on the smooth blue material.

He returned to the garden looking somewhat harassed.

'I've never seen sheep like that before,' he said as they peered at him over the gate, and he tried to tidy his papers into some kind of order.

I made him a cup of coffee to placate him, and he drove

away smiling, promising 'an early sale', and no doubt to take his suit to the cleaners.

I thought with dread of a succession of prospective purchasers wandering round the house. When we had moved there I had fondly imagined that I would be able to live there for ever. I loved the house and I loved where it was, in the middle of the fields, and more than anything I wanted to stay there. But it was impossible. I could not buy Gerald out. I did not have a knight in shining armour to rescue me and save my little castle. So I would have to go, but I knew not where.

I had found the visit of the valuer from the estate agent's office very depressing. Soon the house would be sold, and I knew that I had to make some effort to sort out the rest of my life. But I did not know where to begin. My mind seemed to be numbed to the future.

I decided to go to Ely, to the cathedral. It was a place to which I went occasionally, like a pilgrimage. At times, when life seemed dark and all the rainbows had gone, I would go there and sit in the great stone building. I did not go very often, as somehow I felt that it would be wrong: it would be asking for something too many times, too much.

I drove through the fields with their neat hedges and then to the flat Fenland. Suddenly ahead of me, rising out of the dull, level landscape, was the great grey cathedral. A band of mist in the middle distance gave it the appearance of a castle built in the clouds.

Ely has always been one of my favourite towns, with its beautiful fifteenth and sixteenth century timbered houses, like an oasis in the black peat Fens. Childhood stories of Hereward the Wake, living on the Isle of Ely as it then was, a brave and clever man standing against the Norman conquerors, had always leant a certain romanticism to Ely.

I left the car in a narrow side street and walked across the grass, criss-crossed by people, towards the huge stone doorway. It never failed to amaze me that nearly a thousand years ago, when men were poor and had so little resources, they could build such a magnificent monument to their belief in God.

Inside it was cool and dark compared to the brightness of the day. The flagstone floor echoed with the feet of pilgrims and tourists, mingling together and admiring the wonderful building. In the centre a mirror was placed to reflect an intricately carved and painted ceiling, so high that it strained one's neck to look at it.

I walked along one of the side aisles, touching the great stone columns as I went, feeling for comfort from the age-old building. In a side chapel candles were burning. There was a supply of new candles and a box in which to put money. 'Every candle is a pilgrim's prayer,' was written beside it. I took three candles, placed my money in the box, and lit them slowly: one for Katy — 'Please, God, take care of Katy,' I whispered as I placed it beside the others; one for Tom — 'Please, God, take care of Tom'; and then one for myself. 'Please, God, help me, make me strong,' I whispered into the silence. I sat and looked at the candles for a long time. The flames were golden and burning brightly as I watched them. I wondered who else had placed candles there. Had they too felt the despair that now seemed to engulf me, and also asked for help?

I thought about our little house in the cornfields and how happy we had all once been there. This time next year, where would we all be? Where could I go, and where would I find a home for my sheep? The candles burned very slowly and I watched them, as if our lives were slowly burning away like the candles.

I do not go to church in the ordinary way, but I love churches as buildings and find a certain peace in them. I believe in a God, but I do not find Him in a church full of people. The God I believe in is part of the fields and the mist and living creatures; a God, a Spirit within ourselves. But the prayers of all the people through the ages give a feeling to a church, an awareness of some presence, of not being totally alone.

But that day in the cold emptiness of grey stone I felt nothing but my hopeless despair. Somehow life had to go on, but at that moment I did not know how.

'Please help me,' I whispered again into the silence, 'help me to be strong.'

Perhaps God had heard me after all. Watching the warm flames from the candles I began to feel more hopeful. I knew then that somehow I would survive. One day, perhaps years from now, life would be all right again. We would all survive.

I ran my hands along the stone columns as I walked out of the cathedral, out again into the sunlight and the warmth of the afternoon. Nearby was a craft shop which also served coffee and home-made cakes. I went in and bought some postcards and sat beside one of the windows that looked out onto the cathedral and the smooth daisied grass around it. As I drank my coffee I wrote a postcard to Katy. Then I posted it and bought a copy of *Dalton's Weekly* from a newsagent. When I got home I would go through it and write to different estate agents all over the country. Somewhere in England, Wales or Scotland I should find my cottage and a field for my sheep.

As I drove home again through the flat Fenland, then through the narrow lanes with their tall hedges, I felt almost light-hearted. Life would begin again somewhere else.

*  *  *

Some weeks later I paid a visit to London. As the fields rushed past and the train hurried on its way, I lay back against the scratchy seat coverings. I remembered Katy's description of Berkeley just after shearing — 'she feels just like bus seats'. She also felt just like the seats in the train. I hoped that I had left everything for Tom. Alex was staying the night with him and they had promised to see to all the animals for me. I had left a long list on the dresser, including telephone numbers in case the animals were ill or met with some fearful accident, and in case he needed any help. I would be home again the next morning, but I worried about leaving them all.

The train slowed to a halt and finally stopped at Liverpool Street station. I walked along the platform, through the barrier and then to the footbridge. I stopped half-way across the bridge and looked down. David was standing near the clock and watching the steps.

'David!' I called out.

He looked up and grinned. He was looking unusually smart in smooth fawn trousers and a hairy grey jacket, and although he still wore a cap, I saw it was not his usual working farm cap. I ran down the steps into his arms. He hugged and kissed me, and then looked at me and laughed.

'You look nice,' he said, 'I haven't seen you wearing a hat before. It suits you.'

'I could hardly wear my shepherd's smock, could I? I love your jacket,' and I ran my hand along his arm, feeling the rough cloth, like the coarse hair on Galloway cattle.

'You do look smart, David, and you're even wearing shoes.' I was used to him leaving his wellies on the doorstep and then complaining that his socks were covered in dog hairs.

'Right,' he said, 'where do you want to go?'

'It's such a lovely afternoon. Let's go and sit in a park. And let's go by bus, instead of the Underground. It will be much more fun. We can play tourists.'

'No, I don't understand the buses. We'll get lost.'

'It's just the same as the Underground, really. There's a map for each route at the bus stop and you just choose the number you want and then wait for the right bus to come along. Come on, I'll show you,' I said, pulling him by the arm towards the main entrance of the station.

There was a stall outside selling flowers and fruit. David bought a bag of peaches, then we crossed the road to the bus stop and studied the timetables and maps.

'Look, there's Hyde Park. It's simple. Now we just have to wait for the bus.'

I put my hand on his shirt and inside the rough grey jacket. David put his arms round me and smiled.

'It's good to see you,' he said.

Hyde Park was a green beach covered in deck chairs. And daisies. We lay on the grass eating peaches, while above us the planes came and went to New York, Seattle, Dallas. Later we went to Covent Garden and wandered round the stalls and then had a drink in one of the wine bars.

Walking round London that night the air was warm, and it was as light as day from all the neon signs and shops and street lamps. There were people everywhere, all smiling, looking happy. Buskers played under the trees, and David and I walked arm in arm, part of the magical city. I realised then just how important David had become to me, and how empty life would seem without him if I moved far away.

'I'll still see you if you go to Wales,' he said, 'not as often as now, but I'll still be able to see you. I go to Hereford several times a year and I always go to the ram sale at Builth Wells. You can come with me this year if you like. You could have a look round at houses at the same time.'

'I'd love to come, but I'll miss you if I don't see you for months. I'll miss you such a lot.'

'And I'll miss you too,' he said, 'more than you know.'

* * *

A letter arrived from my solicitor, asking me to go to his office as soon as it was convenient. He had received a divorce petition from Gerald's solicitors. I sat in his large first-floor office looking out over the garden full of trees. There was a huge acacia tree with its spreading branches covered with pale green leaves and white scented flowers hanging in clusters, and several rowan trees. He began reading out the petition.

'. . . the house filled up with animals. Lambs were reared in the matrimonial dining room.'

'What?' I asked, incredulous.

'Lambs were reared in the matrimonial dining room,' he repeated.

I began laughing. 'I don't believe it. It's too ridiculous. Does it really say that?'

'Yes,' he said, and began laughing as well.

'Well, that's very novel, I must say. Matrimonial dining room, it sounds so stuffy.' I couldn't stop laughing and he was obviously highly amused.

'But it was a farmhouse kitchen, anyway,' I said at last. 'I remember reading a case in the papers some years ago, about a man who divorced his wife for calling her dogs her babies, and the judge said she had turned the house into a kennel. I wonder what a judge will make of this. He'll think the house was turned into a stable. I'll be able to tell everyone that sheep were cited in my divorce — the guilty party had mud on his hooves.'

'It's based on irretrievable breakdown of the marriage,' he continued.

'You could say that,' I said. 'The marriage has broken down — we have nothing in common any more apart from the children. I want to change my name,' I added. 'I shan't be Mrs Kingstone any more so I want a new name.'

'There are three ways you can do that. First of all by simply using the new name, secondly by deed poll, which is expensive and unnecessary, or you can do it by making what is called a legal declaration. We draw up papers in the name that you want to be known by for you to sign, and then you can have copies to send to the bank, the vehicle licensing centre at Swansea and anywhere else you think you need to send one.'

'That seems the best idea. Can I do that, then?'

'Yes. What name do you want? Are you going to use your maiden name?'

'No. I haven't used that for twenty years and I'm no longer the person I was then. I want something completely different but I haven't exactly decided yet.'

'Well, as soon as you have, you can let me know and I'll draw up the papers for you.'

'Thank you. Do I have to sign anything now?'

He passed the divorce petition across the table.

'Yes, you have to sign this to say that you have received it.'

Driving home I smiled to myself. 'Lambs in the matrimonial dining room' was such a ridiculous phrase.

The problem now was what name I should choose for myself. I asked both Katy and Tom if they would mind if I changed it. It was their name as well, after all. They both understood my reasons. Katy said that she would be changing her name one day anyway, when she got married. Tom made helpful suggestions on a new name. We looked through the phone book but found nothing we really fancied. We thought perhaps a name suggestive of sheep would be fun, but Elizabeth Ryeland or Liz Dorset did not have the right sound to it. I felt Emma Wensleydale was more promising, but Tom laughed so much that I had to discount it.

Perhaps I should choose the name of a place of which I was particularly fond, but Liz Ledbury or Lizzy Leominster did not sound right either. I wanted a name that had some meaning to it — some association with myself. In the end I chose one which did not appear in the telephone directory at all. After much deliberation I decided on Arthursson, which was the name of my Norwegian maternal great-great-grandfather, who went to the Shetland Islands and married a Scottish girl.

The more I thought about it, the more I liked the idea. I had heard tales of our second cousins several times removed who still lived in the islands, and although I had never been there I had a romantic notion that I would like to live in a croft on Shetland with my sheep. The two big disadvantages to this idea were that idyllic lifestyles need a superman to share them, and on the map the Shetlands are so far away — nearer Norway than Scotland.

I arranged an appointment at the solicitor's and went to the office to collect my document. I had already been told it would have to be signed in the presence of a solicitor from another firm, so I took it to a solicitor on the other side of town to complete the transformation. He had the wonderfully Dickensian name of Sneezum. He signed after me, stamped my document with the name of the firm, then said,

'I'm afraid you owe me three pounds.'

I fished the three coins I had ready out of my purse and said, 'Thanks, it's a bargain,' and went away feeling very pleased.

When I told people what I had done I received varying reactions. One friend, a discerning *Guardian* reader, said she thought it was a lovely idea to choose my great-great-grandfather's name. Meg said she thought it was 'incredible' and immediately sent me a CND 'Women for Life on Earth' postcard addressed in my new name 'to celebrate'. (Not as incredible, however, as she found my acquisition of a Berkshire piglet called Beatrice a few weeks later.)

I phoned the office of a sheep society of which I was a member to ask them to change their records. I gave the girl who answered my new name.

'Pardon,' she said, 'could you spell it?'

I spelled it out for her.

'Bloody hell,' she said, 'you should have stayed single.'

'I was married *before*,' I replied.

A few weeks later I bumped into a friend I had not seen for some time, but she had heard of my change of name.

'Oh, Lizzy, what fun, are you living with a nice Swede? Or is he Danish?'

I laughed and explained where the name had come from. On the way home I wished I had simply said,

'No, he's Norwegian.'

## CHAPTER THIRTEEN

David's friend Arthur, who kept the Herdwick sheep, lived in Surrey on the edge of the downs. The fields sloped gently round the farmhouse, their edges shaded by large oak, ash, and beech trees. Arthur came out of the kitchen door as I drove into the cobbled yard. It was surrounded on three sides by buildings, the house one side, and long, brick-built stables adjoining along the other two sides.

Arthur came up smiling, holding the car door as I stepped out. He was a tall, strong man, with a handsome face and light brown hair.

'Come in and have a cup of tea,' he said, 'then we'll have a look at the sheep.' He led the way back to the house and in through the open kitchen door. Jane, his wife, was pouring boiling water into the teapot. I had met her, with Arthur, at the Royal Show, and she looked up and smiled.

The far wall of the kitchen was hung with red and blue rosettes, won by Arthur's Herdwicks at the various shows, and photographs of some of the prize-winning beasts.

While we drank our tea I told Arthur about Adam's unhappy demise, and asked him about the Herdwicks' temperament. I did not want to bring up another little ram lamb and find that it was turning into an uncontrollable monster. He assured me that the Herdwicks were the most gentle of sheep.

The Herdwick ewes were pale grey, some of them almost white, but the lambs were all jet black. They skipped and jumped near the ewes in the sunny meadow near the house. There were a few sets of twins, but most of the ewes had single lambs, as is usual with hill breeds of sheep.

The main bulk of Arthur's flock of over a thousand ewes and several dozen rams, was Suffolks and Mules. The Herdwicks, numbering about eighty, were an indulgence, he said, because he particularly liked the breed. They were no good for fat lamb production as the animals took so long to mature, but he managed to sell the lambs on in the autumn as stores, and watching the gentle grey sheep wandering about now in the pasture, I remembered how they had first enchanted me at the Royal Show.

They seemed very quiet, none of them dashing madly away as we approached. The ewes just looked up with their pale eyes as we walked past them, and then went back to their grazing.

'Herdwicks are quite remarkable sheep, really,' said Arthur. 'They have amazing homing instincts, and will stay on the same area of the Fell all their lives, keeping to definite boundaries, even though they are unfenced. They are also very long-lived.'

'I'm glad about that,' I said, 'I hope I shall have my little Herdwick for many years. I'd love to see them in Cumbria all over the hills. I keep meaning to go up there, but haven't got round to it yet.'

'I always go in the autumn to the big sales at Kendal. You'd like that. There are thousands of Herdwicks. And Kendal Roughs. I bought fifty of them last autumn and put them with my Teeswater ram. They've just started lambing, producing some good lambs, with nice speckled faces. The more marked the face, the better, although it can't really make any difference to the sheep's ability to mother good lambs. But buyers just look for dark faces. Anyway, I'm hoping to have some good Mashams by the autumn.' (Mashams, like Mules, are a first cross between specific breeds)

We came up to a ewe with twins near her. Arthur picked up one of the lambs and handed it to me.

'You can have this one if you like,' he said.

I held the small black lamb against me. It felt warm and its wool was very soft. It pushed its nose into my neck.

'It's beautiful, Arthur, thank you. How old is it?'

'They were born yesterday afternoon, so it's one day old.'

I had brought a cardboard box in the car, with straw in the bottom, so I lifted the tiny lamb into it. The box was on the floor in the front on the passenger side, so I would be able to keep an eye on him as I drove home.

The lamb stood up in the box as I left the farmyard, but by the time I had driven up the lane and back to the village, he had curled up in the straw. He was soon asleep.

It was a long journey home, and there seemed to be a good deal of traffic on the M25, with long queues for the Dartford tunnel. But my precious little passenger stayed asleep until I turned into our drive and the noisy dogs ran out barking to meet me.

I decided to call the new lamb Nigel. All the others had been adorable as tiny lambs and had followed me everywhere, but Nigel was especially enchanting. He was so small and so completely black, and loved sitting on my knee. He would sit quietly for hours while I knitted or scribbled letters. Most of the letters I wrote for the next few weeks ended, 'Please excuse writing, but Nigel is sitting on my knee.' Rather unfair to blame him for the somewhat illegible scribbles, as my letters were always like that. I never seemed to be able to write down fast enough everything that I wanted to say.

Nigel followed me round the garden. When I did the washing he would run in and out of the back door after me as I carried things out to the clothes line. One afternoon, when I decided to weed the flower bed under the kitchen window, he came and watched me for a while and then sat on the doorstep in the sun nearby. He was the most wonderful little creature I think I had ever had. I loved all the sheep, but I knew then that the Herdwicks were just a little more special than the others. There was an indefinable quality about them and I might easily never have known how appealing they were.

One morning, when Nigel was three weeks old, I noticed

that he seemed a bit snuffly and didn't appear to be as hungry as usual. In the end he finished his bottle of milk, but I was worried about him, so I took him in to the surgery to see Will.

Will examined him carefully and took his temperature. His temperature was up and he had signs of fluid in his lungs.

'Oh no,' I said, 'I can't bear it if he dies. He's the most wonderful little lamb I've had. Can't you help him?'

Will smiled. 'Don't panic, Lizzy. You've brought him in straight away. I'll give him an injection of long-acting antibiotic. That will last for 48 hours. Bring him back the day after tomorrow and I'll have another look at him.'

I took Nigel home feeling very despondent. I knew only too well how vulnerable lambs were, especially those being bottle-fed. But by lunch time he was really hungry and quickly downed all the milk in his bottle. He seemed to be making a miraculous recovery.

When I took him back to the surgery his temperature was normal, and Will said that all traces of fluid had gone from his lungs.

Tom and Alex had both taken a great liking to Nigel. He nosed around them while they polished Tom's motor bike. Tom often picked him up, too, and on Saturday morning when I went out to the garden with mugs of coffee for elevenses, Tom and Alex were sitting on a large log near the barn with Nigel between them.

By the end of the following week Nigel had grown considerably from the tiny lamb I had brought back from Surrey four weeks earlier, and white hairs were beginning to show against the black ones on his face. They appeared first around his eyes, giving him from a distance a rather ghostly look.

I watched him constantly for any signs that his illness might return, but he seemed strong and lively. He ran around the garden, jumping and skipping after the cats or Tom and Alex. He followed me round the house. He had soon learnt his name and ran up immediately when he was called.

He was the most affectionate and lovable creature. He still sat on my knee every evening, although he was now growing quite large. He had all the endearing qualities of a puppy, without any of its tiresome habits.

As well as writing to Sheila, on the Isle of Man, I had been corresponding with a farmer's wife in Yorkshire. She and her husband Frank lived on the moors of North Yorkshire and kept four hundred Swaledale ewes. Ellen wrote now to say that they were busy lambing and she was bottle-feeding quite a few lambs. She also said that if I wanted one I could have one with pleasure and they would look forward to meeting me at long last after all the letters.

Tom and Alex were now studying for their 'O' levels. The exams were imminent and there were very few formal lessons at school. Most of the time was spent in the school library or working at home. They would happily look after Nigel for a day, they said, and give him his bottles at the right times, while I went to Yorkshire.

I set off on a beautiful cloudless day of buttercups and daisies along the roadside, and yellowhammers calling from the tall hedges each side of the lane. It was the last day of May and already summer.

I drove through Wetherbury and joined the M11 which took me on to the A1. A large green road sign said 'The North', and I felt again the excitement that those words always gave me. At the end of this road was Scotland, the land of mists and heather; of harebells, moors and mountains; a magical place in my imagination.

I liked motorway driving for long journeys. It was a fast, efficient way of getting from one destination to another. As the place-names came up on the signs, with their distances, I could predict the exact time of reaching each one, being able to keep a constant speed. I stayed in the outside lane, keeping a wary eye for police patrol cars. I already had one speeding endorsement and did not want to collect another.

At last I reached the turn-off sign for York, and took the road north-east to carry me across the moors. The wide, rolling moors dotted with tufts of cotton grass and heather, not yet in bloom, were exhilarating. The landscape was so different from the narrow hedged lanes and tidy cornfields I had left behind, and now, looking at these empty expanses, I thought just how claustrophobic north Essex really was. Yorkshire was where I had been born, and driving across the moors I felt that it was where I belonged.

There were sheep everywhere, grazing off the rough vegetation or wandering at the side of the road. They were all Swaledale sheep and some of them had tiny black-faced lambs at foot. The ewes had thick, shaggy white fleeces looking like walking rugs, and black faces with distinctive white muzzles and eye patches. These white markings come to the sheep as they mature in the same way that the Herdwick lambs change their colour as they grow older, so the Swaledale lambs had completely black faces. And the ewes, of course, were all horned.

I stopped the car and watched a group of them for some time. They wandered among the heather clumps with the tiny lambs trotting after them. There was no sign of any human habitation: the only living things here seemed to be the sheep as they picked their way across the moor, down age-old paths.

Ellen had given me excellent directions to their farm. I followed the track winding across the moor and found the grey stone house surrounded by stone-walled paddocks and sheep. Ellen and Frank were so welcoming, it was like meeting old friends again. The house was a traditional stone farmhouse with three-feet thick walls and beamed ceilings. Ellen had made a lovely Yorkshire tea with lots of cakes and scones.

After tea I was taken to see the sheep. We walked across the moor that stretched away behind the house. Frank had some magnificent Swaledale rams with great curling horns. They came towards us and stood and stared at me, viewing the stranger with disapproval down their elegant noses.

'When we came here there were two hundred ewes with the farm,' said Frank. 'The flock has been here for generations and each flock knows its own part of the moor and seldom strays far. If we move we have to leave the same number of ewes here to carry on the flock, ewes that were born and bred on this hillside.'

'Do you have any problems with rustling?' I asked.

'Yes, we've had sheep stolen. Everyone's lost sheep off the moors. The rustlers come at night with cattle floats. They park on the moor and leave a trail of bread leading up to the back of the trucks. The sheep follow the trail, eating the bread as they go, then they are herded into the trucks and driven away to somewhere like Birmingham. By the next morning they have already been sold and butchered.'

'That sounds awful,' I said.

'It's very well organised and very difficult to stop unless the rustlers are caught red-handed. I've stopped a few, but the sheep are away and killed and jointed so quickly that there's no way of tracing them.'

The rams continued to stand their ground and stare at me. They were very handsome beasts and looked as if the moor did indeed belong to them.

Ellen had been mixing the milk for the bottle-fed lambs and now we all went over to the long stone barn.

There were about a dozen lambs there, varying in age from a few days old to a few weeks. Although the Swaledale lambs were white with black faces like Suffolk lambs, there was no mistaking their breed. The white baby wool already had the coarser hair-like quality to it, and their faces were rounder, looking almost triangular. And instead of the long black ears of the Suffolk lambs, most of these lambs had ears that were speckled black and white, or pure white.

We began feeding them and they sucked eagerly at the bottles, flicking their tails vigorously as they fed. Ellen went to one corner of the barn and lifted a tiny lamb out of the straw. She supported his body with one hand while she held the bottle for him with the other.

'We found this poor little chap on the moor last night,' she said. 'His mother had abandoned him. We managed to find him before the foxes. See his legs? He can't stand up, that's why she must have left him. The ewes do if they know there is something wrong with their lamb.'

His front legs were swollen at the joints and his feet looked twisted. Ellen took her hand away from him and he crumpled down into the straw. She picked him up. He was the most pathetic looking little creature. Two large lumps on his head, the beginnings of his horns, were still smeared with dried blood from the afterbirth. His legs were horrible to look at with the large, swollen knee joints. He was not a lovely cuddly lamb, but looked rather repulsive.

'What will happen to him?' I asked.

'Sometimes their legs get stronger as they grow. But he may die. Poor little fellow.' She held him tenderly in her arms. I remembered Will's advice: 'Choose a strong, healthy-looking lamb,' he had said.

'Could I have him?' I asked.

Frank was shaking his head.

'He'll be no good to you,' he said. 'There are plenty of good strong lambs you can take home. As many as you want,' he added.

'Please let me have this one,' I said, taking him from Ellen. 'I promise I'll look after him. Perhaps he'll get better.'

'He may,' said Frank, 'but it's taking a chance. One chap came to us for a lamb last year and took one like this. Swaledales are renowned for jumping over walls. He said he wanted one that wouldn't get out.' He laughed. 'In six months it was jumping over everything. Trouble is, though, that as they can't get about the lungs stagnate and they get pneumonia. Then that's it.'

The dreaded pneumonia — the death knell for lambs.

We put the lamb into a cardboard box with some straw and Frank carried him to the car for me. I thanked them for such a pleasant afternoon and my new lamb and drove back across the moor. Ahead of us was a three-hour journey, back to the cosy commuter country of the Essex-Suffolk border. I stopped on the way to get more petrol and telephone Tom.

'Have you got a lamb?' he asked.

'Yes, a lovely little one,' I lied. 'It's only one day old! Is Nigel all right?'

'Yes, fine.' He was in high spirits. He had spent the afternoon fixing a new exhaust system to the beloved bike, to increase performance, speed and, no doubt, noise.

'Wait till you see it now, Mum,' he said.

It was dark by the time I reached home. The front door opened as I drove up and Tom and Alex stood in the doorway, silhouetted by the light. Tom came out to the car and carried the box inside. Nigel ran up to me and I went to find the milk and bottles to feed both the lambs. The new lamb struggled in the box, trying to stand, but falling back against the sides of the box.

I lifted him out. Tom looked at him in horror.

'My God, Mother! What have you brought back this time? Whatever's wrong with it? It looks awful.'

'He was abandoned on the moors by his mother,' I said. 'There's something wrong with his front legs so he can't stand up. Perhaps it's just a deficiency and some vitamin injections will make him better. Will you give Nigel his bottle while I feed him? He must be so hungry now.'

I held him on my knee while he had his milk, the poor useless legs hanging over mine. He pushed his little face up to get at the milk which was soon finished. He was stronger at sucking the bottle than any of the other lambs had been. He seemed determined to stay alive, but looking at his deformed legs and feet I wondered how much of a battle it was going to be.

Next morning I half expected to find him dead, but he was pushing about in the cardboard box in the corner of the kitchen, trying to raise himself. I mixed the milk for him and Nigel, fed Nigel first and then lifted the new lamb out and held him on my knee. He was really hungry: this lamb did not want to die.

After breakfast I telephoned Mrs Pembridge who lived near Wetherbury and held the open farm weekends where I went to spin every summer. She was a lovely lady who kept four hundred sheep and cared for them all with selfless devotion. At lambing time she never went to bed, but kept a constant watch on her ewes in case they should need any help. Every year she reared several bottle lambs and was extremely knowledgeable where the sheep's welfare was concerned.

I told her about my little foundling and his useless front legs.

'We've had lambs like that, my dear,' she said. 'What you need to do is make splints for his legs from cardboard. Cut four strips for each leg to cover the whole length of them, then bind them up with bandage, two first each side of the leg, and the other two pieces at the front and back of the leg, so that his legs are encased in long cardboard boxes.'

'Oh, I see, thank you. Do you think his legs could get better? I've been told he might get pneumonia.'

'I've had lambs just the same that have had their legs bandaged up for a few weeks and then been able to walk all right. I'm sure you'll get him better,' she said.

'Thank you, I'll certainly try.'

'Let me know how you get on with him, and if you want any more help, do phone again.'

Tom, having recovered from the initial shock of seeing the unlovely lamb, was extremely concerned about him. He stood next to the cardboard box, bending over and stroking his back.

'We'll get you better, mate, don't you worry,' he said.

'Mrs Pembridge said we need to make splints for his legs. Will you help me? First of all we need some bandages.'

'I'll go to the village on my bike and get some,' he said. 'Come out and see it now I've got the new exhaust on.'

He was soon into his motor cycle clothes and crash helmet and we went to the barn. He wheeled out his pride and joy and roared away down the lane. I found a large box and cut the strips of cardboard. Tom was back shortly.

I got a bowl with warm water and sponged the top of the lamb's head to get rid of the blood, then, holding him across my knee, Tom and I splinted and bandaged his front legs. Nigel was skipping about on the front lawn in the sunshine. I carried the new lamb out and stood him on the grass. Nigel ran up to us and then sniffed at the new lamb's face. He stood very still, looking around him, on his strange new legs. Then he moved first one leg, then the other, shuffling forward on the rigid splinted legs, but moving.

'Great stuff,' said Tom, 'look at that.'

'Well, at least he'll be able to move around, but we'll have to watch that the dogs don't knock him over.'

'What are you going to call him?'

'Fabian,' I said.

'Fabian? I think he should be called "Merrick the Elephant Man",' said Tom.

Fabian shuffled slowly towards the flower bed under the kitchen window and sniffed at some yellow daisies, then turned and started to follow Nigel who was dancing about near the hedge. His progress was very slow, but at least he was trying to walk.

Tom and I sat on the doorstep and watched the lambs. It was a beautiful cloudless day — the first day of June. One of the cats was stalking along the base of the hedge after a group of noisy sparrows tumbling about in the branches above her. The dogs dozed in the sun near us.

'I was going into Fordington later to do some shopping,' I said to Tom. 'I've got to get some food for the weekend. Do you want to come in with me?'

'All right. But I'll go on my bike and follow you.'

I gave the lambs another bottle of milk each and then shut them in the kitchen with the dogs, lifting Fabian into his cardboard box and lying him down so that his front legs were stretched straight out in front of him.

Tom and I wandered round Fordington and did the shopping and then went back to the car park.

'See you at home, Mum,' said Tom, putting on his helmet again.

'Do be careful, promise me.'

'Of course,' he laughed, 'I'm always careful. You go first, or I'll leave you behind.'

I watched him get onto his bike and start the engine, sitting there looking so happy in the June sunshine. I followed the one-way system through the town. Every time I pulled up at traffic lights, Tom drew level with me, grinning, then waved me forward when the lights turned green.

Out of the town the road home was narrow and winding,

through hedged fields. I saw Tom in the driving mirror, disappearing from view and then reappearing as we negotiated the corners. About a mile from home I saw that he was no longer visible in the mirror, so I stopped the car and got out to pick some of the red campions growing by the roadside while I waited for him to catch up with me. There was complete silence. I listened for the sound of his engine but there was nothing. I had passed a turning to Castle Monkton about a mile farther back and guessed that he must have taken it without my noticing. He had mentioned in the morning that he was going to Castle Monkton later to see his latest girl-friend.

I drove on down the lane and turned into the gateway. Tom still did not appear, but I went and opened the door and let the dogs and the lambs out into the garden and put the kettle on for a cup of tea. I had just made a mug of tea when the telephone rang.

It was the police station in Fordington, My skin went cold with fear. Something had happened to Tom, when I had least expected it. I had spent many worried hours in the evenings waiting for him to come home, but now, on this hot June day, it had never occurred to me that he might have a crash.

'It's your son, Tom, there's been an accident, I'm afraid. He's not badly hurt, but they've taken him to hospital.'

I stood there holding the phone, thinking of Tom as I had seen him standing in the car park in Fordington, happy with the day and his beautiful machine. Only half an hour ago, and now he was being taken to hospital. I had been picking flowers in the lane while something awful had happened to Tom, and I hadn't even realised. Why hadn't I gone back to look for him? Why hadn't I followed him instead of going first?

'Are you all right?' asked the voice. I realised I hadn't made any reply to him.

'Where did it happen?' I asked. 'Which hospital has he gone to? I must go and see him.'

'The ambulance is taking him to Chelmsford. He'll be all right, my dear. They'll just want to make sure and give him some X-rays.'

'Poor Tom,' I sobbed, 'I can't believe it. I've been dreading him having an accident, but this afternoon I didn't think of it. I was just waiting for him to come home. I thought he'd be back any minute.'

'Are you all right to drive to the hospital?' he asked.

'Yes,' I sighed, 'I'll be all right.'

I dialled the number of Gerald's flat, but there was no answer. I shut the dogs and the lambs back inside and set off for the hospital. I kept thinking about the afternoon. If only I had gone back to look for him. It seemed unthinkable that I had been picking flowers in total ignorance not more than a mile away from the accident.

When I reached the hospital Tom was shut away behind closed doors and I was told to sit in the waiting room. I sat on a bench in the corridor. After what seemed hours one of the doors opened and a nurse called me inside. Tom was lying on a table propped up with pillows. His face was pale with shock and pain.

'I'm sorry, Mum,' he said faintly.

'Oh, Tom, I was so frightened,' I said. 'Where have you hurt yourself? Can you come home?'

'He's had some X-rays and nothing's broken,' said the nurse. 'But he's badly bruised and shaken. You can take him home now.'

She helped Tom off the table. I put my arm round him and he leaned on my shoulder.

'I'm so glad you're here,' he said.

'What happened?' I asked when we had got back to the car. 'And what about your bike?'

'The police said they'd get it moved to a garage. I was just coming round a corner and the next thing I knew the road seemed to be filled with a bloody great Granada. I went into it head-on, and got thrown right over the top of it and landed in the middle of the road. I reckon my bike's a write-off.'

'The thing that matters is that you are all right. Oh, God, Tom, you could have been killed. I'm sorry about the bike, I know how important it was to you, but you can always get another. You can't replace people.'

'It was the worst moment of my life,' he said. 'I really thought I was going to die. I couldn't move one of my legs first of all and they thought it was broken, but it's just badly bruised. I ache all over and I've got friction burns on my leg — where I was thrown along the road.'

'Oh, my poor darling,' I said, putting my arms round him.

'Come on, Mum, let's get home. But please drive slowly and try to avoid any bumps in the road.'

It was dark and late when we reached home. Tom went and lay on the sofa and I found him a blanket and some hot water bottles and made him a cup of tea. Gradually the colour came back to his face. He cheered up and began talking about the accident again, but more light-heartedly.

'Rushed me off with flashing lights and bells ringing,' he said as I gave the lambs their bottles. 'Lucky I haven't got my leg in plaster — we've got enough with Merrick.' He laughed. 'He looks much better now, he's actually standing up to have his bottle.'

Next morning Tom was very stiff and could hardly walk from the bruising. He was obviously still very shaken by the accident. 'I thought I was going to die,' he kept saying. It didn't bear thinking about.

I telephoned Alex and he came down to see Tom straight away. They went out onto the lawn and lay in the sun. Soon afterwards there was the sound of motor bikes in the lane and three of Tom's friends arrived. The five of them sat on the grass and I took them some coke. Tom was now looking much happier with his friends around him, and was telling them all the details of the accident. They listened in silence with a mixture of admiration and horror.

Nigel sat with them and the boys took it in turns to lift him onto their knees. Little Fabian shuffled about near them on his stilt-like legs. As sheep sit down by bending their front legs first, he was unable to sit down. He had to wait until we picked him up and then put him on the ground with his front legs stretched out before him.

I tried to phone Gerald again several times that Sunday, but there was still no reply. I phoned Katy and told her about Tom's accident and she was very upset and in tears on the other end of the line.

'He's all right now, my darling,' I said, 'he's just very badly bruised.'

'Poor Tom, poor Tom,' she kept saying. 'I wish I could come home now but I haven't got any time off till the end of the week . . . I'll be home on Friday, sometime in the afternoon.'

Tom spent the next few days dosed with pain-killers. We went to the garage near Fordington to look at his bike. It was a twisted heap of metal.

'When they brought that bike in,' said the garage owner, 'I thought whoever had been riding it must have been killed. I certainly never thought he'd be walking about like you are. How did the accident happen?'

'I took a corner and went head-on into a Granada,' said Tom.

'You were lucky, son,' he said. 'I wouldn't have believed it if I hadn't seen you with my own eyes.'

'My beautiful bike,' said Tom as we drove home. 'That can't be mended. I just keep seeing that car again in my mind, seeing it happening all over again.'

I took Fabian to the surgery to see Will. He resisted any comments about my preference for the walking wounded. After all, with a three-legged dog and a one-eyed cat, a crippled lamb was an ideal addition. We unbandaged Fabian's legs and Will examined them carefully. It was not a simple deficiency, but a congenital malformation. Will was impressed with Mrs Pembridge's advice and said that with care the lamb would survive and might walk in time. He gave him an injection of multi-vitamins and then bandaged his legs up with green plastic splints and thick, sticky bandage.

'You will need to undo the bandages every few days and then redo them. Make sure the skin doesn't rub at all on the splints.'

'How long d'you think he'll need to keep them on?'

'Three weeks should be long enough. He seems quite a healthy little lamb apart from his legs. He may have a tendency to arthritis later on, but we'll sort out one problem at a time.'

Fabian was becoming quite adept at walking now on his splints. He hobbled after Nigel and the dogs. He had also found a way of sitting down. I watched him in surprise one afternoon. He backed up against the wall of the house and then managed to slide his bottom to the ground, then pushed his front legs forward and sat down altogether, with the splinted legs sticking out in front of him. I wondered if he would be able to get up on his own, but that seemed easier for him than sitting down. He leaned his head back while pulling his front legs up and then got his bottom off the ground. A complete reversal of the way that sheep normally sit down and get up, and I was amazed that he had worked it out for himself. So much for sheep being stupid — not that I had ever believed that.

On Friday morning Nigel wouldn't take any milk from his bottle and his nose appeared to be running slightly. I rushed him in to the surgery, afraid that the lung infection was returning. But Will said his temperature was normal and that his lungs sounded clear. I drove home again, but I felt uneasy. I

tried him with some milk again and this time he drank it. It was almost as if I had imagined it all.

Tom was now feeling a lot better although his legs and ribs were still bruised. I tidied the house for Katy's visit home. It was another hot summer day. In the afternoon Tom sat on the doorstep while I trimmed the honeysuckle bush around the front door.

'Katy should be home soon,' said Tom, 'I can't wait to see her.' He stroked Nigel's back, as he stood near the steps and watched Fabian shuffling around in the flower bed.

'He gets around on those splints quite well now,' he said. 'It's funny to watch him trying to sit down, though, the way he always backs up to something first to lean against. How are you doing, Merrick?'

Nigel suddenly crumpled up in a heap into the flower bed next to Tom.

I rushed to pick him up.

'He's going to die,' I said to Tom. 'I've got to take him to the surgery quickly.'

Tom carried Fabian inside and fetched the car keys. I scribbled a note for Katy and Tom stuck it to the front door, which we left unlocked. We drove down the lane, Nigel lying across Tom's knee. I looked at him. The black wool was turning dark grey, his face had white streaks of hair all over it now. He was nearly six weeks old. I knew that rearing bottle lambs was difficult, but the hardest time was the first two weeks. Every week that they lived after that, they had more chance of surviving, but I thought now that Nigel had been slowly slipping away from me all the time.

At the end of the lane we met Katy, coming in the opposite direction. She stopped her car when she saw us.

'What's happened, Mother? You look dreadful.'

'It's Nigel,' I said, 'I think he's going to die. We're just taking him to the vet. I'm sorry, love, we left you a note on the door. Can you make yourself a coffee and we'll be home soon?'

As we drove to Wetherbury I thought of the weekend before and Tom's accident. I knew, in a strange acceptance of fate,

that Nigel would die now, almost as if he had to, because Tom
had been saved. My beautiful little Herdwick lamb lay so quiet
and still on Tom's knee that I thought he had stopped breathing.
I slowed the car to a halt.

'He's still breathing. Come on, Mum, step on it,' said Tom.
Perhaps if I could get him to Will in time, he would, by some
magic power, be able to save him.

Will saw us straight away and I carried Nigel into the consulting room. He suddenly seemed to come alive again. He walked
round the floor as if there was nothing wrong with him. Will
examined him and took his temperature.

'He has some fluid in his lungs again,' he said, reaching for
a syringe and drawing up some antibiotic. 'I think the best thing
is if you leave him with us for tonight. Bring his milk and a
bottle in first thing tomorrow morning, and we'll keep him over
the weekend. We'll give him some glucose solution tonight.'

'I don't want to leave him,' I said.

Tom put his arm round my shoulder.

'Come on, Mum, I think that's the best.'

'The nurses here will look after him,' said Will. 'Come back
in the morning with his milk.'

We drove home. Poor Katy, arriving home to disasters. She
was sitting on the doorstep when we got back, with the dogs
running about outside. She and Tom hugged each other.

'You are an idiot, little brother,' she said fondly. 'You could
have killed yourself.'

Next morning I put Nigel's bottle in a bag with some milk
powder, and fed Fabian. Tom and Katy were sitting at the table
having breakfast.

'I won't be long,' I said as I found the car keys.

Just as I was about to go out of the door the telephone rang.
It was one of the nurses at the surgery.

'I'm sorry,' she said, 'but I'm afraid I've got some bad news
for you. The lamb is dead.'

'I'm coming in to fetch him right away. Don't you dare do
anything with him. I want him back,' I shouted angrily. 'I'm
going to bury him at home.'

I knew it was not the girl's fault, but I felt angry that Nigel was dead, and most of all with myself. I wished that I had kept him at home. If he was going to die I hated the thought of him dying there with people he didn't know.

'Nigel's dead,' I said to Tom and Katy, 'I'm going to fetch him.'

'Oh, Mother, I'm sorry,' said Katy. 'Shall I come with you?'

'No, it's all right. You stay and talk to Tom.'

When I arrived at the surgery it was still early. Morning surgery had not started and Will was not yet there. The nurse I had spoken to on the phone took me through to the animal hospital. Nigel was lying on his side in one of the white wire cages. I hated myself for leaving him there. My poor little lamb who had followed me around so faithfully and loved sitting on my knee. Now he was lying dead in a cage. The girl opened the wire door and I lifted him out onto a blanket I had taken with me and began to wrap him up. She bent to help me.

'I'll do it,' I said crossly, hating her and everyone else at that moment. I picked him up.

'Will you give Mr Allen a message for me?'

'Yes, of course,' she said.

'Well, you can tell him that I wish I had never left him here. I wish he had died at home with me, not shut up here in this horrible metal cage.'

I turned and walked out and cried all the way home.

Alex dug a hole behind the lilac bush and we stood round while he measured it to make sure it was deep enough, then I fetched my little bundle from the car and put him into the grave. We threw the earth in on top of him.

Tom put his arm round me.

'I'm sorry, Mum,' he said, 'he was a lovely little lamb.'

'Thank God it wasn't you,' I said. 'I don't know what I'd have done.'

## *CHAPTER FOURTEEN*

Fabian was growing quickly. The horn bumps on his head had turned into thick black and cream horns, already two inches long. I kept undoing the bandages and looking at his legs. The knee joints were still misshapen, but his legs looked straighter, although they were very thin. His horns, at the base, were thicker than his legs.

After three weeks I took the bandages off and Tom and I looked at him standing up in the kitchen without his splints. He stood perfectly still for two minutes, then his legs crumpled up and he fell to the floor. I splinted his legs again. I began to think that I was going to have the only ram in leg irons.

I thought about poor little Nigel. I had wanted a Herdwick lamb so much, but I decided then that I would have no more bottle lambs. If Fabian survived he was going to be the last one. I was tired of all the tears and the deaths — the cats that had been run over in the lane; the old spaniel that I had had to have put to sleep the first winter we had moved here; the very first lamb I had been given, before Pandora, which had died; Adam, and now Nigel.

In four years we had lost seven cats on the road, although others had come to take their place. There was so little traffic along the lane, but they kept getting run over, perhaps because the lane was too quiet. They would sit in the middle of it, washing themselves. They had acres of fields to hunt in, but for some perverse reason they preferred the mice that lived on

194

the bank outside the gate. The few cars that did use the lane always drove fast, because they probably did not expect to meet any others.

In the end I phoned Arthur and told him what had happened. He had some more lambs, he said, and if I wanted another I could go and fetch one. So I drove back to Surrey, the long journey through the clutter of south-east traffic and the Dartford tunnel.

The lambs were in a small enclosure behind the farmhouse. There were several little black lambs of two or three weeks old, and one that was now seven weeks. Its face was greying and the black wool on its back had taken on the purple-grey tinge that Nigel had been showing before he died. This lamb looked exactly like Nigel.

'His mother died,' said Arthur, 'and he was a very unhappy lamb for weeks. He didn't want to feed properly. He just survived on fresh air and cuddles.'

So I took home yet another lamb. This one was going to be called Barnaby, and he was just as quiet and adorable as Nigel had been. He followed me everywhere. If I sat on the doorstep with a mug of coffee, he sat next to me, chewing his cud. He wandered quietly round the garden, nibbling at the hedge or the rose bushes, with Fabian shuffling after him.

I tried taking Fabian's splints off again. He was now five weeks old. His legs were still very thin compared to normal legs. They looked like human limbs which have been encased in plaster for any length of time — shrunken and withered. But this time they did not fold up. He took a few halting steps and walked across the lawn. He swayed as he walked, like an old sailor. But he could walk. And without his splints.

We began to have a steady succession of prospective purchasers for the house, sent by the estate agents. It seemed that every time I had unrolled a fleece all over the kitchen floor and started spinning, the telephone would ring. The agent had someone in his office who wanted to view the house as soon as possible, which usually meant within the next half-hour. So I

would have to bundle the wool away again and rush around with a duster.

Some of the people were pleasant and interesting. Some of them were extremely boring. Sometimes they did not bother to arrive, which I found very annoying, wasting an afternoon when I wanted to get on with my wool. One day a Japanese woman came to look at the house with her English friend. She was very surprised with the sheep. She said she had never seen sheep in Japan, and was fascinated when I explained about shearing and spinning their wool. She did not know that they would grow more wool by the following year. Barnaby and Fabian followed her round the garden. She was delighted and asked if she could come back to see them again and bring more friends with her.

The insurance company had been to inspect Tom's motor bike and declared that it was beyond repair. He waited anxiously for the claim to be settled as he wanted to buy himself another one. He had been back on a bike again, the week after the accident, riding one belonging to one of his friends.

'If I don't get on one now,' he had said, 'I'll never have the nerve to ride one again.' He had admitted afterwards that he had felt very nervous as he set off down the lane, but after a while he had regained his confidence. I admired his courage. After such a terrifying crash, which still gave him nightmares, I had thought he might give up ideas of riding bikes and wait until he was old enough to drive a car. But he was determined. He wanted another bike.

We sat at the breakfast table drinking coffee. Tom was absorbed in a manual for Honda motor bikes, with glossy pages and intricate diagrams of the inner workings of a Japanese two-cylinder engine. I was reading the monthly *Ark* magazine from the Rare Breeds Survival Trust, which had just arrived in the morning post.

I turned to the classified advertisements at the back and read through the usual list of rare breed sheep for sale — always small and semi-wild. I was not tempted by them as I was by the sight of a day-old lamb, of some perfectly ordinary breed, but warm and helpless and mine for the asking to bottle-feed. Then my eye was caught by — 'Berkshire weaners for sale, 8 weeks old, outdoor-reared', followed by a telephone number.

'Look at that, Mum.' Tom held up a poster of a gleaming black and white machine being driven round a race track at forty-five degrees to the road. 'Isn't it beautiful? I'd love to go bike racing.'

'Yes, it's great, looks rather like yours. What is it?'

'It's a nine hundred.' He sighed. 'As soon as I've passed my bike test I want a two-fifty. Andrew's got a nine hundred Kawasaki. I've been on the back with him and it's brilliant. There's so much power you wouldn't believe it. That's what I'd really like, but I'll have a two-fifty first.'

'How do you fancy a trip to Northampton? There's an ad here for Berkshire weaners. Wouldn't it be fun? I've always wanted a piglet.'

He laughed. 'Leave it out, Mum, you're not serious?'

'Well, why not? A Berkshire would be perfect. They're small and friendly, little black pigs like the one in Beatrix Potter.'

'Mum . . .'

'Oh, do let's go and get one. Will you come with me?'

'All right. Phone up first and then I'll give Alex a ring. I expect he'd like to come, too.' He got up and gave me a hug. 'Why not? You're a crazy old mother, but yes, let's go and get a piglet. Just the day for it.'

I dialled the number and spoke to a girl who obviously knew nothing about pigs and appeared to be the *au pair*. She said that the pig's owner was a teacher and would be in after school, and suggested that I phone later that afternoon. I tried three times between 4.30 p.m. and 5.30 p.m. and finally spoke to the owner of the pigs. He had six piglets for sale, two gilts and four boars. I wanted to set off to collect one that evening, but the licence to move them, which he had to obtain and then give to me with the piglet, came from his local police station and that closed at 5.0 p.m. in the evening. He said he would get a licence the following day, and if we arrived in the afternoon at about half-past four I could choose which of the piglets I wanted.

The next afternoon Tom, Alex and I set off after lunch for Northampton. It was a beautiful hot July day and we drove along happily, anticipating all the fun we were going to have with our new piglet.

We came to the house, a lovely old building of yellowing stone. The large windows were stone mullioned and in front of the house was a walled garden of daisies and irises. At the side was a drive which led round to a stable yard and a paddock. We stopped next to a large iron gate and got out of the car, walking through the gate and into the cobbled yard as the back door of the house opened and a man stepped out into the sunlight.

He took us first to the paddock behind the stables to see the piglets' mother. We followed him into what looked like a mock battlefield — mounds of earth and trenches dug in the grass. But there was no sign of a small Berkshire pig. At one side was a small open-ended barn with a heavy iron water trough half sunk into the ground.

'They knock the water over if it's not in a heavy container,' he explained. 'Mildred! Mildred!' he called.

A large grey-black shape appeared from behind the barn and started walking slowly towards us. She stopped about four yards away and put her nose up, wrinkling it backwards and forwards, and then advanced again. She looked huge. Her skin had the texture of an elephant's hide and there were coarse black hairs along her back. She came up to us and stood looking at us all with interest. Her owner rubbed her head behind her ears and she gave some appreciative grunts. 'Pigs eat dogs and babies', I remembered from some far-back childhood fear. I wondered fleetingly if I was doing the right thing.

'She's so big,' I said to Tom. I suddenly realised I knew absolutely nothing about pigs.

Tom took a step forward and rubbed the pig's head.

'She's a nice friendly old pig, aren't you, girl?' he said. He smiled at me encouragingly. Considering that he had spent the first part of the day trying to dissuade me from buying a piglet, he was doing his best to be helpful. Mildred seemed very docile and friendly and her owner obviously had no fear of her. A few years ago I had known nothing about sheep, but I had learnt through keeping them. So I would learn about pigs.

We left Mildred to her excavations and returned to the yard. The piglets were together in a straw-filled pen in one of the outbuildings. They were lying dozing in an untidy heap on top of each other, but jumped up, instantly awake, squealing and darting around in the straw when we went in with them.

If Mildred had been larger than I had imagined, I still expected the piglets at eight weeks old to be small. But they were about the size of a large dog with short legs and looked heavy. No chance of simply tucking one under my arm and carrying it to the car.

Tom, Alex and I looked at the two gilts in turn as they ran about in the straw, squealing their protests at having their afternoon nap disturbed. All the piglets had white noses and feet and white tips to their tails. The tails were all straight, not curly, corkscrew fashion, as I had thought piglets' tails to be, but they flicked and curled as they ran about. I had read somewhere that pigs and elephants came from the same primeval ancestors, and watching these creatures with their thick dark skin and even their noses looking like the end of an elephant's trunk, it was easy to see their common ancestry.

The piglets retreated to a corner and stood staring at us, their eyes inquisitive, their ears pricked and framing their faces.

'What do you think?' I asked Tom. 'I don't know which one to have.' I knew nothing about the finer points of Berkshires, except that they should have the white points, but I did not want a pig for breeding anyway.

Tom approached the mass of piglets and put his hand out to one of the females, who shied away immediately. The second one stood her ground and wrinkled her nose backwards and forwards at his hand held a few inches away.

'She seems friendly,' he said, 'let's have this one.'

'Come and have a cup of tea,' said their owner, 'and we'll get the licence sorted out, then I'll put her in the car for you.'

'Will we remember which one we're having?' I said.

'Her face is not as fat as the other one's,' said Alex, 'and she's got more white on her nose.'

We went across to the house and into a large high-ceilinged hall, with cream-painted panelled walls and a long Indian rug on the floor, in shades of red and blue. We were shown into the sitting room and his wife appeared with a tray of blue and white thin china cups. Their son, a tall fair-haired boy of about Tom's age, was sent to the police station with my name and address, for the licence.

When he returned the piglet was loaded into the back of the car and we set off home again. She seemed quite happy in the back with Alex, and kept looking out of the window, sticking her nose against the glass, much to the surprise of other motorists. We stopped in a small town on the way home and Tom and Alex got out to get some chips. The piglet sat up in the back of the car on her haunches. I rubbed the top of her head and she made low grunting noises, obviously happy.

The boys were soon back and we sat and ate the chips, sharing them with Piglet. Curious passers-by stared at us and then at our strange passenger. She seemed to be enjoying herself. She certainly liked chips.

When we got home we carried her between us with some difficulty to the barn. I took her a bowl of food and then we made a partition in the pen with straw bales, to separate her from the sheep. When they came in for the night they peered over the bales in surprise and she stared back at them, wrinkling her nose and making inquisitive squeaks. The next morning she had pushed the bales over and was lying asleep in the middle of the straw surrounded by the sheep, who were sitting and chewing their cud. Piglet had joined the flock.

I let her out with them and she spent the day in the garden, running about in great excitement, pushing her nose into the flower bed and the lawn. She seemed to love everybody and quickly made friends with the dogs and the lambs, but her special favourite seemed to be Barnaby. In the afternoon she lay in the sun by the doorstep, and he sat next to her chewing his cud.

We decided to call her Beatrice Trotter. She very quickly learned her name and would come running up with happy squeals whenever she was called. She loved the field and followed the sheep about, grazing with them, eating the grass and the clover.

Next time Meg came to see us, she stood at the gate in amazement as Beatrice came running down to see her.

'Oh, my God,' she said laughing, 'now I *know* you're crazy.'

David was amused by Beatrice and pronounced her 'quite a good little Berkshire'. She responded by trying to eat the toes of his wellies. She was very interested in shoes in general, and if we all sat on the doorstep she would sniff at our shoes and pull the ends of any shoelaces that she found, to undo them.

The would-be purchasers continued to plague us. How easy it was for Gerald, I thought, not having to show them all round and be polite to them, but just phoning up now and again to demand why I hadn't sold the house. Some of the people who came to view the property were the most unlikely candidates for a cottage in the country.

One afternoon a Volvo stopped at the gate and two women got out. The older of the two, a woman of about sixty with carefully waved, blue-grey hair and a plain dark red dress, emerged from the passenger seat The other, who had been

driving, was some fifteen or twenty years younger and wearing a brightly patterned dress with a wide gathered skirt, a straw hat with pink ribbon and a pair of thin white strappy shoes with very high heels. I wondered how she was going to negotiate the gravel drive and front door steps. I could hardly imagine her walking about in the meadow in shoes like that.

'Oh, it's charming, quite charming,' she gushed, stepping in through the doorway and looking up at the dark, heavy beams on the ceilings, 'and what little doors. How quaint.'

She tripped lightly from room to room, looking out of the windows, fingering the curtains. She managed to climb the narrow winding staircase and cooed over the sloping, beamed ceilings of the bedrooms. I found it very hard to be pleasant to her, walking about in my house, staring at everything in her ridiculous clothes, but was consoled by the thought that she was probably terrified by the views from the windows — only grass and trees, not a house in sight, and a million miles away from Sainsbury's and Marks and Spencer's and the rest of civilisation. That at least, I felt, would ensure that she never set foot in the house again.

We went downstairs and back to the still open front door.

'Would you like to see the barn?' I asked.

'Oh, yes, of course,' she said, without the slightest enthusiasm.

I hoped that Gilbert might be lurking in there and give her a peck on the leg. Beatrice had been dozing in the straw and she jumped up and came to the gate of the sheep pen. I leaned over and put my hand to her warm nose, which was wrinkling backwards and forwards as she inspected the strangers with inquiring squeaks.

The woman stepped back in horror.

'Oh, oh, you've got a peeg!' she exclaimed.

'Yes, Beatrice. She's only a piglet, actually.'

'A peeg!' she said again, dismayed. I imagined the nearest she had ever been to a pig before was the bacon counter at Sainsbury's.

'She's usually running around in the garden,' I said, 'but I put her in this afternoon as you were coming. She's fond of nibbling shoes.'

She retreated hastily out of the barn.

'I'll show you the meadow,' I said.

She followed bravely, tottering across the lawn in her silly shoes. Gilbert and Polly had been lying in wait under the lilac bush and Gilbert flapped out now, honking and scolding, stretching out his long neck and orange beak. I kept myself between him and the strangers and took them into the meadow through the little gate by the apple tree. The sheep had been grazing near the gate and came running towards us. But the visitors had had enough. They made for the safety of their Volvo.

I went to the barn and let Beatrice out into the sunlight. Tom and Alex were sitting on the doorstep laughing as the car disappeared down the lane.

'I wonder what they think living in the country is all about,' I said, 'certainly not mud and animals.'

## CHAPTER FIFTEEN

If we had some unlikely house-viewers, we also had some who were seriously interested. One afternoon a couple came to the gate. They apologised for arriving unannounced. Barnaby, Fabian and Beatrice had been sitting on the lawn in the sun, and Beatrice ran up to greet them, squeaking excitedly and sniffing at their shoes. But instead of being horrified they thought she was great fun, and rubbed her head between her ears. I showed them round the house and the garden and then took them to the meadow. We walked about in the clover with Beatrice and the sheep following us.

They said that they had been looking for a cottage like ours for some time and wanted to keep some donkeys and chickens. I made them a cup of coffee before they left and they asked if they could come back in a few days to look round again. Late that afternoon there was a telephone call from the estate agent. They had been to his office and wanted to buy the house.

Tom and I had long discussions about moving. He was undecided about living in Wales, but was keeping an open mind on it, and thought that I should go and at least have a look there to see what was on the market. The ram sale at Builth Wells was the following week, so I arranged to go to Wales with David, while Tom and Alex looked after the animals.

David and I left early on Sunday afternoon. David was a careful and confident driver and had a large two-litre car, which diminished the miles with satisfying speed. We were soon away

205

from East Anglia and driving across the open countryside of the Cotswolds. The villages with their wide sunlit streets and tall yellow stone houses were so different from the thatched cottages and narrow lanes we had left behind.

It was a beautiful afternoon, with a golden haze over the wolds. The corn had all been cut, but fields of yellow stubble dotted the landscape. Then we reached Herefordshire, home of the woolly Ryelands and the black and white timbered houses. Soon ahead of us were the dark blue mountains of Wales.

We went straight to the saleground. The sale started the next morning, but already the rams were there for viewing.

There were seven thousand rams in the sale, and they were penned in open-sided marquees. I had never seen so many sheep at one time — row after row of magnificent beasts. There were splendid Suffolk rams with great black heads and drooping ears; Wiltshire Horns with elegantly curling horns, and plenty of Welsh rams — Beaulah Speckle Faced, Welsh Mountain and Hill Radnor, brown faced sheep with creamy horns. There were no Herdwicks or Swaledales here, but most other breeds seemed to be represented. David went carefully from pen to pen, checking his catalogue, marking any that particularly caught his fancy.

'You can have the car tomorrow while I'm at the sale, if you like,' he said later as we sat eating dinner in the hotel dining room. 'Then you can spend the day going round some of the estate agents.'

'Oh, lovely, thanks. That will be fun. It's very trusting of you to let me have your car.'

'Not at all. That's why I brought the Renault, and not the old farm car that I cart the sheep round in. If I buy any rams I'll have to get someone else to take them back for me.'

'I've really got to find somewhere else to live now,' I sighed. 'It's very daunting. And I've got to get all the animals moved, the sheep and pig.'

'Well, you needn't worry about them. I'll move them for you. How is that pig?'

'She's fun, she really is.'

'That's good. Pigs *are* fun. Mind you, she'll probably end up thinking she's a sheep.'

Next morning we were up early and as soon as we had finished breakfast, David drove down to the saleground.

'Right, all yours,' he said, getting out of the car. 'See you back here at half-past four. Have a good day.'

'Thanks, David, and you. Oh, where's reverse?' I called after him.

He came back to the car window.

'Push it down, then over to your left. Take care,' he said, 'I'll see you later.' Then he was gone, mingling into the crowd of cloth-capped, wellie-booted farmers.

There were several estate agents' offices in Builth Wells. I went round them, collecting details of anywhere with a few acres of land. Then I drove out of the town to try and find some of them. The car was a joy to drive, and the scenery was wonderful. The road snaked over moorland and up the sides of mountains. I found a woollen mill with a coffee shop and went in to have some elevenses and look through the estate agents' particulars. I sorted them into some kind of order, the most likely ones at the top of the pile.

I followed winding tracks over hillsides and got lost several times, but I found at least three little cottages that would make a home for us all. One in particular I liked. There was a wonderful view across a valley and, round the cottage, three little stone-walled fields. I stood looking at the view, trying to imagine myself living here, so far away from everything and everyone that I knew.

The landscape had a wonderful wild quality to it: sweeping expanses of moor and heather, great blue-grey mountains, and everywhere there were sheep. They walked beside the road, nibbling at the rough vegetation, or sat against the stone walls, idly chewing their cud and watching the passing traffic.

'How did you get on?' asked David later when I met him at the saleground. 'Did you find anything suitable?'

'There were several cottages with a few acres. I think I could find somewhere I'd like. It's wonderful here, the mountains and the sheep. They're everywhere, just walking about beside the roads. I went through a village called Beaulah, and there were actually Beaulah Speckle Faced on the hillside there. I'd never thought of them coming from a real place like that.'

David laughed. 'Do you think you're going to buy somewhere here, then?' he asked.

'I'd love to live in Wales. It's just that it seems so far away. I don't know what Tom wants to do yet. How was the sale? Did you buy anything?'

'No, I didn't, although there were some rams I thought of getting. Good prices, not too high, but fair. It was a good day. Come on, we'll get a drink and something to eat, then home.'

*  *  *

Fabian was growing well in spite of his legs. The knee joints were still misshapen, but not as swollen as they had been when he was born. His hooves were twisted, but Will told me to keep them well trimmed, and never let them get overgrown. He still had his rolling gait, but could now run after the other sheep. He and Barnaby had joined them in the meadow. He still sat down bottom first, but once on the ground I saw that he folded his front legs up underneath him, so he could bend them all right.

Barnaby was the most adorable and devoted creature. As soon as I went into the meadow he would come up to me, pushing his nose against my hand. If I sat down in the grass, he would immediately sit down next to me and start chewing his cud. He also seemed particularly attached to Beatrice. They were never far from each other. It was quite amusing to watch the sheep and pig moving across the meadow together in a line, grazing as they went. Beatrice chewed away at the clover, her tail flicking about, making happy little grunts to herself. She had not mastered the art of cudding, so when the sheep sat together near the apple tree or the hedge to ruminate, there would be a grey-black shape lying in the middle of them all, asleep in the sun.

209

Katy came home for the weekend. She was amazed at how quickly Beatrice was growing. Piglet loved everybody. She ran up to Katy, wrinkling her nose backwards and forwards, pressing it against the girl's legs. She left little round circles on people's jeans or skirts from her nose, and Katy always referred to her as 'Muddy Circles'.

Katy had a week's holiday and offered to go house-hunting. I showed her all the particulars I had collected from Wales.

'Wales is so beautiful,' I said, 'but I don't think Tom wants to go there. He's talking about staying here in the village with the Lawrences, and staying on at school to do 'A' levels.'

'Yes, I know,' said Katy. 'Father's buying a house in Fordington, but Tom says he doesn't want to go and live there. He'd rather stay in Castle Monkton.'

'All his friends are here. He and Alex are like brothers. I can't go to Wales if Tom stays here, I'd never see him. But I can't afford to buy anything round here. It's all right for your Father with his job at the College. Oh, Katy, I don't know what to do.'

'What about Norfolk?' she asked. 'We could go and have a look tomorrow. I'll help you find something, Mother, don't worry.'

Katy and I set off for the Fens the next morning. We went first to Ely and toured the estate agents. We sat in the coffee and craft shop near the cathedral, looking through all the sheets while we ate doughnuts. Through the window I could see the beautiful grey stone building.

The prices were much more reasonable than near Castle Monkton, but there was very little that was suitable. Having asked expressly for 'something old with land', I had been given anything that fell within my price range. Most of them were modern houses, either in the town or on an estate on its outskirts — hardly the place for sheep and a pig. They would not be popular with the neighbours.

One cottage, which was very cheap, had an acre and a half of land, but no roof. It needed totally rebuilding. I was tempted to consider it. Perhaps I could live in a caravan and have it rebuilt by local builders, but Katy persuaded me that it was not a good idea.

There were two other old cottages. One sounded charming. It was supposed to date from the middle of the sixteenth century. The middle cottage in a terrace of three, it overlooked a common. There was only a small garden, but Katy said that there might be grazing rights on the common. We put that on our list for viewing, and one other which had three acres of land and was on the edge of a village some ten miles from Ely.

We returned to the estate agent's office and made an appointment to view the cottage on the common. The other one was empty and he gave us the key to go and look at it. We found it easily. The land stretched behind it with a dyke on each boundary. The grass was tall and overgrown and we waded about in it. There would be plenty of room for my beasts here. The flat Fenland stretched away from us, skylarks were singing overhead and it seemed as if it was just what I had been looking for. The roof looked as if it needed some attention, but I would have enough money to get that repaired. Inside was an old Rayburn and a lovely beamed kitchen, the ceiling beams lime-washed. There were two small bedrooms, looking out over the fields at the back of the house. Everywhere needed repainting, but apart from the roof it was in a good state of repair.

We hurried back to the office only to be told that it was actually sold subject to contract. I was furious.

'Why did you give us the sheet on it if it's already sold?' I asked. 'We've wasted a lot of time going to look at it. What about this other one? Has that been sold as well?'

'There has been an offer on it,' he said, 'but the owners haven't accepted it. They want the full asking price.'

I felt like telling him what he could do with all his houses and dumped the pile of sheets he had given us earlier onto his desk.

'Let's go and have a look at it,' said Katy. 'We might as well, now we're here.'

There was a rough track around the side of the common, leading off a quiet lane. Several ponies were tethered on the grass, and a pair of goats. The cottage itself was perfect inside. There were beamed ceilings and small pine doors with eighteenth century latches. Behind the cottage was a small sunny garden full of lilies and delphiniums. It would be a lovely place to live with a few cats, or even an old dog, but there was nowhere for a pig and some sheep.

'Perhaps you could find some grazing nearby,' said Katy, 'maybe talk to some of the local farmers'.

I knew that many people kept horses away from their homes, renting grazing that might be up to several miles away, and visiting their animals once or twice a day. But that was not how I wanted to keep my sheep. I wanted them outside my back door. I wanted to be able to go into my garden and see them whenever I wished. I wanted them with me. It was getting late in the afternoon.

'We'd better get home now,' I said. 'Let's think about it this evening. We can always come back tomorrow.'

We drove home feeling tired and despondent. Our day's house-hunting had not been exactly a success. The next day we set off again, this time farther north of Ely to the market town of Downham. Again we went round the agents. They had plenty of properties for sale, but most of them were either modern with no gardens, or falling down. One village, on the edge of Black Fen, had several houses for sale, but the whole of the village seemed to be slowly sinking into the Fen. The houses all had cracks in their walls, some of them had one end of the house several feet lower than the other. These were not ancient timbered houses that lean at all angles. They were built of brick within the last one hundred and fifty years. They were simply disappearing into the Fens.

'What a place,' sighed Katy. 'I'm not surprised there are so many houses for sale.'

We went to the village pub for a lunchtime snack. The landlord told us of a couple from London who had bought a large house in the area. It had a cellar, which kept filling up with water, so they decided to fill it with concrete. They watched

in horror as the house was dragged down into the Fen by the weight of the concrete in the cellar.

I thought of the mountains of Wales, the beautiful moors and winding roads across them, and the sheep beside the roadsides. The only animals here were a few ragged-looking ponies in odd fields. Cattle and pigs were shut away from the daylight in barns and sheds. There were long straight roads like causeways above the treeless fens. There were no cornfields, but fields of leeks and carrots.

After lunch we drove westwards to the next large town. The scenery improved: there were pine forests, and commons of scrubby gorse and rabbit holes. We collected more particulars and sifted through them. One house looked promising. It was set in three acres and described as 'secluded'. We made an appointment to view it.

The three acres turned out to be copse-like undergrowth and the house was somewhere in the middle of it, hidden away up a muddy track. A woman came to the door holding a large snarling black dog by the collar. We introduced ourselves and she shut the dog away in one of the rooms to show us round.

'The poor woman was terrified living there,' said Katy as we drove away, 'and I'm not surprised. It gave me the creeps.'

That evening we pored over the map of East Anglia, and

looked again through all the particulars we had collected over the last two days.

'None of them are any good,' I sighed, 'not really. Perhaps I shall have to go to Wales after all.'

'The places do seem to get worse,' said Katy, laughing. 'What about that village disappearing into the Fens like King John's jewels? We could go up towards Lincolnshire. Let's have one more day tomorrow and if we still don't find anything, Tom and I can look after the animals and you can go to Wales for a few days. At least you know you'd find something there.'

'All right, last day of looking in East Anglia.'

We drove first to Cambridge and then north towards The Wash. We left the familiar hedged fields of golden stubble behind and came again to the flat, treeless landscape criss-crossed by dykes and wide rivers. The soil was as black as soot and the fields bordered by dykes were planted with leeks, onions, carrots and cauliflowers. The long straight roads seemed to go on for ever, miles and miles into a forgotten wasteland.

I stopped the car. 'Let's go back,' I said to Katy, 'I don't want to live here. We're just wasting another day.'

'Come on, Mother. We might as well go on now that we've come so far. Just one more day. You never know, we might find something.'

'I doubt it,' I said gloomily.

Eventually we reached Wisbech, described on the name sign as 'Fenland's Historic Town'. The road ran in alongside a wide river where swans were swimming. On the farther bank was a long row of tall town houses, some gabled, some looking very elegant with white-painted windows and magnolia trees growing against the old brick walls. They had a distinctly Dutch look to them, and dated from about the seventeenth century. There was a wide bridge over the river called 'Freedom Bridge'. Wisbech was a great deal more attractive than any of the towns we had seen the day before. Perhaps Katy was right — we might find something after all.

We made the usual tour of estate agents, and then found a

little café in the market square to have coffee and plan our house-hunting day.

'This one looks interesting,' I said. 'It's got an acre of ground, brick outbuildings and is two cottages for renovation.'

'No, Mother, you don't want something to renovate. It's probably falling down.'

'It might not be too bad. It's worth looking at, but we'll leave it till last.'

The first cottage that we went to look at, also described as having an acre of ground, was built beside a ten-foot high bank to one of the rivers. Inside it was painted a vivid bright pink on nearly every wall, and the inside walls on the back of the house had large patches of green and grey mould speckled over them. The acre of ground was nearly vertical river bank.

All the houses we looked at seemed to suffer from damp. Or ugliness. We drove round all day, from one marsh-bound hamlet to another. We looked at, and discounted, everything. Last on our list were the two cottages to renovate.

They were built of brick, and from the road there was a single front door, so that it looked like one house. There was a drive to one side and the brick outbuildings adjoined the house at right-angles, making a small courtyard facing south. The so-called outbuildings were in fact two small cottages, the first having one room only on each floor, and the second two rooms. They had obviously not been lived in for some years, but would make excellent stables. We had a key to one of the back doors of the main house, so Katy and I went in. There were two small rooms and a pantry, and some narrow stairs hidden away behind a door covered with thick layers of yellow paint. We went upstairs.

The stairs opened onto a large landing off which were two rooms. The farthest one had two doors, the second door leading out onto another landing, and three more rooms. There was another narrow staircase. We went down and found four rooms, one of which had an old-fashioned kitchen range. All the floors were laid with flagstones or old bricks. One wall had a door-sized indentation and had obviously once led to the other side of the house, but had been bricked in at some time. There were two hideous fireplaces of nineteen-fifties vintage, and some polystyrene tiles on the ceilings, but parts of the house seemed very old, and it had exciting possibilities.

The land behind the house was covered in rough weeds and dotted with tall sunflowers. In one corner were rows of strawberry plants.

'I like this,' I said to Katy. 'If it was all done up it would make a lovely house.'

'But it needs such a lot doing to it,' she said. 'There isn't even any water in the house, just that tap in the garden.'

'I could get the plumbing done and the wiring, and then do the rest of it a bit at a time — a sort of ten-year plan. What do you think? We haven't seen anything else that's remotely suitable. It's this or Wales.'

'Well . . . it does have a nice feel to it inside. It's not a depressing house like some of the ones we've seen. It could be lovely, but I think it's too much work.'

'Let's go back to the agents before they close. We'll probably find now that it's been sold already.'

The estate agent told us that the house had been sold subject to contract in the summer, but the buyers had dropped out at the last minute. So it had come back onto the market two weeks ago. I agreed to buy it, and he took my name and address and the name of my solicitor.

When we got home, we told Tom about the house and tried to draw a plan of all the rooms, but I found it hard to remember exactly where they had all been. We had been able to walk all around upstairs, but the downstairs rooms had been divided off from each other. We had only reached one side of the house by using the second staircase to get to the downstairs rooms. It would be a simple matter to unbrick the original doorway, so that would be the first priority, after I had found someone to do the plumbing and electrical wiring, and then I would rip out the offending fireplaces.

It was an exciting prospect, and would give me something interesting to do, rather than simply sit in a tidy modern house

and wonder what I was going to do with the rest of my life.
And there would be room for my sheep and pig.

CHAPTER SIXTEEN

The mists of Autumn drifted on the air, and the pale toadstools reappeared on the lawn and in damp corners along the hedge. Spiders spread their cobwebby strands, and myriads of tiny golden baby spiders danced in the centre of the webs. Red and gold leaves floated on the wind and scarlet bryony berries festooned the hedgerows, with the silken tufts of old man's beard. The morning air was sharp and smelled of frost.

The couple buying our house had been back several times, and having expressed a wish to keep chickens I asked them if they would take over ours. Most of the bantams had been hatched there, and all the chickens had their own favourite pecking and scratching places. I was going to have more than enough on my rough piece of ground, and much as I would miss the chickens, I decided that if the new owners would keep them, it would be the best solution.

One of Tom's friends knew a farmer who would take Gilbert and Polly. He came to fetch them one morning and I watched sadly as they were put into a crate and driven away. A few days later we were told that they had been seen happily swimming on the large pond at the back of the farmyard.

The days grew greyer and shorter and moving day came closer. Contracts were exchanged on the house. Now there was no going back. I began packing things into boxes, and Gerald arrived one Saturday morning with a large van to take away the furniture that he wanted. He had bought himself a modern

218

house on an estate in Fordington. It seemed to highlight the differences that we must always have had. He had settled for smooth straight walls and the convenience of modern living. I was buying two old cottages with a large untidy garden full of weeds and sunflowers, and the only water supply a cold tap outside the back door.

* * *

Covent Garden in December was milling with people. Christmas shoppers hurried about with large bags and bunches of holly and mistletoe. The sound of carol-singers filled the square. I sat at a little table outside one of the cafés and listened to them as I waited for David. It was the week of the Smithfield Show and he was staying at Earl's Court, having brought some of his sheep to London for showing.

A huge Christmas tree stood in the square, covered with white birds and silver stars, and the carol-singers were gathered nearby. The tree was beautiful, dwarfing everything around it, and I watched the stars tied to its dark branches catching and reflecting the light. Sitting there, drinking my cup of coffee, I could forget for the moment the problems of the coming week.

I thought back to the first time I had met David — a chance meeting at a village fair — and of all that had happened in between. Then I had two lambs, my first year of sheep-keeping. Now I had a whole little flock, and Gerald was divorcing me for 'rearing lambs in the matrimonial dining room'. Soon I would be living 100 miles away. I would have to start a new life on my own. Worries about the house and the future came crowding back and I tried to push them out of my mind.

Then suddenly David came up behind me and put his arms round me.

'I've been looking everywhere for you,' he said. 'There are so many people about I thought I'd never find you.'

'Oh, David, it's good to see you. I've just been listening to the carol-singers. Isn't the Christmas tree beautiful? I'm going to buy one my first day in Norfolk.'

219

He sat down next to me. 'Is everything ready for the move, then? Which day is it? Did you say Tuesday?'

'Yes, only a week left at Monks Green. You will be able to move the beasts for me, won't you?'

'Of course. I'll be there first thing in the morning. Did you manage to find a plumber and an electrician?'

'Yes. The electrician's doing the wiring this week, so at least we'll be able to make a cup of tea when we get there. I don't know. I hope it was a good idea to buy that house. I'm really worried about moving. Suppose I hate living there.'

'You'll be all right once you're there. Don't worry so much. Come on, we'll go and get a drink. And if you really don't like it, you can always move again. You haven't got to live there for the rest of your life.'

The rest of my life. It was a sobering phrase. I could not even begin to think about it.

We made for one of the wine bars, mingling with the happy crowd of people. David always cheered me up and made me laugh. Perhaps he was right. I might enjoy living in my new house with the straggly sunflowers all over the garden. Only time would tell.

The next morning I caught the train from Liverpool Street station back to Fordington, where I had left my car in the station car park. Before I drove home I walked round the shops to see if I could find any white birds or silver stars to decorate my Christmas tree for my first Christmas in Norfolk. I found some white doves, like birds of peace, and bought twelve of them. There were no silver stars, but I bought some silver balls, and strings of silver tinsel. I took them home and packed them away in one of the half-filled tea chests, labelled 'kitchen'.

Katy came home at the weekend. She had taken some holiday to help me move. We took Tom to the Lawrences, in Castle Monkton. It had been arranged that he was going to stay with them and continue with his 'A' levels. I hugged him.

'Take care, Tom. I'll see you soon.'

'Look after yourself, Mum. Don't forget, Alex and I are coming up on Boxing Day with Terry and Alan.'

'I won't forget. See you all next week.'

'Don't worry about him, Liz,' said Madge Lawrence, standing on the front doorstep next to Tom as Katy and I went back to the car, 'we'll take care of him.'

Katy and I were up late into the night, packing china and books, taking down curtains, emptying cupboards. At last we sat down thankfully beside the fire and opened a large bottle of wine. Then I drank too much of it and cried a lot, and woke up the next morning with a terrible headache. Gerald came over in the afternoon to fetch Henry and Wolf. I was taking the cats and Sophie with me, and Gerald had agreed to keep the two big dogs. I would miss them very much, but they had big, hungry mouths and I would not be able to afford to feed them all. Sophie had always been particularly attached to me, and had always rather resented the other two dogs.She was now ten years old and would probably be much happier as the only dog, and Henry and Wolf would still have each other for company. I watched Henry's black face looking at me out of the back window of Gerald's car, until it turned a corner in the lane and disappeared.

The removal men arrived promptly at eight o'clock the next morning, followed shortly by David. As each room was cleared Katy and I swept the floor and made sure that nothing had been left behind. We had taken the things from Tom's room the night before and shut all the cats in there. Now we had the problem of loading them all into carriers for the journey. I had two wicker cat baskets, and had bought seven specially designed cardboard pet carriers. But as fast as Katy and I put the cats into them, they pushed out again through the top. I tried tying string round the carriers, but cats being the resourceful creatures they are, they managed to drop out through the bottom of the carriers.

The idea had been to give each cat a container to itself. But we had to put two cats into each of the baskets. Then with David's help we put four more into a tea chest and fixed some chicken netting over the top. Ursula alone had remained quiet and still in her cardboard carrier, so we decided to leave her where she was. They were supposed to be for taking cats around in, after all, but the other six carriers were now looking very squashed and useless.

The removal men were ready to leave. The house was empty. I walked from room to room, looking out of the upstairs windows onto the little meadow where my sheep had been for the last five years, where we had sat in the summer and had picnics, where Tom and Alex had made the tree house and camp fires. I ran my hand along the beams on the sloping bedroom ceiling. 'Goodbye,' I whispered to the house that I would never see again.

We carried the cats down to my car and loaded them in. The removal men drove away and David backed his van up to the barn where the sheep and pig were still shut in their pen. He had a special crate for Beatrice and she was loaded up first. Then the sheep followed me into the van, except for Fabian, whom I was taking in the car with me. I squeezed out past them, and David shut the back.

I had put the back seat of the car down and I led Fabian across the drive and lifted him in beside the cat baskets. I wanted to take him separately because of his weak legs, and I was afraid that he might get knocked and hurt with all the others. Sophie was sitting up in the front on the passenger seat, and she looked round at him, growling a little.

I locked the front door and hung the key up in the barn and then we set off in convoy — David in the lead, then me with a car full of animals, and then Katy, her car filled to overflowing with odds and ends and a box with the kettle, mugs and tea bags. No sooner had we turned the corner of the lane than Ursula, having extricated herself from the pet carrier, climbed onto the back of my seat. Fabian nosed forward, leaning his chin on my shoulder, quite happy to be in the car.

I had to stop in Castle Monkton to get some petrol, but dared not open the car door in case Ursula rushed away and was never seen again. I opened the window about an inch and a half and pushed some money out through the crack. Fabian tried to climb into the front seat to sit on my knee. People came out of the garage and stood around looking highly amused. Ursula had vanished again under one of the seats.

It seemed a long journey, partly because, with all the animals, I had to drive more slowly than usual. Every time I had to stop at traffic lights or cross-roads, Fabian tried to climb onto my knee, and Sophie started growling furiously at him. Every now and then there would be a blur of black fur as Ursula darted about.

At last the outline of Ely cathedral came into view in the grey December day, and then we were through Ely and into the cold, flat Fenland, the land of herons and wild swans and black peat soil. Goodbye to the cornfields and the little thatched cottages. Goodbye to Essex for ever.

David's van was already parked outside the cottages as Katy and I drove up. I took Fabian out of the car, taking care not to let Ursula out, and he followed me round to the back door and into the house, where the plumber and his mate were waiting for us. They looked more than a little surprised to see him, but he walked about inspecting our new home and then went outside again and started nibbling at some of the weeds in the garden.

I was most relieved that the electricity had been turned on, so we found the things from Katy's car and made some mugs of tea. David had brought some bales of straw in the van and we spread one out on the floor of the small cottage adjoining the main house. I put some sheep nuts into a bucket and rattled them, and sheep and Beatrice all trotted out of the van and followed me into the cottage. We shut them in with some hay and a bucket of water.

We took the cats up to one of the bedrooms and shut them in with food and litter tray. Sophie wandered around downstairs, sniffing at everything and growling at the plumber. The removal men had arrived before us, unloaded everything through the front door into the first three rooms and then disappeared. David helped us to take the beds upstairs, and then eventually went home. The plumber and his mate departed, promising to return in the morning.

Katy and I made another cup of tea and sat in the middle of the boxes and the tea chests. The plumber had asked a builder friend of his to unbrick the doorway between the two cottages, so we were able to walk all round downstairs. We wandered from room to room, planning what to do with each one, and where all the furniture should go. Then we gave Sophie her supper, checked the cats again to make sure that they were all settled, and drove into Wisbech, five miles away, to get some fish and chips.

It was now quite dark, but the town was full of lights. There were Christmas illuminations strung across the main street at intervals, and nearly all the shops had Christmas trees in their windows. The lights were reflected in the river Nene, which ran through the centre of the town, with the tall Dutch-looking houses on its north bank.

We sat in the car beside the river to eat our chips and watched the twinkling lights on the water. It began to rain and the reflections blurred as the raindrops splashed down. When we got back we heard the steady drip of rain through the roof. We found bowls and buckets and placed them to catch the drips. The roof seemed to be leaking in about twenty places. Luckily the room that we had put the beds in for that night appeared to be under a sound part of the roof. We made a cup of coffee and took it upstairs, sitting in bed to drink it, Sophie curled up on the end of my bed, keeping my feet warm.

'What a day,' said Katy, 'thank goodness it's over. I just hope we don't wake up to find the bedroom flooded.'

'Thanks for all your help, love, I couldn't have managed without you. The journey was the worst part, I think. I had Fabian trying to sit on my knee all the time, Sophie trying to bite him, and Ursula leaping about all over the place. It's lucky I didn't have an accident.'

Katy laughed. 'Did you notice all the strange looks you got from other drivers every time you stopped at traffic lights? It was so funny. One old man in a Metro nearly ran into a lamp-post because he was staring so hard.'

'No, I was too busy just trying to drive. Anyway, we got here.

It's a damned nuisance about the roof. It's just full of holes. Listen to all those buckets filling up on the landing.'

'What are you going to do about it?'

Get someone to mend it, I suppose. Never mind, it may have stopped raining by the morning.'

'We'll do some unpacking tomorrow, shall we?' asked Katy.

'Yes, and let's go into Wisbech and get a Christmas tree.'

It had stopped raining by the morning. We emptied all the buckets from the landing and put them back ready for the next downpour. I let the sheep and Beatrice out into the garden and the sheep wandered about, nibbling at groundsel and chickweed. Beatrice put her nose to the ground and started throwing up earth in all directions, making happy grunts and squeals as she did so. It was a morning of pale, watery sunshine, blue-green sky feathered with clouds. The air smelled fresh after the rain and a heron drifted slowly over the house to land beside a dyke at the farther end of the field on the other side of the road.

We filled the kettle from the tap outside the door and were having some coffee when the plumber arrived. Katy and I spent the morning putting china out on the dresser and dragging the table and chairs through into the room that we had decided to have as a kitchen. The plumber struggled with long lengths of copper pipe and what looked like brillo pads on the roll.

In the afternoon we drove into Wisbech to look around the shops and find a Christmas tree. We bought the largest one we could find and set it in a bucket near the front door. It reached to the ceiling. Then I found the bag of decorations I had bought in Fordington the week before, the white birds and silver balls, and tinsel. That afternoon we had bought some tree lights and green and silver butterflies, as well as three bags of logs from a place selling them at the roadside.

I raked out one of the hideous fireplaces and lit a fire. I wondered if the room would be engulfed in smoke, as it was probably several years since the fireplace had been used. But there was a good draught and the fire was soon burning brightly. I spread some rugs over the flagstones and Sophie stretched herself out in front of the flames.

Katy and I spent a happy half-hour decorating the Christmas tree. Then we sat by the fire and opened a bottle of wine. I held up my glass.

'Happy Christmas, Katy,' I said.

'Happy Christmas, Mother, and Happy New Year,' she said. 'Here's to your new life in Norfolk.'

# *CHAPTER SEVENTEEN*

I stood by the window and looked across to the line of trees in the middle distance. They were barely visible, just dull grey outlines, and somewhere behind them I knew that the flat fields ended and the sky began. But now, in the mist of rain, the whole landscape was simply a blurred mass of uniform grey. In front of the trees, I knew, was a wide dyke where the heron often waited patiently on the bank. Sometimes in the early mornings I saw him drifting low across the fields, with his slow, almost lazy flight — heavy wing beats and trailing legs making his silhouette unmistakable.

But there were no birds to be seen now, and if the heron was there this afternoon there was nothing, from where I was standing, to give away his presence. Winter again. As it had been when I had moved, and yet there seemed to be very little difference in the Fenland summer. There had been few long hot days with skylarks singing, only cold winds from the North Sea and the damp, clinging rain. The only thing that seemed to mark the passing seasons was the shorter days. I had spent so many hours standing at this window, looking across at the bleak landscape and wondering what it was that had made me decide to move to Norfolk.

I knew the obvious reason, that I would not be so far away from Tom. But Tom had now left Castle Monkton, disenchanted with school and 'A' levels, and had got himself a job with a newspaper chain in Fordington. After a few months of working twelve-hour weekdays, and most of his time at the weekends, the company had promoted him to one of their branches in Oxford, and at eighteen they had given him a company car and made him one of their youngest sales managers. Tom had drive and ambition and I was immensely proud of him, as I was of Katy. They had both grown into strong, brave people, and now together in Oxford, sharing a house in the town with four students, their life had become happier and more ordered.

I saw my neighbour walking up the road on her way to the village shop, a basket on her arm, a headscarf tied round her lacquered grey hair. She strode purposefully against the rain, marching along in almost military fashion.

I thought back over the year. I had soon disposed of the hideous fireplaces, and ripped down the polystyrene tiles and ugly wallpaper everywhere. I had stripped layers of yellowing paint from the pine doors. We had taken down one of the walls between two rooms to make a large kitchen running from the front to the back of the house. I had planted the small walled front garden with herbs, and put tubs and pots of petunias and geraniums outside the back door. The roof had been mended, there was hot water in the taps and a bathroom.

But it had not been a happy year. Sophie had died in the summer. She had collapsed one night after I had taken her upstairs to bed, where she had her basket in my room. I phoned the vet and took her in to his surgery at midnight. He was kind and considerate, and put her to sleep while I held her in my arms. I had had her from an eight-week-old puppy, and I cried bitterly when I took her home again, wrapped in a blanket. I went out to the front garden as soon as it was light to dig a hole for her, before the rest of the village was up. I did not want everyone to watch me crying as I shovelled out the earth and then buried her. Now a rosemary bush grew over her grave.

Barrington, too, had died, grown to an old lady, and Ben. I was still haunted by his big, sad eyes as he lay dying. Ursula and Claude had been killed on the road, run over by one of the huge lorries that trundled past at regular intervals from the carrot-canning factory at the other end of the village. Of the cats that we had had in our first year at Monks Green, only Fiona was left.

After Sophie died I decided not to have another dog. I had kept spaniels for thirty years, always getting a puppy when one of them died. But now, out all day, working in a nursery that grew Chinese vegetables, I felt it was not fair to get a puppy and leave it shut in a house all day on its own.

But the house without a dog had seemed so empty. Sophie, being old, had slept most of the day, but she was always there at the door to welcome me, jumping up and down excitedly when I returned home. In the end I decided to give a home to an old, unwanted dog. I had spent the whole of one Sunday morning trying to telephone Battersea Dogs' Home. I was sure they would have an old spaniel that nobody wanted, and I would drive down to London and bring it home. But the number was continuously engaged.

In the end I phoned a local animal sanctuary, and went to see them that afternoon. I would take any old bitch that needed a home, which seemed to like me and would fit in with all the cats and the sheep. When I got there they had a four-year-old cocker spaniel dog, which had been brought in the day before. I was taken to the kennels to look at him. He was very friendly, and a beautiful-looking animal, but somehow he was just some-one else's dog. He bore no relation to the bitch I had loved and mourned.

They had an old spaniel cross who was eight, they said, but she had been with them for three months now, and they had kept her in the house with them, as they had given up hope of finding her a home. Everyone seemed to think she was ugly. I asked if I could see her. She came walking slowly down the path from their house, wagging her tail, while several cats wandered round her. She came straight to me and pushed her nose into my hand. I knew she was just what I wanted.

She was a cocker springer cross and did not look at all ugly to me. She was the colour of new horse chestnuts, with white paws and chest and a white blaze down her nose. Her poor face was covered with scars, but I thought she had a lovely face, and she obviously had a wonderful temperament. It was as if she had been there waiting for me.

'She was in a terrible state when we took her in,' the sanctuary owner said. 'She couldn't open her eyes and had been scratching her face, that's why it's so scarred. And her claws had grown round into her pads. She had been chewing at her feet and they have scars on them, too. But she has a lovely nature. She's one of the nicest dogs we've had. I shall miss her, but I know she'll be happy with you. Lots of people won't take an old dog.'

'I'd rather have an old dog. Having just lost one I want something quiet and gentle; a puppy is such a shock after a twelve-year-old dog. I don't think she's ugly at all. How can people say that?'

I turned to look at her now, lying asleep on the rug before the fire. She had been my dog for the last six months, but it was as if she had always been my dog, as if I had had her from a puppy.

'Dear old Amber,' I said, and she looked up and wagged her tail. She had been a great comfort to me — always there, always overjoyed to see me. I had loved all my other dogs and mourned them greatly when they had died, but I could truthfully say that she was the nicest dog I had ever owned.

I thought of the sheep. I knew they would be standing in their little cottage looking out at the rain, or munching hay. Barnaby and Fabian had now grown into shearlings. Barnaby's first fleece lay in a corner of the kitchen near my spinning wheel, a beautiful purple-grey.

David had given me two more bottle lambs last spring, Ram Friday and April, and they were now nearly a year old. Ram Friday had been born on a day of pale blue skies, when the water buckets in the yard outside had been covered with ice. His mother was what David had called a 'die-er', an old ewe who had seen many summers and had many lambs. Her last effort was to give to the world a tiny fragile lamb with trembly legs and a quavering bleat. He was quite the smallest lamb I

3

had ever seen. His little neck was cardboard-thin and he made pathetic bleating noises.

David stood in front of the fire holding him, while I mixed some milk to put into his bottle. Then I took the lamb from him while David sat by the fire and had a glass of whisky. The lamb began sucking at the bottle with surprising eagerness for something so small. The whole of his tiny body trembled all the time, but the milk was soon gone. I sat opposite David and held the lamb against me to warm his frail body, but the trembling continued.

'Do you think he's cold? Should I wrap him up?'

'I expect it's the move. Put him in the pen with the others and see how he is.'

'The 'pen', made from straw bales, was in the room next to the kitchen, reached through a brick archway under the back stairs. I had great plans for this room. There was a glazed door to the garden, and the old flagstone floor. I imagined it full of plants and white-painted furniture, hanging baskets suspended from the old meat hooks in the ceiling. But having moved in only three months previously, the room still held half-unpacked tea chests, and the 'pen'.

I had been feeding a pair of pure-bred Ryeland ram lambs for David from three days old. They were then eight weeks old, robust and healthy and ready to go back to the farm. They peered over the bales with interest and then backed away as I put the tiny newcomer down in the straw beside them. Next to them he looked smaller than ever. After a few minutes he folded his legs and sat down. David was pleased with the way the first two had grown and we took them out to the car to go back with him.

I went inside to my new lamb. He was crumpled up in a corner against the straw. I found an old jersey and cut the bottom off one of the sleeves, made two holes for his front legs and pushed it over his head. It gave him the appearance of an organ grinder's monkey — all spindly arms and legs. But at least it would keep him warm during the night without his mother to cuddle against.

Next morning I had been woken early by the sparrows scrabbling about under the tiles. I lay in bed waiting for a sound from downstairs. It was very quiet and I wondered if the tiny lamb had died. Then came the unmistakable cries of a lamb hungry for his breakfast.

By Sunday some of his newness had disappeared and he had stopped trembling all the time. He had quickly learnt to associate the sound of my footsteps with food. I had only to walk into the room to start him quivering his tail insistently and bleating that he was hungry. David had phoned later that morning: 'Do you want another lamb to keep that one company?'

If Ram Friday was the smallest lamb I had ever seen, this next one was certainly the largest. A cross from two of the biggest breeds of sheep — a Lincoln Longwool ewe and an Oxford ram — she was twice as tall as my little scrap in the monkey vest. His back was a little higher than her knees, his ears came to the top of her shoulders.

She was just two days old and very beautiful. She had a lovely pale grey face and long, silky ears. Her back was covered in tiny tight curls and she had fluffy brown moon boots — she shuffled around in the straw as if they were too big for her. Her bleat was low and soft, while Ram Friday's voice had the piercing, high-pitched wail of a human infant. He put his little nose up to sniff at her and seemed quite pleased to have some company, tossing his head and doing the beginnings of a lamb's jump for joy. I gave them both a bottle, and half an hour later they had curled up together and gone to sleep.

A week later the wide Fenland skies had been grey with rain. The weather was more like November than April and even the weeds had stopped growing. But Ram Friday was growing bold and strong. Not exactly larger as yet: something so small had a long way to go. But he jumped and turned in the straw like the best acrobat and downed his bottle in forty-five seconds. April in the moon boots plodded after him. She reserved her energies for getting larger. She was fast approaching the proportions of a donkey foal.

Then I found that Ram Friday had a lump. I was not unduly

worried as I imagined it to be an umbilical hernia. But I wrapped him in a blanket and took him to the surgery. We sat in the waiting room surrounded by dogs. He pressed his little body against me, his eyes large as tea saucers, and he started his trembling again.

He had a temperature of 105°F. He did not have a hernia, it was an infection. I apologised for his silly monkey vest, but the vet said it had probably saved his life. He gave him an injection of antibiotics and told me to keep him feeding.

When I had first seen Ram Friday I had not expected him to survive. Then he had seemed to be getting stronger. Now it seemed as if I might lose him after all. I could only hope that he had grown strong enough to resist the infection with the help of the antibiotics. All I could do was stay up all night and keep feeding him every two hours. It was a long, cold night. I sat by the fire with a blanket wrapped round me and Ram Friday. But he stayed alive, and he stayed hungry.

Soon after half-past five it had begun to snow. Large, soft flakes quickly put a white covering everywhere, but after about twenty minutes they stopped.

I went to the door and opened it. It was already quite light and the cold morning air rushed at my face. But the wind of the night before had dropped, the clouds were moving away. I heard, far away, a cockerel crowing, and the sound of geese and wild swans calling. In the ash tree near the house a pair of turtle doves were cooing to each other. It was the beginning of a perfect day and Ram Friday had survived.

Now he had grown considerably. He was still a small sheep, but no longer a lamb. Now, until shearing, he was a hogget, and as greedy as the proverbial pig. April would eventually become a large sheep, probably the largest in the flock. She was already the size of Barnaby and Fabian, although she was not fully grown. The sheep seemed to grow for about three years, although Rupert, now five, still seemed to be spreading outwards. He looked like a beached whale when he sat down to chew his cud. He, too, had been a tiny lamb, a 'little runt' as David had called him.

I saw Dorothy coming back from the shop. She paused near the gate and then walked up the path beside the house and round to the back door. I went to open it and she came in, smiling cheerfully in spite of the wretched day.

'Hello, Liz.' She set her basket on the kitchen table. 'How are you?'

'Fed up. Come and sit by the fire, Dorothy. Would you like a cup of coffee?'

'Oh, thank you, I'd love one.' She sat down and lit a cigarette, while I switched on the kettle, then joined her by the fire.

'All it ever seems to do is rain,' I said. 'I've had enough of Norfolk.'

'Oh, we love it here,' she said. I had heard her say that so many times, almost as if she was trying to convince herself that she did. 'You're not really thinking of moving, are you? Where would you go?'

'Wales,' I said without hesitation. 'I nearly went to Wales instead of coming here. Now I wish that I had.'

She laughed. 'It will rain in Wales, too, you know.'

'It can't rain any more than it does here. And at least there'll be mountains to look at, and room for my sheep.'

'Oh, Liz, you're not serious?'

I got up to make the coffee. 'I'm thinking about it,' I answered.

'What will Tom and Katy say if you move? How are they both, by the way?'

'They're fine. They'll be here next weekend. If I go to Wales I won't be much farther away from them than I am now. They won't mind at all, if it's what I want to do.'

After Dorothy had gone, I went out to the sheep. Barnaby and Fabian were standing in the doorway of their cottage, looking at the rain. The whole of the garden was water-logged. The land here was below sea level and the water table was so high that when it rained there was nowhere for the rain to sink away. It just stayed on top of the ground in great marshy pools. It was not good sheep country at all. They hated getting their feet wet, and I had spent days over the winter trimming and spraying their hooves to prevent them getting foot-rot.

They all pushed up to the doorway, looking at me with their pale, melancholy eyes. They looked most unhappy. I had taken them away from their meadow full of lush clover and long grass, and brought them to this flat wasteland of mud and rain. I had sown grass seed in the spring, but the weather had been so cold and wet that only half of it had germinated, the rest of the seed rotting in the ground.

I went into the next-door cottage, now used as the hay shed, and carried out armfuls for them. They pushed and jostled each other, munching at the sweet-smelling hay. Pandora looked up at me, tufts of hay sticking out of the side of her mouth. I stroked her soft ears and she tossed her head a little. Barnaby came up to me and rested his head against my arm. I rubbed his head, and stroked his smooth face.

It was already getting dark. I refilled their water bucket and said goodnight to them, then went back into the house. Amber was still lying beside the fire, but she looked up as I opened the door. The cats were milling about, getting impatient for supper time.

That evening I sat by the fire and watched the logs burning brightly in the hearth. I thought of my dream of a little cottage on the side of a mountain, with space for the sheep, and sweet mountain flowers and grasses for them to eat. It was a dream I had held in my heart for so long, even before I had owned the sheep. Away at the back of my mind the dream had always been there.

I did not belong in this desolate place, and I knew I would never be happy here. In the morning I was going into Wisbech to the estate agent, to put the house on the market. I would take the sheep and go to Wales and find a new life there. I would try and find my dream.